PRAISE FOR USA TODAY AND WALL STREET JOURNAL BESTSELLING AUTHOR JAN MORAN

Seabreeze Inn and *Coral Cottage* series

"A wonderful story… Will make you feel like the sea breeze is streaming through your hair." – Laura Bradbury, Bestselling Author

"A novel that gives fans of romantic sagas a compelling voice to follow." – *Booklist*

"An entertaining beach read with multi-generational context and humor." – *InD'Tale* Magazine

"Wonderful characters and a sweet story." – Kellie Coates Gilbert, Bestselling Author

"A fun read that grabs you at the start." – Tina Sloan, Author and Award-Winning Actress

"Jan Moran is the queen of the epic romance." —Rebecca Forster, *USA Today* Bestselling Author

"The women are intelligent and strong. At the core is a strong, close-knit family." — Betty's Reviews

The Chocolatier

"A delicious novel, makes you long for chocolate." – *Ciao Tutti*

"Smoothly written…full of intrigue, love, secrets, and romance." – *Lekker Lezen*

The Winemakers

"Readers will devour this page-turner as the mystery and passions spin out." – *Library Journal*

"As she did in *Scent of Triumph*, Moran weaves knowledge of wine and winemaking into this intense family drama." – *Booklist*

The Perfumer: Scent of Triumph

"Heartbreaking, evocative, and inspiring, this book is a powerful journey." – Allison Pataki, *NYT* Bestselling Author of *The Accidental Empress*

"A sweeping saga of one woman's journey through World War II and her unwillingness to give up even when faced with the toughest challenges." — Anita Abriel, Author of *The Light After the War*

"A captivating tale of love, determination and reinvention." — Karen Marin, Givenchy Paris

"A stylish, compelling story of a family. What sets this apart is the backdrop of perfumery that suffuses the story with the delicious aromas – a remarkable feat!" — Liz Trenow, *NYT* Bestselling Author of *The Forgotten Seamstress*

"Courageous heroine, star-crossed lovers, splendid sense of time and place capturing the unease and turmoil of the 1940s; HEA." — *Heroes and Heartbreakers*

BOOKS BY JAN MORAN

Summer Beach Series

Seabreeze Inn

Seabreeze Summer

Seabreeze Sunset

Seabreeze Christmas

Seabreeze Wedding

Seabreeze Book Club

Seabreeze Shores

Seabreeze Reunion

Seabreeze Honeymoon

Seabreeze Gala

Coral Cottage

Coral Cafe

Coral Holiday

Coral Weddings

Coral Celebration

Beach View Lane

Sunshine Avenue

Seabreeze Honeymoon

USA TODAY & WALL STREET JOURNAL BESTSELLING AUTHOR

JAN MORAN

SEABREEZE HONEYMOON

SUMMER BEACH
BOOK 9

JAN MORAN

SUNNY PALMS

PRESS

Library of Congress Cataloging-in-Publication Data
Moran, Jan.
/ by Jan Moran

ISBN 978-1-64778-107-1 (epub ebook)
ISBN 978-1-64778-109-5 (hardcover)
ISBN 978-1-64778-108-8 (paperback)
ISBN 978-1-64778-111-8 (audiobook)
ISBN 978-1-64778-110-1 (large print)

Published by Sunny Palms Press. Cover design by Sleepy Fox Studios. Cover images copyright Deposit Photos.

Sunny Palms Press
9663 Santa Monica Blvd STE 1158
Beverly Hills, CA 90210 USA
www.sunnypalmspress.com
www.JanMoran.com

For my beloved family of readers, and all who value the meaning of family and friends.

1

"You shouldn't wait any longer to go on your honeymoon," Carlotta said, lifting an eyebrow at Ivy in reproach. "It's been delayed enough as it is."

"Between the inn and City Hall, Bennett and I have been swamped with work," Ivy said. Still, coming from her mother, that comment stung. She lifted her face to the fresh breeze cooling the patio of the Seabreeze Inn, where she was gathered this afternoon with her family. They were having a barbecue to send off their parents after the large family reunion they'd had.

"Which is why you must get away," Carlotta replied, framing Ivy's face in her hands. "You and Bennett hide it well, but I can see the signs of fatigue in both of you."

"I didn't want to leave while you were visiting," Ivy said. "Or with Shelly and the new baby, or during our busy summer season."

Carlotta sighed. "I'll grant you that, but you must promise to take time off. You've been working relentlessly since you arrived in Summer Beach."

"That's what it took to get the inn to this point, Mom."

Ivy's face burned with the memory of that difficult time. Learning of her late husband's adultery and intention of hiding this asset from her had fueled her determination. "I stood to lose everything after Jeremy's death."

"And you did an incredible job. But your health and your marriage are far more important. Shelly is feeling better now. She and Poppy can look after the inn. And Sunny will pitch in. I've had a talk with her."

"We'll think about it," Ivy promised, although she didn't know how they could manage it. As for Sunny, Ivy couldn't count on her youngest daughter, not while she was finishing her last year of university study. It was important that Sunny complete her degree. She had changed her major, and as a result, the projected cost had escalated.

Every time Ivy got a little ahead financially, something unexpected arose, like an expensive plumbing or electrical failure at the inn that couldn't wait. As much as Ivy loved the old house, sometimes she wished she'd been able to sell it right after Jeremy's death. She had tried. Still, she wanted Sunny to find her path.

Her mother had always been astute; the stress was wearing on Ivy, much as she tried to hide it. The next day will be better, she told herself every evening when she fell into bed, utterly exhausted.

Her sister Shelly loped across the patio toward them with Daisy bouncing on her hip. "Hey, why the glum looks?" She elbowed her sister. "Come on, Ives, this is supposed to be a party."

Carlotta and Sterling had stayed a little longer than they'd planned. They were booked on a flight to Australia that evening, so this was the last time the family would be together for a while. Her parents had left their boat in Sydney. In just a few days, they would depart for the next leg of their round-the-world voyage.

Carlotta hugged her youngest daughter. "We were just

talking about making time to get away." She kissed Daisy's silky-soft forehead. "How's my precious little one?"

Waving her hands, Daisy cooed and laughed.

"Look at her," Carlotta said. "Not a care in the world. We could all learn a lesson from her."

"Until she's hungry, wet, or tired, that is. Then, watch out." Shelly pantomimed a scream, and Carlotta laughed.

"Are you ready to continue your journey?" Ivy asked her mother, trying to keep her voice from cracking. Her parents were adventurers, and they led by example. Yet, she would worry about them alone on the open seas.

Detecting Ivy's emotion, Carlotta put her arm around her and drew her in, the familiar sound of her silver bangles tinkling as she did. "We love the freedom, the wind on our faces, and fresh discoveries every morning. At our age, we won't have many more chances like this. But it's always difficult to leave you and the family. And the grandchildren."

Shelly leaned in for a group hug. "Especially Daisy, right?"

Her eyes sparkling, Carlotta tilted her head. "She might be the newest addition to the Bay family, but you're all my favorites."

Shelly laughed as she shifted her daughter, who was nearing her fifth-month birthday. "That's what you always said, Mom."

"And it's still true."

A deep voice boomed behind them, and Ivy's lean, silver-haired father joined them. "Can't stay away from my latest favorite grandchild for too long," Sterling said, bending to tickle Daisy's chin.

Daisy gurgled with laughter, and they all joined in.

"That's a promise, *mi amor*." Carlotta kissed her husband's cheek. "We plan to fly back occasionally to break up the trip. And check on all of you." She stepped aside, the breeze sweeping her dark, silver-threaded hair from her shoulders.

Wide-eyed, Daisy reached for Carlotta's turquoise necklace and gnawed on the beads.

"Watch out, you'd break your teeth if you had any," Shelly said, gently removing the polished stones from Daisy's mouth. "I should feed her, or she won't be your golden child anymore. Her scream is so shrill, dogs run for cover."

"You both need to eat," Sterling replied. "I'll bring you a plate from the grill when you're finished."

"Thanks, Dad," Shelly said, beaming at the offer. "We sure will miss you." She started toward an outdoor sofa so she could nurse Daisy.

Ivy sensed that Shelly would miss their parents the most. Carlotta had returned the day Daisy was born and helped Shelly through a rocky adjustment to motherhood. With proper treatment, Shelly's stormy clouds of post-partum depression had lifted, and her usual irreverent attitude was returning. Her patience had also increased, especially around Daisy. Shelly and Mitch could manage on their own now.

Ivy's brothers and their children were chatting and exclaiming over the buffet that Shelly's husband, Mitch, had prepped in his kitchen at Java Beach. He had fired up the grill on the patio and drafted Bennett to help. The aroma of grilled pineapple, pulled pork, garlic shrimp, and roasted vegetables permeated the air.

It was still warm at the beginning of October, though the inn had few guests. Two women were out exploring Summer Beach. A third one in their party had stayed in.

Mitch's favorite Hawaiian playlist rose against the sound of the ocean waves. Izzy's rendition of "Somewhere Over the Rainbow" was playing, and it was all Ivy could do to contain her emotion. When she and her siblings were young, Carlotta sang that to all of them at bedtime.

Ivy gulped back her feelings. She treasured these precious minutes with her mother.

Ivy's twin brothers were here with their families, and it

struck her that, except for Daisy, all the grandchildren were in their twenties.

How was it that she was closer to fifty than forty? *Blink your eyes, and a decade whizzes by.* She was beginning to feel her years, yet her parents still moved with incredible vitality despite their struggles.

Carlotta turned back to her. "Before I leave, promise me you'll take that honeymoon with Bennett. You've already celebrated your first anniversary."

"Neither of us has much time." Even as the words left her mouth, Ivy knew she was only making excuses to cover up brewing issues.

Her mother shook her head in dismay. "We're all granted the same number of hours in our days, though the number of days remains a mystery. You must live without regrets."

"I don't regret anything I've done," Ivy said. Even her first marriage, as challenging as it had been—rest his soul. She had been young, inexperienced, and with stars in her eyes— perhaps they both had been—yet she had two beautiful daughters.

"That's not what I meant." Carlotta smoothed a hand over Ivy's. "You will regret a trip you missed, a friend you meant to call, a path not taken. At your age, you must seize every day, now more than ever. Don't put off your sweet celebration too long."

Her mother's advice hit a nerve. "Mom, a honeymoon at our age seems a little indulgent, don't you think?" That was another excuse, Ivy knew.

Once enthusiastic about taking a romantic trip, Bennett had become oddly reticent. When Ivy asked, he would only say that it was city business.

"You two are always there for everyone else," Carlotta said softly. "Take your trip, darling."

Ivy drew in her lip. Her mother had always been perceptive. "We've tried before, but that's when Shelly went into labor."

That was several months ago now. Their mini-holiday to Palm Springs had been cut short. Shelly needed her, so they rushed back. Then, there was the busy summer season. Maybe they had missed their chance. Ivy sighed. A honeymoon almost seemed silly now. Still, she longed to get away with her husband.

Even when the inn wasn't fully booked, she still worked. Something always needed repairing or repainting.

As if reading her mind, Carlotta shook her head. "You've performed an amazing feat with Shelly and Poppy in turning this old home into an inn, but it's your turn for a break. Do it now, during the slow season."

"We don't have too many of those weeks anymore, thank goodness."

The theme weeks they'd added—cooking classes, spa weeks, writer retreats, holiday shopping—were booking up fast, thanks to Poppy's ads and Shelly's video posts. Guests who'd stayed with them before were returning, too.

Carlotta pressed a hand to Ivy's shoulder. "You might ask yourself why you think you can't break away, *mija*."

Ivy glanced away, and as she did, she caught Bennett's gaze across the patio. Could he tell what they were talking about? She rolled her shoulders with unease. "It's not that I don't want to take a trip—"

"A *honeymoon*," Carlotta interjected. "Your marriage needs this. Promise me you won't miss the opportunity. A couple we know did, and to this day, it's a sore topic between them. They put everyone but themselves first, and now they can't seem to break the cycle."

Ivy winced. She didn't want to be that woman.

"I love being an innkeeper," she said with reflection. "Although it seems like I'm on an endless treadmill."

"Then step off." Carlotta kissed her cheek. "Cherish each

other, *mija*. Between family and work, being alone together is rare. Having raised five of you, I should know."

"And now I've traded up to a houseful of perpetual guests." Ivy lifted a corner of her mouth in a wry grin.

She glanced at Bennett again. They rarely had time alone. Usually, it was a guest who needed a toilet unclogged or a party that was a little too loud. But now, Bennett was dealing with an outsider who was petitioning the city of Summer Beach for a nightclub in the village. Though the zoning variance had been declined, Bennett told her the guy wasn't giving up.

"Go before the spring rush arrives," Carlotta said, lightly pressing her fingers on Ivy's forearm. "Regrets are a sour swill from this cocktail of life."

Ivy relented. "I'll visit the travel agent this week."

"Hey, Mom. Got a moment?" Ivy's brother Flint swooped in to pull their mother into another conversation about sailing.

Carlotta left her with a satisfied look of approval.

Ivy slowly exhaled; now it was up to her. She watched Bennett cooking with Mitch. Outwardly, her husband looked happy enough, manning the grill and chatting with her family. But lately, his usual positivity seemed slightly forced.

Once, he had talked about needing more adventure in their lives, and she had joked about taking ballroom dancing lessons.

They hadn't done that either.

Ivy crossed her arms. Dancing on the beach shouldn't be a once-in-a-lifetime event. She'd told him that, too.

She recalled how her life with Jeremy had turned into a predictable existence that revolved around their children. For her, at least. Her husband had traveled regularly for his work. But then, he had dallied with another woman.

Not that she was concerned about Bennett in that way. She trusted him, and there were no red flags. Yet, she wondered—and not for the first time—if he thought their life had become mundane? He had also turned down a lucrative position in another city to stay in Summer Beach. Could that be weighing on his mind?

Her mother was right. Somehow, they would make this trip—this *honeymoon*—happen this time.

Poppy dashed toward her. "Aunt Ivy, you have a phone call inside. It's that strange man again. The one that sounds like he's from New York."

"Would you take a reservation or a message, please? I don't want to leave the party."

"I tried, but this guy is awfully insistent and won't leave a message. He wants to speak to you personally."

It was late afternoon, so technically, it was still office hours. Although at the inn, it seemed every waking hour was a working hour—and even some in the middle of the night.

"He might be calling about booking an event," Poppy said. "Some people just want to talk to the boss lady."

Ivy smiled at Poppy's term for her. "We could use that business. But come get me if he turns out to be a talker."

She started for the door. As she passed Shelly, her sister reached out and grabbed her skirt.

"Hey, what's up with you, Ives? You look like you need some of my happy therapy."

Ivy paused. "I'm glad you're doing better, but I have a lot on my mind. Mom and Dad are leaving, and I have a call waiting."

Shelly scrunched her nose. "Ivy?"

"What now?"

She pulled Ivy closer by her skirt. "You haven't called me Shells in a long time. If you need to talk, I'm here."

Ivy mussed her sister's hair, touched that she cared. "I'll remember that, Shells. Thanks."

After making her way inside, Ivy picked up the landline. She leaned against the reception desk, said, "Hello, this is Ivy. Who's calling, please?"

A man's slightly rough voice came onto the line. "This is Milo Rivers."

Ivy wanted to make this quick, yet she was courteous. "I'm glad you called. Are you planning an event, or would you like a reservation?"

"Neither. I'm the head of Redstone Investments." He paused. "Have you ever thought of selling the Seabreeze Inn?"

"If you're calling about a listing, my husband is a real estate agent, and I have no intention of selling—"

Ignoring her comment, Milo cut in. "My investment group and I are interested in acquiring the property at much more than it was listed before."

Surprised, Ivy was momentarily at a loss for words. She'd tried to sell the house right after Jeremy died, but it was so run-down there were no offers. Compounding that was its historic designation, which limited what owners could do. Her only option had been to move in and rent rooms. After a family painting-and-repair party, the old grand dame now had a shabby chic style that worked at the beach.

The property wasn't just an old house; it was a profitable business.

Still, it couldn't hurt to hear his proposal. Ivy shifted the receiver and turned away from the party commotion. As she listened, she focused on the medallion on one side of the stairway's newel post at the bottom. She traced a finger over the intricately carved wood design, which had always fascinated her. A matching finial crowned the sturdy base. At a hundred years old, the finely crafted mahogany staircase was still solid, if a little creaky.

"Do you realize there is a historic designation that limits use and appearance?" she asked. The city won't let you tear this down for a new resort if that's what you had in mind."

"Not at all. We think it has great potential as it is."

"It would need some updating." He should know that upfront.

"We have plans to do that."

Ivy glanced around the entryway that she had spackled, painted, and polished. She was emotionally invested in this property. "I don't know. This is more than an inn; it's also our home. I'm afraid I'm not interested—"

"With what we're prepared to offer, you could live anywhere you wanted—and very well."

Ivy pinched the bridge of her nose. She should hang up right now, but she was curious. Focusing on the medallion to quell her nerves, she asked, "What are your plans for it?"

Milo cleared his throat. "While that's confidential, I can assure you it would be a luxury destination that would elevate surrounding property values." He paused before quoting a price.

Ivy's heart leapt at the figure, though she remained noncommittal. "I'd have to think about it."

"First, we would need to see inside."

"That can be arranged. But not this week. Or next. We're awfully busy." The truth was, she needed time to consider this.

"Then I will mark my calendar to call back in two weeks. In the meantime, I'll send a letter of intent."

Before Ivy could get his number, he hung up. Milo Rivers of Redstone Investments. That's all she knew. A shiver raced along Ivy's spine. Was this a coincidence or providence? Maybe it was a little of both. She touched the medallion for good luck.

As Ivy walked back to the party, she tried not to think about the call. This wasn't the time to tell anyone, and who knew if the guy would be back in touch.

When she stepped onto the patio, her brother Flint stopped her. "How are you holding up?"

"Seems like Mom and Dad just arrived, and now they're taking off again."

"Yeah, I know." Flint rocked on his feet. "If you'd told me as a teenager that I'd be so attached to them now, I would've laughed."

"I hope our kids feel that way someday."

Flint chuckled. "I won't make any bets on that, but they're all good kids. We're lucky." He paused and tapped his watch. "We should leave for Los Angeles soon. Mom and Dad need to be at the airport in plenty of time, and I don't trust city traffic."

"Are you still picking up Honey and Gabe from Elena's?"

"It's not much out of the way," he replied. "None of them have much luggage, so I can fit them all into the SUV."

Their sister and her husband had also flown from Sydney for the reunion. They'd stayed on in Los Angeles to see their daughter, who was making a name for herself as a jeweler to the stars.

Ivy watched her parents with a stab of longing for more time. As much as she would miss them, she was happy for them, too.

Flint watched their parents as they regaled the grandchildren with stories. "When I'm in my early seventies, I hope I'm still active enough to pursue my dreams like they do."

Ivy prayed they were still up to it. Carlotta and Sterling had planned this round-the-world trip as their last major voyage on their boat. Not that they were slowing down, but as her mother said, they were simply being realistic. They couldn't foresee accidents or illnesses, and the sheer physicality of such a long, arduous journey might be beyond their reach in a few years.

Ivy turned to her brother. "I'm glad they're doing this now, just the two of them." Even after fifty years of marriage, Carlotta and Sterling still enjoyed being with each other.

"It's very cool." Flint nodded. "Honey told me she and Gabe will crew for them if they want to sail again later. I wish

I could get more time off. But maybe some of the kids could go. Rocky and Reed are good sailors."

"Think we'll be like our folks someday?" Ivy asked.

"I'll hold you to it," he replied, slinging his arm around her.

A little while later, after everyone had eaten their fill and had their last conversations with Carlotta and Sterling, it was time to say goodbye. The family gathered in the car court behind the inn.

"My darlings," Carlotta said as she and Sterling hugged each child and grandchild: Ivy and her daughter Sunny, then Bennett, Shelly, Mitch, and little Daisy. Forrest and his wife and their grown children, and Flint, along with his wife and their brood. Ivy's other daughter, Misty, would see them off in Los Angeles with her cousin Elena. A chorus of laughter, tears, and promises to stay in touch rang out.

At last, Carlotta smiled and held her arms out to Ivy. "My beautiful, brave daughter. Be well and keep your spirit. What we discussed—promise me again?"

"I will, Mama," she said, reverting to her childhood name for her mother as she fell into her embrace. She swallowed against the lump in her throat and fought back the tears that stung her eyes.

Sterling hugged her next, and Ivy smiled up at him. "Be careful, Dad."

"Chin up, kiddo. We're all on a voyage," her father replied, tapping her nose as he used to do when she was young.

Sterling embraced Bennett and held up a finger. "Remember," he said, and Bennett nodded. And then, with a last wink at Ivy, he helped Carlotta into the SUV and closed the door.

"Oh, Mom," Sunny said, leaning against Ivy. "I'm going to miss Nana so much."

As Flint turned the SUV onto the street, Ivy put an arm around her daughter, who was sniffing back tears. "We all will, but just imagine the stories they'll have to tell when we see them again."

Bennett stood next to them with his hand lifted in farewell. "I wish that were us taking off," he said softly.

"Someday soon," Ivy said, squeezing his hand.

Bennett's expression held sadness and regret. "It seems *someday* never comes."

His words were barely audible and spoken more to himself than to her, but they sliced through her. After his first wife died, he'd lost her and their child. Ivy knew Bennett had been devastated. Her husband had missed out on the opportunity to be a father.

Though Ivy couldn't give him that, this was his second chance at marriage. She would not put off their life. Not anymore.

She slid her arm around him, feeling the beating of his heart. He needed this as much as she did. Maybe more. "Let's take that trip we've been talking about."

"I don't know," Bennett began, sounding tired. "I'll believe it when we're actually in the air."

Sunny leaned forward. "You two shouldn't let anything stop you this time."

"You sound like Nana." Ivy smiled at her daughter. "Are you trying to get rid of us so you can throw a party here?"

Sunny's face flushed. "It wouldn't be a huge party, Mom. Nothing that would bother the guests."

"We still have that zoning issue, I'm afraid," Bennett said, putting his arm around Ivy. "Now isn't a very good time."

"Isn't that Boz's department?" she asked gently.

"It's liable to get touchy with residents over that request for the zoning change."

"Last time I checked, most resorts have telephones and internet." Ivy stroked Bennett's hand. This undercurrent of malaise and hesitancy wasn't like him, and it worried her. She wondered if he was telling her everything. "Let's talk about it this evening in the treehouse. I have some ideas."

They had built a large balcony onto the rear of the chauffeurs' quarters above the garage where they lived behind the main house. Surrounded by palm trees and overlooking the ocean, they could be alone and watch the sunset. It was their magical retreat.

Bennett still looked doubtful. "Remember what happened in Palm Springs? Between the city, the inn, and our families, it's nearly impossible for us to get away."

Ivy bit her lip. This wasn't like Bennett, her perennially optimistic husband. Last year, Ivy had been the one complaining that she was too busy to leave. She recalled her mother's admonition as she tilted her chin...and something else. "What did Dad mean when he told you to remember?"

Bennett drew a breath to reply, but just then, her niece Poppy interrupted them. "We have so much yummy food left over. Should I see who wants some?"

"I can always use a good meal," Reed replied, and his brother Rocky was right behind him.

Poppy motioned to them. "Then you'll help me. Let's go."

"I should clean up, too," Bennett said, turning toward the grill.

Ivy pushed her curiosity aside; they could speak later. She caught her daughter's hand. "Come on, Sunny. Help me in the kitchen. Call some of your cousins, too."

Ivy opened the rear door to the kitchen, and before she realized it, she stepped into a soggy mess.

The entire kitchen was flooded with dirty brown water.

2

"*W*here did all this water come from?" Ivy cried, backing out of the kitchen.

"Ick," Sunny said, recoiling. "That's nasty."

Ivy looked up. The ceiling above them was dripping. Earlier, she had gone through a different door to take that phone call. She wished she'd come this way. Maybe she could have caught it earlier.

"I'll see what's going on upstairs," she said to Sunny. "We keep a squeegee in that closet over there. Would you start sweeping this water out?"

"Me?" Sunny's eyes widened.

"Sure. Just slip off your flip-flops and wade through."

Sunny recoiled. "I'm not letting my toes get anywhere near that stuff. I just had a pedicure."

"Don't be so dramatic," Ivy said. "The water can damage the floor if we don't get it cleaned up right away."

Sunny made another face. "Mom, really? Can't you ask someone else? I don't know how to clean up a mess like that."

Ivy sighed. Sunny was her spoiled daughter, thanks to her father. "It's time you learned."

"It's gross." Sunny shivered. "Why should I?"

"Because sooner or later, a little dirty water flows into everyone's life. You can wash your feet later."

Sunny rolled her eyes. "Get one of the guys. They won't care about gross water."

"Then you can do that," Ivy said, trying to keep the exasperation out of her voice. "I have to go upstairs to cut off the water."

"Can you tell them on your way? Or ask Poppy to come in?"

Ivy threw up her hands. "Just do something, Sunny, and don't act helpless. I won't always be here, you know. You're the one who just told me to take a trip." She backed out and shook off her sandals.

After going through another door off the patio into the rear hallway, Ivy made her way upstairs. She paused at a room right above the kitchen and tapped on it. "Hello?"

When there was no reply, a sense of unease seized her. She knocked harder. "It's Ivy Bay, the proprietor. I need to check your water. We seem to have an overflow downstairs, and it might be coming from this room." It wasn't the first time this had happened. "Are you okay in there?"

Silence.

Ivy wondered if the woman who'd checked in was out. She banged on the door. "Hello?

Still nothing. She pressed fingers to her temple, worried something serious might have happened.

Racing back downstairs, she ran into Poppy.

"What's going on?" Poppy asked. "Sunny is having a fit in the kitchen."

"Cleaning isn't her thing." Ivy patted her pockets. What if someone had drowned in a tub? They had to act fast. "I need a master key. Could you get one and bring it up? I should check the adjoining room, too. I hope we don't find something awful…"

"Oh no," Poppy replied, her brow creasing with alarm. "On it."

"Please hurry." Ivy ran back up the stairs, her heart hammering.

Upstairs, she knocked on the adjoining room. As she waited for a reply and tried to remain calm, she decided her mother was right. The inn really did have a hold on her. Ivy loved being an innkeeper, and she was good at it. Still, the responsibility could be overwhelming at times.

Now, it could be a matter of life and death.

"Hello? Hello?"

Ivy prayed the guest was okay. Or simply out. They'd left the water on, she told herself. That's all. As Poppy's footsteps pounded down the hallway, Ivy chewed her lip.

Panting, Poppy appeared in the hallway, holding the key like a prize. "I ran all the way. Here you go."

"Thanks, sweetie. I don't know what I'd do without you." Her hand wavering, she took the key and thrust it into the lock.

"Tell your guests to turn off the water before they fall asleep in the tub," Forrest said, leaning against the kitchen counter.

"I'm so glad I didn't have to resuscitate a guest. Or worse." Ivy shivered at the thought. They'd never lost a guest. She was so relieved the older woman was still alive that she almost didn't care about the flooded kitchen.

When Ivy burst had into the guestroom, she'd thought the woman was dead. Fortunately, the guest was only sound asleep with headphones on, the water cascading merrily over the edge of the old clawfoot tub. When Ivy touched the woman's neck to test for a pulse, she screamed and flopped like a fish.

Ivy sighed and wrung out her wet towel over the sink. Her brother was a contractor, and his son Reed had a wet vacuum in the back of his work vehicle. While she wiped down the splashed cupboards and counters, the two men cleared the flooded kitchen.

Reed was in his mid-twenties now, the same age as her daughter, Misty. He'd filled out, and with his muscular build, he looked even more like his father. Ivy had another vision of life speeding past her.

Forrest gestured toward the soggy ceiling. "I think we can dry that out with some large fans, but if this had happened during the night, you would have had to replace that ceiling for sure."

This wasn't the first time a tub had overflowed and leaked, but each time it was worse. "What's a repair job like that run?" Ivy asked.

"Expensive." Forrest stepped to one side as Reed siphoned up the water. "For starters, you'd have to replace the flooring, ceiling, and everything above that's damaged. But that's not your biggest worry."

"Whatever it is, I don't want to think about it right now."

Forrest shrugged. "This house is about a hundred years old. You're going to have some costly repairs."

Ivy wiped down the cupboards and gazed from the kitchen window with dismay. Sunny had left the squeegee and a pile of wet towels on the back porch and was hanging out with her cousins near the pool.

She scooped up the towels and dropped them into the washing machine in the laundry room off the kitchen. The smell was sour and musty.

After Reed finished, Forrest unplugged the wet vacuum and retracted the cord. "We had another job where the owners had been on vacation when a pipe ruptured."

Ivy couldn't imagine the damage that would do here. "What happened?"

"It was a mess." Forrest grimaced. "The owner had to gut the place and rebuild. Good thing you caught this right away.

You also need to check your roof and windows before the winter rains."

"I'll be sure to have someone do that." The thought of an extensive remodel was sobering.

Forrest hitched up his jeans. "This place is a big commitment. People who live in these old homes do it out of love. They're committed to preserving them."

"Sounds like a marriage."

Forrest grinned. "Some people spend more time and money on their house than their marriage. I worried about you taking on such a responsibility when you moved in."

"Like I had much choice?"

He hesitated. "You might not want to hear this, but now that it's turning a profit, have you thought about selling it?"

Ivy fought the urge to share the call she'd received. The figure that Milo of Redstone Investments had quoted sprang to mind. If the offer was genuine, she should consider it. She needed a life, and the offer was tempting.

"I'm an innkeeper," Ivy replied, biting her lip. "This is my job." For now, anyway.

Forrest looked uneasy, but he forged on. "I've seen places like this practically bankrupt the owners. The reason you couldn't sell it was because buyers knew what an undertaking this would be. I see it all the time in my business. With its historic designation, buyers couldn't demolish the house and build something new unless they could prove it was beyond salvageable."

Ivy shifted with discomfort.

Forrest went on. "It's not that I don't think you can handle this, but after what you went through with Jeremy, I'd feel terrible if I didn't speak up. When the time comes—and it will —the labor can get awfully costly. And if the health department shut you down…"

"Okay, I get the picture." Ivy shuddered at the thought. That last scenario hadn't occurred to her.

Forrest spread his hands in apology. "You might not want to hear this, but you need to be prepared. I only want to see you succeed."

"I know, and I appreciate that," Ivy said. A sense of unease grew within her, and she recalled the conversation they'd had some time ago. "How long do you think the plumbing and electrical systems have?"

"Hard to say," Forrest replied. "But planned renovation is always better than an emergency response."

Ivy cringed. That didn't really answer her question about the house. But it might impact the honeymoon Ivy was now hoping to take. The place was becoming a money pit.

She saw another drip and wiped down the counters. "How much are we talking about?"

Forrest stroked his chin. "I'll give you supplies at cost, but you'll have to cover labor."

Ivy appreciated what her brother was offering. "We've had a good year, but I'll need to plan for this."

"Of course." Forrest quoted a price she should be prepared to spend. "That includes the roof, too."

The cost was sobering. Much more than Ivy expected. "I thought the estate's management company had kept up repairs."

"That's been a few years now." Forrest shook his head. "Management was probably putting off the inevitable as well."

Ivy looked down at her skirt, which was now wet and stained. "And if I did sell the place?"

"A boutique hospitality company would have deeper pockets. You could probably get a good price. I hear there's a guy in town looking for investments."

As Ivy wrung out the dishtowel, a sense of dread washed over her. The amount her brother had quoted was far beyond her ability to pay, especially if she couldn't keep the inn open during the renovation. She flung out her towel again, soaking up more water on the counter.

"Maybe I could get a loan for the repairs."

"You might have to raise your rates to cover the payments," Forrest said. "Or cut some costs."

"We run pretty lean already." She would have to discuss this with Bennett, but in his current frame of mind, she was hesitant to do so.

Maybe after they took their honeymoon. She thought about that, feeling dismayed. After talking to Forrest, she thought this might be their last chance for a trip for a long, long time.

She considered the phone call she'd taken. Ultimately, the decision to sell the inn would be hers as it was her separate property. Still, she wanted to consider Bennett's view as well.

Despite the stress of running the inn, she loved the life they had built here. Living here and welcoming guests brought her joy and provided a place for their extended family. She also employed Shelly and Poppy, and she loved hosting events for the community here. And then there was the responsibility she felt to preserve the inn for Summer Beach and the memory of Amelia Erickson.

But none of that would pay for a leaky roof.

She squeezed out her damp rag over the sink again. Had the time come to sell the Seabreeze Inn?

3

*I*vy was arranging fruit in a bowl for the breakfast buffet when Shelly bounced into the kitchen in a tiger-striped spandex outfit that reminded her of Tigger from Winnie-the-Pooh. Ivy wouldn't dare wear that, but it looked made for her sister.

"Fancy—is that new?"

"Isn't it fabulous? I got it when I was out shopping with Mom. She says you only live once, so I thought, why not?"

"Suits you," Ivy said, smiling. Shelly was teaching the morning yoga classes at the inn again. "Did you have a good class this morning?"

Shelly brushed her chestnut hair back into her careless topknot. "Small, but the best group ever, Ives. Those guests we have are awesome."

Ivy smiled at her sister's enthusiasm. It was good to have the old Shelly back after what she'd been through. "So, what makes them awesome?"

Shelly leaned on the counter. "They've been practicing for thirty—no, probably forty years. They had moves I didn't know existed." She plucked an apple from the bowl. "So, are you going to tell me what's bothering you before I have to rescue Daisy from Poppy?"

"I thought it was the other way around."

"You're probably right. But don't avoid my question this time. You and Bennett both look like your goldfish just died." She bit into her apple.

"That's not a very nice thing to say." Ivy stalled as she thought about how to answer her sister's question. She hadn't slept much last night, thinking about her relationship with Bennett and the phone call that had come in.

Shelly swallowed. "Think about the poor goldfish. Come on, spill it, Ives. I know you too well." She took another bite.

Ivy couldn't avoid her sister, but she hadn't told Bennett an offer had been made for the inn. She eased onto a stool and began to peel an orange. "What would you do if you could do anything you wanted?"

"Wow, that's a pretty broad question." She gazed through the window toward the ocean. "Fly, I guess. I'd love to soar over the waves and watch the dolphins play out there."

"No, that's not what I mean. Something reasonable." Ivy nibbled at an orange slice.

"That's probably what people said to the Wright brothers, too. Dare to do the impossible—that's what Mom and Dad always told us."

"Shells, will you be serious?"

Her sister crunched her apple. "That's what's wrong with you. You're way too serious. Like you're contemplating a life upheaval of some sort." Her eyes grew wide. "Oh, my gosh. You and Bennett aren't—"

"What? No, of course not. Whatever you're thinking."

"I was going to say pregnant, but if you thought something else, then we really need to talk."

Ivy glanced down, studying her orange as she thought. "Seeing Mom and Dad off to continue their voyage around the world got me thinking. I'm curious; what would you do with your life if you didn't work here?"

Shelly narrowed her eyes. "Did you win the lottery?"

"I don't even play the lottery."

"Well, you ought to. Could be the best two-dollar investment you ever made." Shelly glanced around the spacious kitchen. "Although you haven't done too badly by this place."

"This was my retirement money, and I had to make it pay for us. But really, what would you do?"

Shelly stretched to one side and then the other. "Be a digital nomad and visit every country on earth."

"Seriously?"

"Mitch and I have talked about it. We could take Daisy and have someone manage Java Beach. Why do you act so surprised? I could film and post about our adventures, maybe get sponsorship." Shelly finished her apple in one bite. "Your turn."

"Paint more, I suppose."

"That's not very original. You could do that now."

"I suppose I could if I didn't have a thousand other things to do."

"Hire a manager. Hey, is that what you're thinking about?"

Ivy shook her head. She hated not confiding in Shelly, but she hadn't received the letter of intent Milo promised, and it had been a couple of days now. This might all be a dream. But it was an option. "I am thinking about our honeymoon, though."

"It's about time." Shelly tossed the apple core into the trash can. "Where are you going?"

"We talked about a few places, but nothing seemed to excite Bennett. I think he's worried about leaving."

"Poppy and I will take care of the inn. We'll watch Sunny, too. Not that she needs watching. Much, anyway."

Ivy smiled at that. This might be their last chance for a

while. She would have to find an inexpensive, off-season trip. "I thought I'd drop by Get Away and talk to Teresa. She'll have some ideas. You don't think it's a silly indulgence for us?"

Shelly reached for her hand. "I think both of you really need it. You haven't taken a mental health day off in a long time. You guys aren't as young as you used to be. Stress will get to you, especially as you get older, and it builds up."

"So noted, Dr. Shelly. I'll keep that in mind."

"Anytime. Now, are you going to eat that orange or just play with it?"

Ivy took a slice and tossed the rest to her. "Thanks, Shells." She picked up the bowl of fruit and headed toward the dining room to serve their guests.

AFTER BREAKFAST, Ivy whisked toward the front door. "I'm off to the post office."

Shelly and Poppy were reviewing reservations for the coming week at the front desk.

Shelly looked up and grinned. "I hope you have a good trip. So to speak."

"Hey, what's going on with you two?" Poppy narrowed her eyes and looked from one to the other.

Ivy adjusted her cross-body purse over her white cotton shirt and jeans that she wore with espadrilles. "Poppy doesn't miss anything, Shelly."

If Bennett couldn't make the trip Ivy wanted to plan, she hated to broadcast that through the family. But her niece was different. "You can tell her."

Poppy grinned at that. "I can hardly wait to hear this. Oh, wait a minute." She pulled out a small stack of letters from beneath the desk and handed them to Ivy. "I have more thank-you cards for guests. I'm including a list of our theme weeks, along with a discount invitation."

"That's a nice touch." Ivy had been impressed with

Poppy's idea. It only took her a few minutes to write each note. "Any response from the others you sent?"

Poppy beamed. "In the last few days, I've booked three return guests. Our email newsletter helps keep people informed, too."

"Very impressive." Along with tending to guests, keeping the house in good repair, and managing the finances, they had to make sure they were attracting guests. Poppy was a whiz at marketing. "Shelly, why don't you help her on a few more?"

Her sister made a face. "Poppy's handwriting is a lot better than mine. Besides, I have a lot of work to do in the garden, and I need to make a new batch of videos for our social media channels. Anyone want to help me with that?"

"I have to finish the bookkeeping," Ivy said. "But Sunny can help. Those garden signs she made for you are cute."

"If only your highly educated daughter would actually read them," Shelly said, pursing her lips. "She yanked out my parsley the other day while telling me about her new classes. First, it's my bulbs, now my herbs. I suggested a horticulture course, but she didn't pick up on that."

"At the rate she's going in school, she might get around to that major, too," Ivy said. "But don't encourage her. This is supposed to be her final year."

"Again?" Shelly asked.

Ivy cast a warning look her way. Sunny had been close to graduating, but when she changed her major to hospitality, she had more courses to take. At times, Ivy suspected that Sunny wanted to stay in school as long as possible.

But at least her daughter was studying and not traipsing around the world, racking up credit card bills as she once had. When she looked at it that way, Sunny's annual tuition was less than the first-class airfare addiction she'd once had, thanks to her father's spoiling of her. Sooner or later, she would have a degree or some knowledge to show.

Her older sister Misty was proving herself in acting. She

was making a living now in Los Angeles, but Sunny was proving more difficult to launch into adulthood.

Shelly sighed. "I'll grab Sunny this afternoon to help me. She can video. Hey, maybe that will be her forte. She could be the next Steven Spielberg."

Poppy looked up from her writing. "Or Alice Guy-Blaché."

"Who's that?" Shelly asked.

"An early filmmaker," Ivy replied. "Megan once mentioned her." She'd been meaning to check with her friend about her progress on the Amelia Erickson documentary. However, she knew Megan's film projects often took time to fund and produce.

Poppy's eyes lit with excitement. "I watched a documentary about Alice. She was incredibly talented and the first person to put stories on film. She started in France before she came here."

Shelly looked at her niece in amazement. "The first?"

Poppy nodded. "In 1896. She was often erased from history the way women were back then. But Alfred Hitchcock talked about her and how much he learned from her. She made more than a thousand films. And the old boys' club conveniently forgot her. Sort of like the woman who designed this house."

Ivy tucked the letters into her bag. "Mention that to Sunny, would you? An idea from an aunt or cousin might be better than the same from Mom. I'm not sure she's cut out for hospitality."

"Or horticulture," Shelly added.

"Everyone had hidden talents," Poppy said. "It's just a matter of finding them. Nana says a person's true path might be what they're the most modest about. If they're creative, anyway."

"Your grandmother is pretty wise," Shelly said. "That's like Mitch. He knew he could make a killer cup of coffee and serve people, but Bennett gave him the confidence to believe in himself and open Java Beach."

"Mitch is talented in many areas," Ivy said. She recalled other stories she'd heard about Bennett. Even before he became mayor, her husband had encouraged people to start their own businesses in Summer Beach.

No time like the present, he still told people.

"But it all started with his passion for coffee," Poppy said. "I think Sunny will find her way."

"I hope you're right," Ivy said.

She believed in her daughter, but Sunny also had to believe in herself. Her father hadn't helped in that regard. Jeremy had made Sunny think all problems were solved by throwing money at them.

Ivy shut the door behind her and glanced back at the house, which was the picture of shabby chic. She'd done the best she could with what she had. Was she ready to leave it?

She enjoyed working with Shelly and Poppy but worried about this business holding them back.

As she walked in the sunshine, Ivy tried to shake off her concerns. This was one of her favorite times of the year. The early fall was still warm in Summer Beach, and the village was a little easier to navigate. She couldn't imagine what it would be like if that guy everyone was talking about opened a club that backed up to residents' homes.

After mailing the letters, Ivy left the post office. Since arriving in Summer Beach, she had become friendly with the shopkeepers and enjoyed seeing them. She often sent guests to their stores. In turn, the shop owners referred their customers to the inn.

She loved taking short breaks during the day to run errands in the village, but today, she was on a mission.

She waved at Imani, whose flower stall was busy this morning. At Java Beach, people lingered outside with coffee and pastries. Usually, she would stop and talk, but not today.

Ivy slowed as she passed Pages Bookshop and approached Get Away, their local travel agency. The owner, Teresa, was seated at her desk on the computer. She looked up when she saw Ivy outside and gestured for her to come in.

The more Ivy got to know Teresa, the more she liked her. She was the type who always did a little extra for her customers. Ivy was happy to send business to her.

"Glad you called this morning," Teresa said, motioning to a chair by her desk, which was filled with whimsical items from her clients' travels—miniature wooden clogs, an Eiffel tower, a tiny red telephone booth, a stuffed kangaroo. The travel agent wore a brightly patterned summer dress with sandals.

"Have you found anything interesting for us in Hawaii?" Ivy asked.

"I have," Teresa replied with a slight frown. "But when you told me this was your honeymoon, I thought we should explore different itineraries." Teresa tapped her keyboard.

Curious about Teresa's shift in attitude, Ivy leaned forward. "I'm open to anything that makes Bennett happy."

"That should always work both ways." Teresa peered over her reading glasses. "When he first stopped by, I gave him all sorts of ideas. Paris, African safaris, Nordic adventures. Did any of those interest you?"

"As I mentioned, I've been trying to interest him in Hawaii. I thought that might entice him." She didn't know how to explain Bennett's sudden reticence.

Teresa's eyebrow twitched. "And has it?"

Ivy sighed. "Not really."

Teresa nodded thoughtfully. "You're both busy and giving a lot back to the community. You should take time for an occasional trip."

"My mother said something like that. On the other hand, we don't have to go on an extravagant vacation to have a good marriage. Or any trip at all."

"Of course not," Teresa said. "I have told young people to save money and go camping instead. What's important is the time you spend together and the plans you make for your lives together."

"Well said." Still, Ivy thought about the years that Jeremy traveled for business while she stayed home with the girls. While she hated admitting it, she had felt a little left out. Is that what Bennett meant when he said his life lacked adventure?

With a sigh, Teresa reached across the desk and touched Ivy's arm. "May I be honest with you?" When Ivy nodded, she went on. "The Hawaiian Islands are beautiful, but I used to arrange tickets and hotels there for Bennett and Jackie. He probably has a lot of bittersweet memories. They were there on a babymoon—their last trip together before the birth of their first child—when Jackie's health issues arose. The trip had to be cut short, and they returned right away. Neither of them imagined it would be their last one."

"Oh, my goodness, that must have been so sad." Ivy pressed her fingers to her temple. Maybe that was why Bennett's enthusiasm about their trip had waned. "He told me about their first honeymoon in Baja. And their second honeymoon to Europe."

"They couldn't afford much when they first married. I planned the European trip for them and found some great deals," Teresa added with pride. "I was always glad they had a chance to go."

"I am, too." Ivy had heard people talk of Jackie, especially Bennett's sister and her husband. Jackie sounded like someone she would have liked very much. But this was a new chapter for Bennett. And for her, too.

"Is there another place you might suggest?"

Teresa nodded knowingly. "You'll want a clean slate to make fresh memories. How about Paris? That wasn't on their itinerary."

Ivy wrinkled her nose. "I love Paris, but my first husband was from France. His family still lives in Paris."

Although it was a large city, she couldn't imagine running into them. After Jeremy passed away, his parents practically disowned her and the girls. Their actions cut deep, but Ivy never had a close relationship with them. Jeremy once explained that Ivy was too American and casual for their taste. She suspected he'd married her as a rebellion against their ideals.

"I might have an idea." Teresa's eyes brightened with a smile. She tapped a few more keys and shifted the computer screen toward Ivy. "What do you think about this place? It's a five-star hotel with a rich, fascinating history. I don't think Bennett has been to the Mediterranean."

Ivy peered at the screen. Palm trees swayed above a clear turquoise sea, and a castle turret rose from a green hilltop. The interior photos of the hotel revealed what looked like masterpiece oil paintings. The entire setting was so lovely and serene that it filled her heart with longing.

"It looks amazing," Ivy said, wishing they could afford a trip like that. "But I'm sure it's way out of our price range. I've had some unexpected expenses at the inn. And possibly more to come."

Shifting her glasses, Teresa nodded. "Old houses can be money pits. At least that's a business expense for you." She leaned forward with an eager, conspiratorial look. "I have a special invitation from the manager that I think I could pass along to you. I'm a little busy anyway. Just bring back photos that I can share with other clients. He's an old friend, so I think he'll agree. And you've sent me so many customers."

A surge of hope filled Ivy. "I'm sure we could do that. I'm always taking photos for my paintings anyway."

Teresa flipped to another screen and tapped a few keys. "It's off-season, so airfare will be less than the peak summer period. This is such a perfect honeymoon setting. I'll reach out to clear it with the hotel manager right away." She opened an email and began to tap a message.

Ivy hardly dared to hope. "I'll have to mention it to Bennett, though we haven't discussed anything so far away." From where they were in California at the farthest southwest tip of the continental United States, Ivy imagined such a journey would require a full day of travel.

Teresa shrugged away the comment. "What's a few more hours on a flight? You'll sleep anyway. It's a rare opportunity, and you could be on your way next week. Just get Bennett to agree."

"Next week? I don't even know what I have to wear."

Teresa laughed. "Everything is casual there, and the shopping is fabulous. All you need are swimsuits, negligees, and sundresses. Stop by the boutique next door." She sent the email and turned back to Ivy. "I'll let you know."

A flutter of excitement filled Ivy, and she could hardly wait to share this idea with Bennett. She never imagined they might have the chance to visit such a beautiful island.

If Teresa received approval from the hotel manager, that is.

4

"Good morning, Mayor," Nan Ainsworth called out when Bennett stepped inside City Hall. Her eyes darted toward a younger, angular man dressed in black jeans, a T-shirt, and a black knit cap seated in the waiting area. "Dirk Wilder says he has an appointment with you."

Nan's expression was clouded and somber, a departure from her usual friendly countenance.

Immediately, Bennett felt his skin bristle. Dirk was a hipster who ran clubs in Miami and Las Vegas. Why he wanted to do that in Summer Beach was beyond Bennett, but Dirk was no slouch when it came to attracting young party crowds to his latest venue. He had to have an angle for Summer Beach.

Of course, the real estate prices were lower. And it was an easy drive from Los Angeles unless you encountered traffic on the highway. Still, it didn't make sense to him.

Dirk stood and started toward him.

"He doesn't, but I'll make time." Bennett gestured for the younger man to follow him to his office. "This way, Dirk."

"Wise decision. And call me Blaze."

"Excuse me?" Bennett winced inwardly.

"That's my club name. You're cool. You might as well use it, too."

Bennett shook his head. "Dirk is fine."

Dirk grinned as he glanced around City Hall. "Pretty cool mid-century modern design. You can see all the way to the beach and marina. If the city ever needs to sell, this place could make a great nightclub. I could get you a good price."

"City Hall is not for sale."

"Come on, man. Everything is for sale." Dirk chuckled. "Actually, I've bought a lot of city halls, now that I think about it."

"Maybe you have, but not here."

Bennett wasn't rising to the bait. As the mayor of Summer Beach, he was here to serve his community. Unfortunately, that now included Dirk Wilder. He had bought an estate on the ridgetop not far from singer Carol Reston. The local celebrities here enjoyed quiet lives far from the paparazzi in Los Angeles.

But it didn't seem that was the life Dirk wanted to live.

Bennett walked into his office and gestured to a table and chairs. "Tell me how I can help you today."

Dirk sat down and scratched the scruffy growth on his jaw. "Summer Beach needs a place for young people. Many in the community are against it, but they don't understand how my plan will increase their property values."

Bennett leaned back. "Most of our residents are happy where they are."

"For now. But think about how much money they'll need for long-term care." Dirk splayed his hands on the table. "Most people underestimate that. Like my grandparents. From my clubs, I pay their tab at the best facility in Boca. You might say I'm here to do community service."

"That's a real stretch, Dirk. And hardly a selling point."

Bennett crossed his arms. "Most residents like Summer Beach just the way it is. A club that runs until two in the morning—"

"We need to make it four," Dirk cut in. "The after-hours crowd is huge." He spread his hands as if this were obvious. "We make non-alcoholic craft cocktails designed to ease hangovers. Very popular and an enormous margin."

That's not exactly what Bennett had heard. Dirk's clubs had been busted for serving alcohol after legal hours—and for serving under-aged kids. But the real question gnawed at him. "Why are you interested in Summer Beach? This is hardly your usual habitat."

Dirk held up his hands. "Look, Los Angeles is pricy and competitive, Orange County is uptight, and North San Diego County is sleepy. Summer Beach is right in the middle of it all, poised to blow up. I can turn this town into the latest destination playground. You're in real estate; you know it's relatively cheap. And with your connections, you could make a fortune here. Am I right?"

"You might think so, but residents will fight this." Bennett shifted in his chair. Dirk had done his homework.

"It might be a sleepy beach town now," Dirk said, growing more animated. "But here's the deal: We'll attract every college kid in easy driving distance in California, Arizona, and Nevada. Give me one season, and this will be the new spring break destination. I'll get sponsors like Red Bull and pull in social media influencers. Just look at that beach out there." He spread a hand toward the window. "We'll throw up some cheap motels until we can attract major hotels. Real estate will blow up. And you'll be in on the ground floor. Everyone will want these little bungalows. And the houses up on the hill—"

"The ridgetop, you mean. That's what locals call that neighborhood."

"Yeah, yeah. Whatever. Amazing views, way underpriced."

"That so?"

"If I were you, I'd buy up everything you can. Get a franchise on some fast-food drive-throughs. Summer Beach is the next destination party town. And it all begins with the Wilder Beach Club and my growth team. So, are you with me?"

Bennett ran a hand over his face. "I appreciate your visionary abilities, but the zoning doesn't permit—"

Dirk chuckled, dismissing Bennett's comment. Leaning forward, he lowered his voice. "Come on, what will it take to push this through?"

"A deviation from the zoning plan, but I don't think—"

"Look, I've got a friend whose company makes the sweetest boats up in L.A. You should see them." Dirk snapped his fingers. "Bring your zoning guy. We could be there this afternoon on my plane. Maybe you'll see something you like."

Bennett steepled his fingers and glared at Dirk. "If I'm not mistaken, that sounds like a bribe."

"What?" Dirk threw a hand up. "No way. I give a lot of gifts to friends. I never expect anything in return."

"I'm not your friend, Dirk." Bennett clenched his jaw. This guy was exhausting.

Dirk leaned on the edge of the desk. "Are you kidding? Everyone wants to be part of the Wilder world. Maybe you want to join me on a trip to Belize. Just the guys. Or you could bring your wife. Some of the older guys do. The girls always have a good time. My girl can arrange some shopping and spa time."

"We don't do business like that." Bennett stood abruptly, bristling at his comments. "Our head of zoning, Jim Boz, will review your most recent request."

"I need that variance." Dirk tapped the desk, emphasizing every word.

Bennett's patience was being tested. "All requests will be presented to the community in a forum. We'll have a chance to hear all sides."

"Yeah, yeah." Dirk laughed and smacked his hand. "Like I

said. Everything—and everyone—is for sale. People will see it my way. We'll wake up this town. Everyone will make more money than they know what to do with. The shopkeepers stand to make a fortune, so they'll get on board first."

Bennett walked to the door and opened it. "We're finished here, Dirk."

"What happened to your sense of adventure, man? This is the opportunity you've been waiting for."

"Dirk, you need to go through the process, just like everyone else."

"We'll see about that." Dirk stood and stuck his hand out. "Partners?"

"I'm not your partner, and don't call me that." Bennett didn't have to like everyone, but he did have to represent their best interests. While Dirk had some points, he was overestimating his ability to sway the residents of Summer Beach.

At least, Bennett hoped so. Progress and improvements were expected, but changing the community's ambiance was another matter.

Still, a certain amount of progress was inevitable. But surely Summer Beach could do better than Dirk Wilder.

After Dirk left, Bennett made his way to Boz's office. His head of planning had been with the city for years, and he served Summer Beach well. Boz was heavily involved with the community, from surfing with guys half his age and volunteering in schools with young parents to speaking at the senior community center. The women there called him a silver fox, which Bennett ribbed him about.

He stopped at Boz's office. "Got a minute?"

Boz looked up from a set of plans. "What's up?"

"Dirk Wilder."

Boz drew a hand over his face. "The guy has been at Java Beach telling everyone about the millions he'll make here, and all the residents who support him will, too."

Bennett frowned. "Are people falling for it?"

"He's got old Charlie convinced."

Some people were gullible. "Charlie will bet on anything," Bennett said. "I hope he's not betting on this."

"Talk to Mitch," Boz advised. "See what he's overheard at Java Beach. I don't think the guy has a chance with the community, but if we're wrong, his plans would change Summer Beach as we know it. And not for the better, in my opinion."

Bennett rapped his knuckles on Boz's desk. "Keep me informed if you hear anything."

"Will do."

Bennett didn't have a good feeling about Dirk Wilder. After leaving Boz's office, he headed to the front reception area.

"Nan, I'm going out to check on a few things."

"I hope it's to sort out that Dirk." She shivered at his name, her red curls quivering. "If I need you, where can I reach you."

"Java Beach. Need to get information."

"That's the place to do it. Say hello to my other half."

"Want one of Mitch's caramel macchiatos?"

Nan grinned. "You sure know the way to a woman's heart. Lucky Ivy."

"I don't know about that."

Nan looked surprised. "I hope you're not having problems."

Bennett hadn't meant to say that to Nan, who wasn't known for her discretion. Still, her loyalty was never in question. Instead, he said, "You know that Dirk is a real thorn in my side."

"Don't let him get into your head. You and the missus should go somewhere for the weekend. That always helps Arthur and me when we start getting cranky with each other. We lock up Antique Times and escape to the mountains to clear our minds. You should try it."

"It's a little hard to close up the inn, but I appreciate the suggestion." Bennett smiled. "One caramel macchiato coming up."

Overhead in the village, palm trees swayed in a light breeze, and the weekend weather forecast was for clear skies and calm waters. This weekend would be an excellent time to take his boat on the water, but his schedule was already full of city business. Ordinarily, Bennett didn't mind, but it had been a long time since he'd had a free weekend, mostly because of Dirk Wilder and how residents were reacting to his plan.

As mayor of a small town, Bennett accepted that the job was more than full-time. However, he still needed the occasional time to decompress.

Maybe Mitch could offer some insight. Bennett opened the door to Java Beach, and a cheerful island reggae beat spilled out. He noticed a new vintage Polynesian travel poster Mitch had found and more Tiki-style decorations.

"Hey, Mr. Mayor," Mitch said, lifting his chin toward him. He ran a hand through his spiky blond hair, which was still wet and a little long. "Missed you this morning on the beach. Yesterday, too. Going soft on me?"

"There has been a lot of city business lately." Bennett had been skipping some of his morning runs, which wasn't like him. "Thought I'd give you a chance to get a haircut, too."

"I hear you." Mitch grinned and angled his head toward a group of men at a table. "Lot of talk going on."

"Yeah?"

"How about a coffee? I need to take a break anyway. We can go outside."

"Sounds good. Don't let me forget a caramel macchiato for Nan."

"I'd never hear the end of it." Mitch nodded toward his employee. "Whip up the mayor's special brew, then cover for me. Thanks."

A few minutes later, they made their way outside and

settled into a pair of Adirondack chairs on the sand that faced the ocean.

"This is what I've been missing," Bennett said, lifting his face to the sun.

"Sounds like you've got some problems at the city."

"I didn't want to talk about it at the party," Bennett said. "But I hear Dirk has been drumming up support for his plan here."

"The guy's a promoter," Mitch said. "A lot of what he's promising is unrealistic, but some people don't realize that. Dirk throws around a bunch of big figures, and people salivate. Sure would change Summer Beach. If you ask me, they'd be selling out."

Bennett sipped his coffee, grateful for the caffeine. "You'd benefit from the extra business."

"I do just fine as it is, and I don't have to deal with a bunch of rowdy spring breakers. Or the rest of it."

"What do you mean?" Bennett asked.

"The drugs and all the craziness that goes along with that. Vagrancy, theft, troublemakers." Mitch shook his head in dismay. "Dirk's plans are much bigger than a club on Main Street, although that's the kick-off. He wants to use the public beaches for parties, and he's targeting alcohol sponsors. Not that there's anything wrong with that, but kids go overboard. There are plenty of other places they can go."

Bennett didn't like the sound of that. "The city will have to draw the line."

"You should know that it's not just spring break, which would be a month-long party. He's talking about turning Summer Beach into an all-summer party town, a little like Coachella or Woodstock but ongoing."

"We'd lose a lot of residents over that," Bennett said. "At least, the ones who could afford to move."

"About that," Mitch said. "Dirk is talking about forming a venture fund to buy people's houses and turn them into short-term party rentals. I like our neighborhood as it is. I don't want Daisy growing up around all-night parties."

"I don't blame you," Bennett said, growing more concerned. "And Summer Beach would need more services. A larger police force and more emergency medical services. Thanks for the update."

"Wish I had better news for you," Mitch said. "I'll make Nan's coffee to go for you."

The prospect Dirk had in mind was worse than Bennett realized, so he had to work fast. But he couldn't do it alone.

5

When Ivy returned to the inn, Poppy told her another couple had arrived, and they'd received a reservation from a returning guest.

"That's good," Ivy said. "Need help with anything?"

"It's all under control," Poppy said. "And Shelly just left for the day."

Shelly was working a flexible schedule so she could tend to Daisy, which Ivy was glad she could do.

"I have a lot of work to do in the library before the afternoon reception," Ivy said.

She had a multitude of tasks she'd been putting off. Bookkeeping, ordering extra blankets for the newly renovated attic rooms, and so on. The days slipped away from her.

Poppy leaned over the desk. "If you'd like, I can oversee the afternoon tea and wine reception in the music room."

"Would you?" Ivy beamed at her niece. "I'd appreciate that. I'm really swamped."

After making her way to the library, Ivy opened her computer and slid on her new, bright yellow half-glasses. She was long overdue in posting her cash expenses to the bookkeeping program.

As she typed, her mother's advice echoed in her mind. She paused, rubbing her eyes and yawning. Numbers were swimming in front of her eyes.

Removing her glasses, she gazed around the library. The wood-paneled walls had been a silent witness to the history of this house. She ran her hand across the old writing desk. Beneath it, she'd discovered the first of Amelia's elusive writings, which she was still trying to piece together.

Between the maintenance required in the old house and the time it took to keep everything in working order, Ivy was often exhausted. If only she could have a crew come in to make all the repairs at once instead of being hit with emergency repairs and scrambling to take care of guests.

As her brother had mentioned, was it time to consider selling this house?

The lights overhead flickered as if in confirmation.

Or warning.

With a weary sigh, Ivy returned to her receipts and online ledgers. Even as she tried to be slow and methodical about it, she still made mistakes that were time-consuming to correct. But it had to be done, or she would regret it during tax season. And if she ever needed a loan for repairs, her banker would need to see her financials. There was no way out of this task.

A little while later, Bennett appeared in the doorway. "Still at it?"

Surprised, Ivy checked the antique clock above the desk. "I lose track of time with this bookkeeping. It's not my favorite part of the job."

He crossed to her and rested his hands on her shoulders. "We both do what it takes, don't we?"

His hands felt warm and reassuring on her shoulders, and she rotated her neck. As she did, he lightly massaged her neck. "You can stop that *never*," she said.

Bennett chuckled. "Life can get pretty intense."

"I thought a sleepy beach town would be relaxing."

"Not with shady characters trying to profit from it."

Detecting a tense shift in his tone, she glanced up at him. "I've heard about Dirk Wilder."

"He doesn't let up." Bennett swiftly changed the subject. "How about some supper?"

Hearing the weariness in his voice, Ivy removed her glasses and pressed a hand to her forehead. "I completely forgot about dinner," she replied, gesturing toward her stack of receipts. "Sunny and Poppy are going out tonight, and this work is endless." Their guests were all out for the evening, too.

"Leave it," Bennett said, massaging her neck. "I don't expect you to make anything. I think I saw a frozen pizza in the fridge that I can work some magic on."

Ivy was relieved. "Fine by me. And I know of a good bottle of wine that will make that taste like Italy."

Bennett finally laughed. "No wine is that good."

Just then, her phone dinged with a message from Teresa. She checked it and smiled. "But my news is," she countered, teasing him.

He raised his brow in surprise. "What's that?"

"Let's wait until we sit down to eat." Excitement gathered in her chest, but she wanted to wait for just the right moment. She breathed out in relief. This could be the fresh beginning they needed.

He held out his hands to her. "Come with me now. I need some good news."

Sliding her hands into his, she rose and brushed her lips to his. "And we're just in time for the sunset."

As they made their way through the inn and up the stairs to the old chauffeur's quarters over the garage, Ivy sensed tension in Bennett's demeanor despite his studied nonchalance. She wondered what had happened at City Hall today.

In the small vintage kitchen, Bennett sliced fresh mushrooms, sweet peppers, and garlic for the pizza, while Ivy opened the last bottle of Sangiovese wine.

"How is that wine?" he asked. "I meant to store it some-where cooler, but I didn't get around to it."

She sniffed the cork and the bottle. "Seems fine. I need to buy more wine."

Ivy made a mental note to replenish. Her endless to-do list was a constant in her life, yet the thought of a sweet escape with Bennett might spur her on to finish what she could before they left. If only he would agree and be as excited as she was.

Teresa's offer was too good to pass up. And it was just what they both needed. Hope surged in her heart.

"How about some fresh herbs on that?" she asked.

"This frozen slab of bread and cheese can use all the help we can give it."

Ivy pinched off a fragrant handful of leafy green basil and small oregano leaves. "Try these. And I think we have some leftover prosciutto." She opened the refrigerator and handed him a thin package.

Bennett opened the prosciutto and topped the pizza with what remained. He tore the basil leaves and sprinkled the herbs liberally over the pizza. "In the oven it goes. Shall I make a salad while we wait?"

"Something simple would be nice. We have romaine." She hummed as she stacked dishes, utensils, napkins, and wine glasses onto a tray. "I'll set up on the balcony."

"You're sounding happy."

"Why shouldn't I be?" Ivy smiled, thinking about her news about the trip. "I love being alone with you."

"All righty, then. Right behind you with the greens." Paus-ing, Bennett added, "I like this. Just the two of us. Even with a somewhat dodgy pizza."

His voice sounded tired, she noted. "No one else has to know," she said, kissing him before she left.

Outside on their new covered balcony, Ivy arranged two place settings on the low table in front of the outdoor sofa. If Sunny and Poppy were home, she usually cooked in the main house, and sometimes Shelly and Mitch joined them, although since Daisy arrived, they didn't come over as much.

Ivy loved gathering everyone for a meal, although dinner time was often hectic. Still, she welcomed drop-ins. Sometimes Sunny brought Jamir, Imani's son, who went to the same school and was studying pre-med.

Since Ivy had arrived in Summer Beach, she'd spent long hours forging a new life for herself and those she loved. Yet, those hours left little time for her new husband.

As she turned on soft music and lit candles for the table, she realized she and Bennett might be at a crossroads in their marriage. She loved this old house, but if it strapped them financially and in terms of lifestyle, then maybe her brother was right, and it was time to let it go.

The inn was her business, but this old house was far more than that; it had become their way of life by default.

They needed time to consider the rest of their future together. The days slid past, and in responding to others, they often lost control of their lives.

They needed this trip for so many reasons. And yet...

Ivy blinked back tears for all this house had meant to her. Jeremy's death had brought her to Summer Beach, Bennett, and a new life. She would always be grateful for that.

She'd learned that life had its phases, but that didn't mean passing through them wasn't painful.

"Here's the gourmet pizza," Bennett said, sweeping onto the balcony. "Such as it is."

Ivy turned from the sweeping view of the ocean and the beach below. "It was fast and prepared with love. What more could I ask for?"

"Edibility would be good." Bennett pressed a kiss to the top of Ivy's head. "Best I could do."

He reached for the wine bottle and filled their glasses. The ruby red liquid shimmered against the flickering candles in the waning light. A light breeze rustled palm fronds surrounding their elevated treehouse, which was bathed in a rosy glow as the sun sank toward the horizon.

"To us," he said, handing her a glass.

Ivy took it and tapped his with a soft clink. "And to all that lies ahead."

As she met his gaze, she fixed this paradise of a moment in her mind. Their family was away, there were no guests for Ivy to tend to, and no urgent town matter requiring Bennett's attention.

That could change in an instant, of course, as each of them was essentially on-call around the clock. The only way to ensure and extend this bliss was to be unavailable.

A week, that's all she asked for.

After they sat down to eat, Bennett devoured the pizza while Ivy nibbled at a slice. She swirled olive oil and balsamic vinegar over crisp romaine spears and the last cherry tomatoes of the season from Shelly's garden.

Ivy noted the crease between Bennett's eyebrows, which became more pronounced under stress. She had to wait for the right time.

At last, he eased back against the sofa and cradled his wine. "Come here, you. I sure missed you today. I could have used your creative problem-solving."

She leaned against him, listening to the steady beat of his heart. "What happened?"

"Dirk Wilder, as I mentioned," he replied, wrapping his arm around her shoulders. "The neighbors that back up to the venue he's leased for a club are waging an all-out war against him, while others are sensing financial windfalls. Petitions are circulating, and now the attorneys are lining up on both sides. The city is caught in the middle, trying to do what's best for the community—and avoid expensive legal entanglements."

"Isn't what's good for Summer Beach pretty clear?" Ivy asked.

"Sometimes only in hindsight." Bennett sipped his wine

thoughtfully. "Do we guide Summer Beach into a new, more vibrant era with younger tourists who might possess more economic buying power but bring a lot of bad habits? Or do we remain as we are, which might leave some residents economically lagging as other nearby communities attract more visitors? It's not an easy decision, and tempers are rising."

Bennett fell silent, and Ivy digested this news, considering how it might impact their plans for the inn. Did she want to deal with that? She leaned against him. The warmth radiating from his body was a soothing contrast to the cool evening breeze.

After a few moments, Bennett turned to her, his eyes reflecting the sunset. "Enough about my worries. You said you have some news."

Ivy looked at him with a smile. "I talked to Teresa at Get Away Travel today."

Guilt washed over Bennett's face. "Before you start, I've been thinking about our trip to Hawaii. I don't think I can—"

"I understand." She pressed a hand to his shoulder to his chest. "But hear me out. Teresa suggested another island."

"In Hawaii?"

"No. It's in the other direction. In the Mediterranean Sea."

Bennett looked intrigued. "I could go for that."

"She had planned a trip to the island of Mallorca, Spain, but she can't make it. So, she contacted the hotel manager, and—" She sucked in a breath of excitement. "It's ours for an incredible deal if we go next week."

Quickly, she told him about the clear turquoise waters, the award-winning chef, and the highly rated golf course. "I'll even take lessons and golf with you if you want."

Bennett smiled for a moment before his expression fell. "I appreciate that, but I don't see how either one of us can manage that."

"If not now…"

"I know, I know," he said, running a hand through his hair.

"Can't Boz deal with the situation with Dirk Wilder until we return? It's only for a week."

"What about you?" he asked. "Poppy is capable, but will Shelly and Sunny be around to help her?"

"I'll make sure of it. I have a few things to wrap up, including the bookkeeping, but I'll figure it out." She clutched his hand. "We need this. Our marriage needs this."

Bennett drew in a breath. "You seem to have your heart set on this."

"I do. I might have been the one who couldn't get away before, but this time, I'm determined. Shelly is doing well with Daisy now, Sunny is back in school, and Poppy can practically run the inn."

"And if you have another flood?"

"They can call Forrest. He'll know what to do." As long as it wasn't too expensive, she thought.

"I know I promised you, but I'm not sure I can disconnect from city business. This is a hectic time right now."

"It always is, for both of us," she said. "I'm not going to beg you. Either we celebrate our marriage, or we just forget it."

A look of shock washed over Bennett's face. "The marriage?"

"The honeymoon," Ivy said, taking his hand. "I'm a grown woman, and I can travel wherever I want. But I'd rather go with you." She slid a hand over his arm and leaned in, eager to make her point. "We need time to ourselves. Like this, only more of it. There's a lot we need to talk about, sweetheart. Now, before it's too late."

"I suppose so," Bennett agreed, shifting on the sofa. He had clearly understood the seriousness of her tone. "I don't like letting people down, especially you."

"You never do. As for others, you should be able to delegate work for a week. Maybe they'll appreciate you even more when you return."

Bennett clasped her hands and brought them to his lips. After kissing her fingers, he said, "I'll talk to Boz and the team. I have confidence in them."

"This is a chance to show them that you do. But we don't have much time to decide." She turned her face to him, hoping they could make it happen.

Bennett touched her chin and brought her lips to his. "You deserve this." He wrapped his arms around her. "Pack your bags, sweetheart."

Ivy flung her arms around his neck, her trepidation dissipating.

The rest of the week was a blur of wrapping up loose ends. Ivy delegated more than she'd thought possible to Poppy and Shelly, and even Sunny agreed to host the afternoon tea and wine receptions. Her daughter promised to do her homework before she left school each day.

Ivy was particularly proud of Bennett, who enlisted Nan to help him revise his schedule and carve out a week from work.

At last, the day of their departure arrived. Nothing could keep them from Mallorca now, Ivy thought as she packed her bags. Soon, they would be on their way.

6

"I can hardly believe we're going," Ivy said to Bennett, her heart filled with excitement. She led the way through the cabin of the aircraft departing from the San Diego airport. After squinting at their boarding passes— her reading glasses were in her purse—she stopped and gestured to two seats in the last row. "I think we're right here."

Bennett swung their carry-ons into the luggage compartment above, and they settled into their seats for their first short trip. They had two connections to make before they arrived on Mallorca.

"How long is our layover in San Francisco?" he asked, easing into the aisle seat.

Ivy fumbled for her glasses to consult the itinerary Teresa had sent her. "Looks like forty-five minutes. From there, we board a nonstop flight to Frankfurt. It's eleven hours, so we have plenty of time for dinner, a movie, and a good night's rest."

For the long flight, she had dressed comfortably in a white knit top, a flowing navy skirt, and white sneakers with glittery silver stars. She had packed light because she wanted to buy a few things once they reached Mallorca. Teresa had told her she could find an array of lightweight cotton dresses and leather *avarcas*, flat sandals that came in a variety of colors.

"Are these seats getting smaller?" Bennett's knees were touching the seatback in front of him. He grinned at her. "Or maybe I've grown."

"Teresa said she'll try to get better seats for us on the long flight, but as long as we get there, I don't care how we do it."

"So true. Thanks again for pushing me to do this."

They were both excited about this trip, and Ivy was glad that Bennett was in particularly good spirits today.

She peered at the itinerary on her phone again, enlarging it to see better. "We're on the ground for about three hours in Frankfurt, then we have a two-hour flight to Palma. There, we can sleep all we want. No guests, no kitchen floods, and no cranky constituents. Just us. Pure bliss."

Bennett took her hand and stroked it. "It's about time we did this. I'm glad you organized this trip with Teresa, and I'm sorry if I was hesitant at first. It's not that I didn't want to go."

"I understand," Ivy said. "We have busy lives. But we're here now, and that's all that matters. We're going to have a fabulous time on Mallorca."

Just then, a tall woman with an unpleasant expression towered above them, glaring at Bennett. "You're in my seat."

"I believe these are ours," he said pleasantly. "But we'll check."

"Just a moment." Ivy took out her phone and peered at the screen. "The type is so small, and I have a hard time making it larger." She tapped the screen, finally getting it to enlarge the text. Immediately, she saw her mistake; she'd looked at the boarding passes for the next flight.

"Oh, dear. Of course, you're right. We're in the row across. I'm sorry about that."

The woman folded her arms while they slid out of those seats and into another pair of seats.

"My apologies, ma'am," Bennett said.

The woman raised her voice. "You should look where you're going so you don't inconvenience people." With that, she plopped into her seat.

Ivy shared a look with Bennett. They both had to deal with rude people like that in their professions, but she'd hoped they could avoid such people on this trip. As if reading her mind, Bennett leaned close to her, lowering his voice. "We can choose how we react. Let's enjoy the journey."

Across the aisle, the woman glared at them.

"I feel like I've been called before the principal at school," she whispered to Bennett.

For whatever reason, the woman continued to stare at them. They had quickly relocated, leaving her standing for only about thirty seconds, but this woman wasn't letting go of her grudge.

"It's not us," Bennett said. "Something else is probably bothering her."

Ivy stole a glance at her. "That's awfully magnanimous of you."

Bennett smiled and kissed her cheek. "That's part of my job."

The flight attendants secured the overhead compartments, and the pilot eased the plane from the gate. As the aircraft began to taxi into position for takeoff, the flight attendants began to perform the safety instructions.

Across from them, the woman whipped out the safety instructions from the seatback in front of her and stood in the aisle holding the card like a hall monitor at school.

Ivy thought that was a little odd, but it wasn't any of her business. Besides, her seatbelt was proving difficult to buckle.

"Can I help you with that?" Bennett asked.

"Thanks," Ivy replied.

"Here's the issue." He removed part of a candy wrapper lodged inside the buckle.

"Excuse me," the woman said in a belligerent tone. "Do you have the safety instructions memorized?"

Bennett looked up at her. "We've flown before."

"Then you'll kindly shut up so other people can hear."

"I beg your pardon," Ivy said. "He's helping me with my seatbelt."

"Stop talking," the woman yelled. "I can't hear the directions. Do you know where the flotation devices are?"

A flight attendant hurried toward them. "Ma'am, the plane is moving. Please sit down and fasten your seat belt."

"I can't see the demonstration if I'm sitting down."

The flight attendant tried to reason with her, but the woman became even more pugnacious and quarrelsome, refusing to sit down before the safety demonstration ended.

Finally, she did, but she immediately began pushing the call button and banging the seatback in front of her, startling the older woman in that seat.

"I want to move," she announced. "I want to talk to your supervisor."

"That would be me, and this is a full flight."

A stream of swear words emitted from the woman's mouth, and the flight attendant stepped into the galley and lifted the phone. Ivy could hear her speaking in a low tone. She caught a few words, *offloading* among them.

"I think we're turning around," Ivy said softly.

Bennett let out a long sigh. "I hope we can still make our connection in San Francisco."

Sure enough, the aircraft turned toward the gate. Across the aisle, the woman continued complaining about various perceived injustices, kicking the seat in front of her for emphasis. The poor older woman leaned forward, jolted with every kick.

"This isn't going to end well," Bennett whispered. "Are you okay?"

"Of course. What a way to begin the journey. But as long as we're together, I'm happy."

Once the plane had returned to the gate, they waited. Flight attendants gathered around to help the other woman from her seat in front of the troublesome passenger. Bennett gave up his seat to the frail-looking woman and went to stand in the rear galley.

The older woman eased into the seat beside Ivy. "Dear heavens, that woman scared the daylights out of me. Please thank your husband for giving me his seat." She straightened her jacket with quivering hands and brushed strands of silver hair that had fallen from her bun.

"The crew is taking care of the situation," Ivy said. "You just stay beside me, and we'll chat. I'm Ivy. Is San Francisco your final destination?"

"Seattle," the woman replied with a shaky smile. "I'm Leonora, and I'm going to see my daughter and grandchildren. They want me to move closer to them. Maybe I will. Flying is becoming more difficult for me. Although it's usually not like this."

The minutes ticked by, and Ivy was growing nervous about their connection. She saw Bennett talking to a flight attendant, but they both looked grim.

Ivy continued talking to her new seatmate until a pair of large men in uniforms boarded the aircraft and made their way to the rear of the plane to confront the cantankerous passenger.

The troublesome woman across from them began to plead her case, shifting her tone and story.

She seemed quite disturbed, and Ivy felt sorry for her, but that was no reason to allow the disruption of fellow passengers. The woman probably shouldn't have been traveling alone. Ivy sensed security was doing their best not to forcibly remove her. Still, the woman wasn't making it easy on them.

Flight attendants gathered around, and one attempted to

reason with the woman. "For the safety and comfort of other passengers, you'll have to find another way to San Francisco. Our gate agent will be there to personally assist you when you deplane."

At last, that seemed to placate the woman, and she rose from her seat to collect her belongings. Ivy heard an attendant call for baggage handlers to remove her luggage. With the woman still complaining, the two men escorted her from the plane. When they did, the cabin broke out in applause.

That surprised Ivy, though she felt like clapping, too.

"Thank goodness she's gone," Leonora said. "It was lovely meeting you, Ivy. I only wish the circumstances were more pleasant."

"I hope you have a good flight now," Ivy said, feeling for her. At Leonora's age, she shouldn't have to endure such treatment.

Bennett helped Leonora back to her seat, and a flight attendant brought her some water and snacks, along with a heartfelt apology.

Bennett eased back into his seat. "It's going to be a tight connection."

"Do you think we'll make it?"

"They can't say."

However, they still had to wait for the woman's baggage to be offloaded. Ivy picked at a thread on her skirt and tried to stay calm.

Bennett gripped her hand. "We'll do the best we can."

When the flight finally took off, Ivy relaxed a little. The crew did what they had to do, and she understood. That was all part of traveling. Still, she was growing increasingly nervous.

About an hour late, the plane descended into the San Francisco airport. Ivy clutched Bennett's hand as they flew low over the water. Just as she was growing concerned, the edge of the runway appeared, and the wheels thudded onto the airstrip. She pressed her fingers against the seatback in front of her as the force pitched her forward in the seat. When the plane eased to a stop, Ivy let out a sigh of relief.

Bennett kissed her cheek. "We made it."

After the flight touched down, they had to wait before they could pull into the gate. Bennett was stoic, but Ivy saw the tension in the flex of his jaw when he glanced at his watch,

She squeezed his hand. "We're going to have to run for it, aren't we?"

"We'll do our best," Bennett said, nodding.

At least she'd had the foresight to wear sneakers. "You're the runner, but I'll be right behind you."

The flight attendant asked people to remain in their seats until those with close connections could leave, but that didn't help much. They were still among the last off the flight. Bennett reached for her carry-on bag. "I'll take this for you."

They had scant minutes to make their connection—if they could. After deplaning into the airport, they broke into a jog.

"We have to change terminals," Ivy said. "Go on ahead, and I'll catch up."

Bennett grasped her hand. "I'm not leaving you behind on our honeymoon."

They raced through the terminal, dodging other passengers. Ivy was beginning to think they could make it when she realized they were still a distance away. The final boarding call rang out.

"Go," she huffed, pressing a hand to her chest. "Tell them I'm coming."

"I'll try to hold the flight."

She nodded, and he sprinted away. This was their only chance. *What a way to start the honeymoon we dreamed about.*

Ivy ran with her skirt streaming behind her until she neared the gate. There, Bennett was alone, leaning against the wall and catching his breath. When he looked up, he shook his head.

She slowed, her heart hammering and her breath coming in short rasping sounds.

Bennett held his hands up. "It was already gone."

"I should have let you go ahead earlier."

"It wouldn't have made any difference," Bennett said, still breathing hard. "There was no way we could have made it."

Ivy glanced around. The gate attendants were gone, and this section was deserted. "What do we do now?"

"We'll get on another flight." He wiped his brow with the back of his hand.

"That inconsiderate woman did this," Ivy cried, suddenly frustrated. She wiped away angry tears. "She's ruined our trip. And maybe countless others."

"Only if we let her," Bennett said, taking her hand. "You're the pro at turning lemons into all sorts of interesting concoctions. I remember when you decided to turn Las Brisas del Mar into the Seabreeze Inn. I admired your resourcefulness, Ivy Bay. You faced a tough crowd at City Hall."

She had to smile at that memory. "It took a major fire to change that stubborn mayor's mind."

"This little blip is nothing for people like us, right?"

"I suppose so," she said. "At any rate, it keeps things interesting."

This was simply another dose of adversity life had dished out, but here they were, despite everything. So many occurrences were out of their control. She still needed to talk to him about the future of the inn.

But not here, and not yet. Not before she received that letter of intent. Until she did, it was like dreaming of winning the lottery. And she wouldn't sign anything unless she was sure of the fair value of the property and the business.

"Teresa can make another reservation," Ivy said, pulling out her phone.

She called the travel agent, who promised to find another

flight for them. After hanging up, Bennett said, "Let's see what happened to our luggage."

After making their way to the baggage area, they discovered their luggage was off to sunny Mallorca without them. Fortunately, they had each packed a change of clothes in their carry-on.

Just then, Ivy's phone rang. It was Teresa, and she answered it. "Any luck?"

Teresa's voice cracked over the phone line. "I managed to get you both on a plane tomorrow evening, so you'll have to spend the night there. I've made a reservation for you at the St. Francis Hotel in Union Square. It's too early to check in, but you can drop your bags there and explore the city. You'll find good food at the pier."

"We sure appreciate that." Ivy didn't mention that their luggage was off to sunny climes without them. There wasn't anything Teresa could do about that, and she had already done so much for them.

After she hung up, Bennett wrapped his arm around her shoulder. "Let's find a taxi. I could use a bowl of chowder by the water."

Ivy managed a little laugh. "I never thought that would be on our itinerary. But it sounds good."

When they stepped outside of the airport, Ivy shivered. San Francisco was a lot chillier than where they had planned to go.

Bennett put his arm around her again. "Do you have a jacket?"

"I have a windbreaker in my carry-on bag." While Bennett engaged a taxi, she pulled out her thin jacket and a scarf she'd tucked in, just in case.

Once inside the taxi, Bennett directed the cab driver. "Pier 39, please. Lots of great clam chowder there. Best there is."

"I don't know about that." Ivy arched an eyebrow in a challenge. "As good as Boston's?"

"Well, I haven't been back east in a long time."

"This might be a worthy contender," Ivy said with a sniff. "But nothing beats a steaming bowl of New England clam chowder at Faneuil Market."

"You're on," Bennett said, chuckling. "Let the chowder wars begin."

The cab driver glanced at them in the rearview mirror. "You're both wrong," he said with a thick accent. "Give me Manhattan red clam chowder any day. That other stuff pales in comparison. Literally."

In the back seat, Ivy and Bennett laughed. She tucked her arms through her husband's. As exasperating as the flight had been, she could appreciate this unplanned side trip. This would be a memorable part of their honeymoon story.

"Despite a detour, this is sort of exciting," she said, drawing close to Bennett. "I've always loved visiting San Francisco. I brought Sunny and Misty here once. We rode the cable cars and stuffed ourselves with sourdough bread and crab."

"Has to be Scoma's for Dungeness crab," Bennett said with a fond smile.

"Then you've never been to Crustacean," she said in mock horror. "Unless you have something against garlic crab."

"Aw, you're both wrong again," the taxi driver interjected. "Alioto's is the wife's favorite, and I do everything she says. Happy wife—"

"Happy life," Bennett finished. "Did we mention that we're on our honeymoon?"

"Hope springs eternal," the cabbie replied, and they all laughed. "What else is on your agenda?" Before they could respond, he rattled off the highlights, ticking them off on his fingers. "There's the Presidio, Chinatown, and North Beach. And you've got to see Golden Gate Park and Telegraph Hill. Incredible museums, too. You name it, we got it."

"You're a real ambassador for the city," Bennett said, grinning.

Just then, a thought struck Ivy. "Oh, my goodness. Gustav and Amelia Erickson's main residence was here in the city. I wonder if we could find it."

That sparked interest sparked in Bennett's eyes. "Let's do it. Who might know where it was?"

"Megan Calloway," Ivy replied, pulling out her phone. "She's done a lot of research on the Ericksons for her documentary. I have her number, but I'm not sure I can reach her. They left for a film festival somewhere in Europe to present another documentary they just completed."

"How are they coming along on the Erickson project?"

"Slow. Megan said documentaries often require extensive research, and the Ericksons, while prominent, didn't leave many historical details that she could verify."

"Other than what you've found," Bennett added, stroking her hand.

Ivy smiled, recalling the old masterpieces they'd found on the inn's sealed lower level, as well as part of the German crown jewels. Those had been stitched into a doll stashed in the trunk of Amelia Erickson's old cherry-red Chevy convertible, which Ivy now drove.

"The stories behind those artifacts have often been difficult to figure out," Ivy said. "Megan is still working on unraveling the couple's history."

"Here's Pier 39," the taxi driver called out. He wheeled in front of a pier bustling with visitors. Buskers were playing music and performing for tips. The area was full of people enjoying themselves on this unusually sunny, crisp autumn day.

Bennett paid the fare and drew a deep breath. "Mmm, just smell that. Sourdough bread, fresh seafood, and the San Francisco Bay. Nothing else like it. That's how I always remember this city."

"There's a lot more to the city than the pier," Ivy said. "Have you been to the Palace of Fine Arts?"

"We could go there. But wouldn't you rather see if the Ericksons' house is still standing?"

"You know I would." Ivy smiled and kissed his cheek. The idea swiftly lifted her spirits. She could wait to have that important talk with Bennett until later. "I'll call Megan. Might as well make the best of our unscheduled stop."

"Wasn't on our schedule," Bennett said, waggling his eyebrows. "But maybe old Amelia had something to do with this."

"Not you, too." Ivy shook her head. "I'm surprised Shelly has you believing in spirits."

Rocking on his feet, Bennett grinned. "It's hard to deny sometimes."

She swatted him playfully on the shoulder before tapping Megan's number. The phone rang quite a few times, although just before Ivy gave up, Megan answered. Ivy quickly told her they'd missed their flight and were in the city. On the other side of the connection, she could hear a low, rhythmic clacking sound. "Hi Megan, it's Ivy. Where are you?"

"On a train somewhere between Hamburg and Warsaw." Megan's voice crackled through the phone. "We're making the rounds of film festivals with our latest documentary. Say, if you're in San Francisco, you should visit the Erickson house."

"That's why I'm calling," Ivy said. "We hoped you would know the address."

"It's in Pacific Heights. But I could never get through to the current owner, which is a trust of some sort. I'm not sure anyone is living there. It was part of the estate and empty for a long time, like your place. But you could try."

"We sure will." An odd sensation prickled Ivy's neck, and a sense of *déjà vu* washed over her as if she'd been here before a long time ago. She shook her head to dispel it, though her neck and shoulders tingled.

Megan's voice floated to her through the phone. "Are you still there?"

"Oh, sure. Just an odd connection." Ivy rubbed the back of her neck.

"I'll text you the address. Would you take some photos for me?" Megan laughed. "And please try to get inside."

Ivy grinned at Bennett. "If no one is there, should we break in?"

"Just don't get arrested," Megan said as the line began to break up. "I'd better send the address before we lose this connection. *Ciao!*"

Ivy hung up, and sure enough, her phone pinged right away. She read the text.

Sliding a hand over his jaw, Bennett shook his head. "I am not hoisting you over the wall of a mansion in Pacific Heights. That's a ritzy area."

"Whoever said that?" she said lightly.

"Ivy Bay, I know how your mind works. I'm a mayor— think about how that would look if a neighbor called the police."

"That sure would make your next campaign more interesting." Kissing him, she added, "I rather like a man with a past."

"I doubt my constituents would."

"You might be surprised. But I promise I'll try not to break the law—very much." Still, she was determined to figure out a way to get into the house. "Let's find some chowder and talk about it." She slung her bag over her shoulder, and they set off.

By the time they found a restaurant with a bar overlooking the San Francisco Bay for lunch, Ivy's mind was whirring with possibilities.

She and Bennett eased onto red vinyl stools at a bar in front of a long window that looked out toward Sausalito and Angel Island. He stashed their bags under the bar.

A server greeted them and motioned to a chalkboard where the day's menu was posted. Ivy and Bennett quickly conferred.

"Two cups of clam chowder," Bennett told the waitperson. "Along with salad and sourdough bread."

"And the Oysters Rockefeller," Ivy added. "It's not often we come this way."

"We should do it more often." He added a half-carafe of wine to the order and turned to her, clasping her hands in his. "Let's celebrate this surprise diversion. San Francisco is a great town steeped in history."

She was growing more excited, too. "Let's make the most of it."

Enjoying the warmth of his hands as they chatted, Ivy recalled a conversation she'd had with her newly found cousin, April Raines, who had been a university history teacher and was dedicated to preserving local history. April had talked to her about California's historical eras of Native Americans, Spaniards, and Mexicans. "Imagine being here during the gold rush of 1849 as the city was being settled."

"We might discover another chapter of Amelia Erickson's life here," Bennett ventured.

Seeing his eyes light with interest, Ivy grinned. "I think you're as invested in her story as I am."

He pulled Ivy close to his chest. "That's because I've always loved fascinating women," he said, kissing her softly. "Happy honeymoon, darling. With you, life is a perennial surprise."

She smiled at his tenderness and trailed her fingertips along his smooth, freshly shaven face. "I'll take that as a compliment."

"It was meant to be."

With his arm around her, Ivy rested her head on his shoulder as they gazed through the wide window and watched ferries plying the waves. Their hearts seemed to beat in unison, and she was comfortable just being here with him. She leaned against him, smiling at their good fortune. Even though they'd missed their flight connection, she would embrace this interesting change of schedule.

Her mother's words floated to mind. Life really was the way you looked at it.

After a while, Bennett spoke, his deep voice reverberating in his chest. "At this time in our lives, we each have a past, but we also have so much more to look forward to. Just when I was feeling like I was on a perpetual treadmill of resident complaints, you came through for us. I'm looking forward to diving into the Mediterranean Sea."

"I'm pretty sure Teresa organized this with you in mind." After his wife's death, the community had rallied around him. "You're a popular man, Mayor Bennett."

"But you were the one who sought her out. And just when I needed this break." He hesitated for a moment. "I hate to admit it, but the stress was getting to me. I guess you could tell."

His admission touched her heart. "You can hide it from most people, but I know you too well now. And I needed the break just as much."

Ivy took his hand and raised it to her lips. This was the first time she'd seen her usually capable husband having issues with the stress of his position. Even he needed to take time off to recharge.

They sat in companionable silence, watching people strolling along the water's edge. Soon, the server delivered piping hot sourdough bread and the half-carafe with a pair of wine glasses. Bennett poured the wine while Ivy sliced the bread.

"That sourdough smells awfully good." Bennett raised his glass to Ivy. "To you, and other unanticipated pleasures in life."

"Those are often the best kind," she replied with a kiss. "Who knew I'd be here with my long-ago beach crush?"

Bennett chuckled. "When you charged back into my life, I was shocked. And intrigued, if I'm being honest." He tapped her nose. "I'm glad we worked it out again."

The clam chowder was next, and it was as delicious as Ivy remembered, putting to rest their disagreement over which coast had the best. Sitting close, they ate and enjoyed the view of the San Francisco Bay, taking their time over the salad and oysters.

After finishing lunch, they called another cab. This driver wasn't as entertaining as their first, but he was quick and courteous. They passed clanging trolley cars before he turned onto a steep, narrow street that led up the hill.

As the taxi driver slowed, curiosity surged through Ivy. She called out the house numbers. When they came to a beautiful, stately old home, she peered from the window. "That's it," she cried. "Stop here, please."

Bennett let out a low whistle. "What a place. There must be a lot of history within those walls."

"Possibly quite literally," Ivy said. Once again, a surreal feeling washed over her. "I wonder if the current owners have found anything Amelia might have tucked away."

*a*s Ivy stood beside Bennett across the street from the Ericksons' former estate, she was awestruck by the quiet grandeur of its architecture. A tower rose above an arched loggia and three stories. Groups of tall, narrow windows flanked the tower, and balconies rimmed each level. Colorful pots filled with well-tended pink geraniums rested on wrought iron plant stands, indicating the house was inhabited.

Ivy's heart quickened at the possibility of seeing the inside of the house. But this was still more than she had expected.

"What style would you call this?" Bennett asked, squeezing her hand. "Besides grand?"

"I'd say it's designed after an Italian Renaissance villa," Ivy replied, growing excited. "In art school, I did a painting of a similar house. This style was popular in San Francisco, but this…" She waved her hand. "It's a masterpiece of design."

She could hardly believe she was standing before Amelia's former residence. Strangely, she could almost feel the woman's presence.

That is, if she believed in such things.

Ivy looked up in awe at the house that rose high on the

hill. Likely, it had expansive views of the San Francisco Bay. She was impressed with the exterior condition of the house.

"It looks like this house was maintained better than her beach house," Ivy said.

Lush gardens surrounded the house, with a variety of palms, Japanese maples, shaded ferns, and other undergrowth. A gate led to a rose garden on one side of the house.

"It's stunning." Bennett snapped a few photos. "In case you want to paint this scene."

"Good idea." Ivy nodded, transfixed.

She felt a kinship with the Ericksons and tried to imagine what they might have been like here in their prime decades ago. She had seen photos of Amelia and Gustav in an old photo album she'd found at the house in Summer Beach, and she'd seen Amelia in an old film reel Sunny had discovered in her room at the inn. Amelia was a formidable presence. Megan had a professional transfer that to video, and a friend read her lips to translate her words.

Ivy still recalled the eerie, prickly feeling she'd had watching the old clip and seeing Amelia on the screen. It was as if she'd been transported back to that time through a rare portal.

Now she pictured the Ericksons in their finery receiving guests at the front door. That image became so vivid in her mind it seemed as if they were reaching through time to welcome her.

Staring at the house, Ivy felt oddly lightheaded.

Or could this be a side-effect of whizzing through the sky at thirty-five thousand feet and having a glass of wine for lunch? She wavered slightly on her feet and reached out to steady herself on an iron fence beside them.

Noticing, Bennett touched her arm. "Are you okay?"

"Just a little overwhelmed," she replied. "This is the last thing I expected to be doing today, especially after rising so early and then sprinting through the airport. If I'd known we were coming here, I would have researched this segment of the Ericksons' lives."

With his arm around her, Bennett rubbed her shoulders. "If Amelia had the same habits here as she did in the Summer Beach property, the current owner might have found some items. We can ask."

Ivy nodded, appreciating that he was as fascinated as she was. "Maybe they've pieced together more details of their lives. Megan would be interested in that."

Even after all they'd found, Ivy was still searching for artifacts and writings that Amelia Erickson might have stashed away to make sense of her life. The woman had been prone to secrecy, but then, she'd had to be.

Amelia had lived through two world wars and helped people escape to better lives. She'd hidden valuable art and artifacts for future generations. Amelia had also converted her beach house into a rehabilitation and recovery facility after the bombing of Pearl Harbor.

That she had dedicated herself to service in times of need was clear. But how much of her secretive behavior in later years could be attributed to habit, and how much to the Alzheimer's disease that gripped her?

Ivy tented her hand against the sun. "I wish we could go inside."

"It's clearly a private residence now."

"We show people around the inn all the time."

"That's different. The Seabreeze Inn is already open to the public." Bennett winked at her. "But we can try."

Just then, a side door opened, and a woman who looked to be about Ivy's age stepped out. She wore casual clothes and gardening gloves and had a basket looped over her arm.

Ivy caught her breath. "Here's our chance. Let me talk to her first." Before Bennett could intervene, Ivy dropped her bag and started across the street.

"Hello," she called out, waving in a friendly manner.

Nervous anticipation welled within her.

The woman looked up as Ivy reached the front gate.

"My name is Ivy Bay," she said. "I'm visiting from Summer Beach. I know this will sound odd, but the couple who lived here also built a summer house there. It's mine now, and I'm very curious about the Ericksons."

The woman smiled with surprise. "Summer Beach. That would be the Seabreeze Inn, right?"

Ivy was surprised. "You know about it?"

"Not long ago, I searched online for information about the former owners. I came across some articles about the artwork you found. What a pleasant surprise to see you here. I'm Meredith, by the way. The house belongs to my aunt."

Ivy stared up at the old home wistfully. "It's beautiful."

"My aunt is quite proud of the house," Meredith said. "I help her look after the gardens when I visit. When the hydrangeas are in bloom, people often stop to take photos." She motioned across the street. "Is that your friend?"

"My husband. We missed our connection at the airport and found ourselves here. The history of Ericksons fascinates me, so I jumped at the chance to see where they lived."

"Oh, that's a shame about your flight," Meredith said. "Have him join us."

Ivy motioned to Bennett while she shared the story of their airport mishap.

Carrying their bags, Bennett jogged across the street to join them. Ivy introduced him and added, "Meredith has read about the inn, or Las Brisas del Mar, as the Ericksons called it."

"That's right," Meredith said. "I'm fascinated with them, too." She smiled at Bennett. "Say, aren't you the mayor of Summer Beach?"

Bennett glanced at Ivy and grinned. "Why, yes, but how did you know?"

"I was searching for information about the architect who

designed the house," Meredith replied. "My aunt prides herself on preserving this house and its history. I discovered a great deal about Julia Morgan, who designed many private residences and public buildings in and around San Francisco. I was surprised to learn the Ericksons had also commissioned a summer home. That led me to an article about Ivy and her sister and the masterpiece paintings discovered there. You were both quoted, and there were photos."

"A lot of reporters covered the story," Ivy said. Shelly had also posted a story and video on her website about it.

Meredith smiled self-consciously. "I shared the articles with my aunt. She keeps copies on her desk and would like to visit your inn someday. The Ericksons had excellent taste and were avid collectors, so she is eager to see it. As am I." She paused, her eyes flashing with interest. "Paintings and jewels—how exciting. Amelia was quite the preservationist."

"She was," Ivy said. "I understand now that Amelia was only trying to salvage and protect these items during the war. If she hadn't, they might well have been lost."

Bennett cleared his throat before speaking. "Have you or your aunt seen or found anything unusual here?"

Almost imperceptibly, Meredith's demeanor shifted. "My aunt doesn't like to talk about it, but I know there is growing interest because of what was found in your home. There's even a documentary filmmaker who has been trying to reach her, but Aunt Viola won't take her calls, even though the woman sounds nice."

Ivy didn't mention that she knew Megan. "I still find things Amelia tucked away, like a hair comb or a page from her journal. We've found most everything of importance, but you never know."

"Unless we start digging up the garden," Bennett said, joking.

Meredith glanced behind her at the house before answering. "Gustav Erickson died in the house. And a few older neighbors told me Amelia's memory was slipping. After her husband passed away, she spent most of her time at her summer house."

Ivy noticed that Meredith didn't really answer her question. Still, she pressed on. "Your aunt must have heard stories, I'll bet. The Ericksons lived such an interesting life."

"Oh, yes," Meredith said, nodding. "Aunt Viola bought the home from the estate after losing her home to a fire. It was offered fully furnished, so that appealed to my aunt. You should see some of the pieces."

"I'd love to," Ivy said, grasping at the chance. "Do you think your aunt would speak to us? We're here only for a short visit. I promise it won't take long."

"I'd have to ask," Meredith said in an apologetic tone. "You two seem nice, and I'd love to show you around. But my aunt is very particular."

Sensing Ivy's disappointment, Bennett caught her hand. "Would you ask her? It would make my wife awfully happy."

"I will, but I'm sure it won't be today," Meredith said.

"Tomorrow would be wonderful," Ivy countered. "We leave in the evening for Spain. If there's any way at all…"

Meredith looked doubtful. "I'm so sorry about your travel woes. Give me your phone number, and I'll see what I can do. My aunt is fastidious about her schedule."

They exchanged numbers, and then Ivy thought of something. "Would you tell your aunt that we've found some of Amelia's personal writings and…" She hesitated, unsure of how this would be received, but maybe Meredith's aunt would be intrigued. "Some even feel they have encountered Amelia's kind spirit."

Beside her, Bennett cleared his throat, and she could feel his gaze on her.

Meredith raised her eyebrows. "I'll certainly let her know that. And I'll call you, regardless of what she says."

Sharing that last bit about Amelia was probably a mistake,

Ivy thought with dismay, but she tried not to let it show. "That's kind of you, and regardless of what she decides, you're both always welcome at the Seabreeze Inn."

The three of them chatted a little longer, and Ivy saw the curtain in an upstairs window part. Meredith's aunt was probably watching them.

"Where are you staying?" Meredith asked.

"Our travel agent reserved a room at the St. Francis Hotel for us," Bennett replied. "We're on our way to check in."

Meredith smiled and nodded. "Did you know Julia Morgan was hired to restore that hotel after the 1906 fire in the city? That's how she got her start as an architect in the city. She had a wide variety of styles but certainly left her mark on the city."

Ivy couldn't help but marvel at the coincidences. "We'll be sure to look for her influence there as well."

Meredith asked, "Have you had lunch yet?"

"We had clam chowder and oysters at Pier 39," Bennett replied. "We love seafood."

"Be sure to have crab or lobster while you're here." Meredith shared a few of her favorite restaurants, some of which were the same ones their chatty taxi driver had recommended.

"If we don't see you again, it's been lovely to meet you," Ivy said to Meredith. "Thank you for sharing, and it's been a pleasure just to see the Ericksons' old home. I'm sorry if we barged in on you."

"Not at all," Meredith said. "I'm glad you stopped to talk. I've been wondering about the Ericksons' summer house. I hope we'll meet again."

Ivy and Bennett thanked Meredith again and left. They hailed a taxi and started for Union Square with their small bags.

"We'll have time to relax and have a leisurely dinner," Bennett said, taking her hand in the back of the cab. "Not quite the dip in the sea we planned, but anywhere with you makes my day."

"I feel the same way," Ivy said. Already, she was feeling more relaxed, even though they'd had to sprint through the airport. As much as she pushed herself to achieve what she needed, there were other situations, like today, when things were out of her control. She could only relax and trust that their trip was unfolding as it should.

Just as they pulled to the front of the St. Francis Hotel, Ivy's phone rang. It was Meredith.

"I wanted to catch you before you checked into your room," Meredith said, sounding rushed. "I just spoke to my aunt. Not only would she like for you to see the house, but she also invited you to stay in the guest wing."

Astonished, Ivy held the phone where Bennett could hear Meredith, too. His face lit up at the offer.

"We'd love that." Ivy was surprised and delighted.

"She is quite interested in what you told me," Meredith said. "This is unlike her, I assure you. She's getting dressed now. How soon can you come?"

Ivy conferred with Bennett, and they decided to turn around. "We could turn around now or wait a little while."

"Come now," Meredith said. "We have a guest room ready, and I can show you around the house. I'm pleased I caught you before you checked in."

Ivy hung up, and Bennett kissed her on the cheek.

"You're a remarkable woman, Ivy Bay." He leaned forward to speak to the taxi driver. "This appears to be a round-trip ride. Take us back to where you picked us up."

Ivy clasped Bennett's hand, pleased to see a smile and a measure of relief on his face. He was looking forward to this visit as much as she was. While they drove back, Bennett called Teresa and asked her to cancel the hotel reservation.

When they arrived at the old home, Meredith greeted them at the front door and invited them inside, where bouquets of roses and lilies scented the foyer. Meredith had changed from her gardening clothes and now wore a crisp Oxford shirt, taupe trousers, and discreet diamond earrings.

"Thank you for your lovely invitation," Ivy said.

Meredith smiled and welcomed them. "My aunt was thrilled you accepted."

"I hope this is not an imposition on her," Bennett said.

"Not at all. She loves having visitors. This way, please. My aunt, Viola Standish, is ready to meet you."

They followed Meredith to a large living room arranged with groupings of sofas and chairs and anchored by a large fireplace. In the background, a soaring song by Andrea Bocelli filled the silence.

An imperious older woman sat in a red-velvet tufted chair, swaying softly to the music.

Meredith approached her. "Aunt Viola, may I present Ivy and Bennett, the couple I told you about. Ivy is the proprietor of the Seabreeze Inn in Summer Beach, the old Las Brisas Del Mar beach house that Amelia and Gustav built."

"I certainly know who they are." Viola impatiently flicked her hand. "They're guests in my home, aren't they? I might forget where I left keys or some such frivolous item, but I remember everything important. I can't say the same for Amelia Erickson; rest her soul."

Viola held herself with an air of authority as she surveyed Ivy and Bennett. She was immaculately dressed in a navy-blue dress with pearls gracing her earlobes and neck, giving her the impression of one born to privilege.

"I'm delighted that you could join us," Viola said. "Now, tell me something interesting about yourselves."

Ivy hardly knew where to start. "My husband Bennett is the mayor of—"

"Summer Beach, yes, yes." Viola leaned forward with an air of expectation. "Better yet, tell me about Amelia. Does she still stroll the garden, too?"

8

When Ivy paled at Viola's questions, Bennett quickly grasped her hand. "I can't say we've seen Amelia there," he said. "But some say her presence has been felt in the primary bedroom, which was hers."

Viola laced her fingers and sat back with satisfaction. "It's as I said, Meredith. Gustav is undoubtedly looking for his wife, don't you think?"

"Or maybe that's why she left for Summer Beach," Bennett said, trying to inject humor into the conversation for Ivy's sake. Whatever she might say, he knew she was still uncomfortable with the concept of otherworldly spirits in residence at the inn. Yet, he liked Viola. She spoke her mind, and she was kind enough to invite them to stay this evening.

"What a good point you make," Viola allowed, continuing in a serious vein. "After all, once a husband dies, you don't expect to see them lingering in the rose garden. Or the library. Although, when I detected his pipe tobacco—"

Glancing at Ivy, Meredith cut in. "Auntie, please don't frighten them. They've only just arrived and might not appreciate your stories yet."

Viola cast a piercing look at her niece. "As I was saying before I was interrupted,

I enjoy a snifter of cognac with old Gustav in the library on the odd occasion. Next time, I shall inform him that I have discovered the whereabouts of his dear Amelia. Although I can't imagine why he wouldn't have looked at their beach house for her. It seems obvious to me." She shrugged as though this was an entirely normal conversation. "But then, he's reticent around strangers."

Looking relieved, Ivy said, "Amelia was a well-respected resident of Summer Beach. I'm sure she was here, too."

Bennett knew his wife was trying to turn the conversation. "Amelia certainly left a legacy in Summer Beach. And here in San Francisco?"

Meredith grasped that thread. "Why, yes. The neighbors still talk about her with reverence. She did so much for the city and the arts here."

Ivy turned to Viola. "Meredith told us that you bought your home fully furnished. When I acquired the beach house, it was almost as Amelia left it. We still use her dishes and flatware to serve guests at the inn. And her silver serving pieces are exquisite."

Meredith turned to her aunt. "You found the same thing here, didn't you?"

"Why, yes, indeed. Most of the antiques here date from the Ericksons' era." Viola turned toward the windows, which framed a view of the Golden Gate Bridge in the distance. "I lost my home in a fire, so I was quite happy to find this."

"I'm so sorry to hear that," Ivy said. "But how did you discover it?"

"My attorney told me of an estate that was finally being settled," Viola replied. "It was the talk of the city for years. There was a clause in Amelia's final instructions about possible heirs, which you're probably aware of. Anyway, the timing was fortuitous for me, and the home was to my liking.

It certainly saved me the trouble of rebuilding or furnishing another home."

"It's such a large place," Ivy said. "You're not afraid to live here alone?"

"I'm hardly alone, my dear. As I mentioned, Gustav is still—"

"My aunt means is that she has many friends who visit, and she hosts quite a few charity functions here." Meredith shot her aunt a withering look of warning.

With a glint of mischief in her eyes, Viola merely shrugged. "As I said, I have Gustav to keep me company."

Listening to the two women, Bennett chuckled. "And I'm sure you keep him company as well."

"I'm glad you understand," Viola said. She turned back to Ivy. "I read that you're a fine artist, too. I'm sure you're eager for a tour."

Bennett squeezed Ivy's hand. He could feel her fairly vibrating with excitement. "You learned an awful lot about us in that article."

"I'm curious by nature," Viola said. "And I appreciate the arts as well as the Ericksons did, although I don't have their expertise. But first, we'll show you to your guest quarters. I understand you've had a rather taxing journey thus far, with a much longer one ahead." She nodded toward two figures who appeared in the doorway.

"I'll show you to your room," Meredith said. "Leon will see to your bags, and Lily will bring a tray of refreshments."

Bennett started to tell the other man he could manage their small carry-on bags, but he understood Viola kept to a certain standard of living. It wasn't his place to question or change that.

Bennett rose and addressed Viola. "Thank you for your hospitality, Mrs. Standish."

"Dear heavens, do call me Viola. We're practically related through the Ericksons, wouldn't you say?" The older woman grasped his hand and squeezed it with surprising strength. "We'll have tea after your tour and dinner at eight o'clock."

Her niece had mentioned that Viola kept a strict schedule, which he respected. This was a different world than Summer Beach, but it had its appeal. He smiled to himself. Maybe he'd even join Gustav in the library later.

"I appreciate your offer of a tour," Ivy said.

She seemed eager to explore, and Bennett was, too.

"Right this way," Meredith said.

She showed them to a suite that was surprisingly light and airy feeling, given the age of the home. The room was decorated in restful shades of white, taupe, and beige. Doors opened onto a private balcony with views of the San Francisco Bay and the Golden Gate Bridge.

On one wall, bookcases anchored each side of a carved marble fireplace. A grand four-poster bed was covered with a snowy white duvet and a bank of pillows. Bennett saw the delight on Ivy's face when she saw it.

"This looks very comfortable," Bennett said.

"It is. Occasionally, I stay in this room. I'm just down the hall if you need anything." Meredith drew the drapery, revealing a broader view. "You can watch the fog roll in from here. It can be quite dramatic. We have an artist friend who loves to paint this view."

Taking it in, Ivy nodded toward a painting as their host spoke. "And is that one of hers?"

"Yes, it is." Meredith gestured to the painting of a fog-shrouded Golden Gate Bridge that hung on one wall. "Every day is a different view."

"Sunsets are like that," Ivy said, approaching the canvas. "No two are ever alike. The artistry of nature is unlimited."

"We have many paintings that the Ericksons acquired here in the house," Meredith said. "They certainly had an eye for art, and Viola is very proud of them."

"Their investments in art were likely based on Amelia's

expertise," Ivy said. "From what we've discovered, Gustav was an investor, though he fully supported his wife's art acquisitions. Did you know her father was head of a museum in Berlin?"

Meredith raised her eyebrows. "Really? I'm not sure Viola knows about that."

"Ivy has quite a lot to share with you and your aunt," Bennett said, clasping Ivy's hand as he spoke.

"This is quite exciting," Meredith said. "I'm looking forward to hearing more about the Ericksons and your home."

The houseman arranged their small bags on a bench at the end of the bed, and Lily delivered a tray with a pitcher of lemonade, fruit, and cheese.

Meredith turned back to them. "Please let me know if there is anything you need. After you're settled, I can give you a tour of the home if you'd like. And later, we can join Viola for tea in the sunroom."

"That sounds marvelous," Ivy said. "Thank you for hosting us here. This is more than we could have imagined. We're so grateful to you."

Meredith smiled as she picked up a leaf that had fallen from a bouquet of roses on an antique desk. "Traveling is often full of surprises, and not all are pleasant. My aunt loves entertaining, so you're welcome here until you can book another flight."

"That's very thoughtful and generous of you and your aunt." Bennett reached for Ivy's hand, which felt soft and feminine in his. "Perhaps another time. We have a honeymoon awaiting us on Mallorca."

He could hardly wait to arrive and have Ivy all to himself. Not that he wasn't enjoying this, too.

"Why, that's wonderful," Meredith said. "That's one of my favorite places. You should visit La Seu, the magnificent cathedral in Palma."

"I believe we're staying quite close," Ivy said. "I've heard the cathedral rivals the great ones in Europe."

"Palma has an extraordinary history. It's such a sunny oasis. You'll love it." Meredith excused herself and shut the door.

The moment the doorknob clicked shut, Bennett swept Ivy into his arms. This was their honeymoon, and he had so much to say to her. He'd thought about it when they were waiting on the tarmac earlier today.

He slid a finger under her chin and tilted her face to his. "What an amazing woman you are. Not only did you manage to have a look inside the house, but now here we are, guests of the owner, thanks to you."

"Can you believe how this day has gone?" Laughing, Ivy kissed him.

He framed her face in his hands and kissed her back. This was the woman he loved. On this trip, he wanted her to understood how much he cared for her. With so much city business on his mind in Summer Beach, he'd sometimes been short with her. He vowed to correct that.

When Bennett pulled away, he tucked her silky, sunstreaked hair behind an ear. "I love you, Ivy, now and forever. Happy honeymoon, my darling."

A radiant smile lit her face. "I fell in love with you on that beach many years ago. I can still remember the song you were playing on your guitar."

So could he. "We've only been married a year, but we've built a good life together," he said, his voice catching on the emotion sweeping through him. "Let's never let that slip away. I watched Tyler and Celia grow apart. They almost didn't make it back to each other. That would devastate me if it happened to us."

Ivy gazed up at him. "We both have a lot of other people and issues to deal with every day. I hate to admit it, but sometimes I feel like I'm serving you the mental leftovers at the end of the day."

"I've felt the same way and am not proud of that." He smoothed a hand over her hair. "But any time with you is a gift. I promised I would cherish and love you every day, and that includes when one or both of us are tired or out of sorts. That's life, too."

After Jackie died, he'd wished for more time with his wife. Everything he had regretted saying or doing—or even omitting—had raced through his mind on a maddening loop for months. He'd sworn to himself he wouldn't make that mistake with Ivy.

"Are you ready for that tour Meredith offered?" he asked.

"I'll freshen up quickly." Ivy looked around the room. "Imagine, this is where Amelia and Gustav lived when they weren't in Summer Beach. I never imagined their home would look like this."

"What did you have in mind?"

"I pictured it as old and dark." She glanced around the room, taking in everything with her practiced eye. "But this is so light, airy, and elegant. This architecture was way ahead of its time."

Bennett thought so, too. "The house wears its age well."

While Ivy was freshening up in the white marble bathroom, Bennett's phone rang. With one glance at the phone, he knew they had a situation.

When Bennett had expressed concern about leaving, Boz had assured him he and his team in the zoning department would handle anything that arose. They wouldn't need his input—unless it was an emergency.

Bennett had appointed another city council member to act in his place, and he had complete confidence in Boz. Still, why was he calling now? Bennett and Ivy hadn't even been scheduled to land on Mallorca for another few hours.

Bennett answered. "What's up, Boz?"

"Teresa told me you had been detained in San Francisco." He cleared his throat. "I realize you're on your honeymoon, so I don't want to keep you. But I thought you would want to know."

So that was it. "And you want to give me a chance to return while I'm still in the country?"

"Wanted to give you the option," Boz said quietly.

Bennett blew out a breath. He wasn't happy to hear this. But more than that, he couldn't do that to Ivy. Unless this were a true emergency, their marriage would suffer for it. Yet Boz wouldn't call unless he thought it important. "I assume Dirk has filed his lawsuit."

"We were expecting that, but the guy is up to something else. I thought you should know."

Nothing would surprise Bennett at this point. He'd encountered plenty of toxic people during his tenure as mayor, not the least of which was Ivy's late husband. That lawsuit had cost the city a lot to defend. First Jeremy, now Dirk. Fortunately, Maeve was serving as the city attorney.

"What's he done now?"

"Something I can't figure out. Unless he wants to spook you."

Bennett chewed his lip. He didn't want anything to come between him and Ivy on this trip. This was their promise to each other before they left.

"Are you sure it can't wait?"

"You can make that call." Boz heaved a sigh on the other end of the line. "Another out-of-towner had been asking about some important parcels."

"A friend of Dirk's?"

"Not sure, but I have my suspicions."

"We've been over this with him," Bennett said, trying to maintain his composure. "He can't turn Summer Beach into a spring break playground. Much as I've enjoyed visiting clubs in South Beach when I was younger, that won't work here."

Mitch had filled him in on Dirk's plan. Just yesterday, he'd learned that one of Dirk's friends had made an offer to another owner on Main Street and planned to file an application for a liquor license. If they had their way, it would be one bar after another and a party every night.

Most residents were against this plan, except for some vocal people who frequented Java Beach. Mitch had promised to report back to him.

Bennett wanted to maintain the integrity of Summer Beach, but he also had to represent what his constituents wanted. That could be a fine line when they were divided.

"Is this about the parcel next to Dirk's? I'm familiar with that situation," Bennett said.

"That's not the one this guy has been looking at." Boz hesitated. "He's asked for details about the parcel that the inn sits on."

Bennett's shoulders tensed. "Ivy's Seabreeze Inn?"

"And Darla's house beside that."

He narrowed his eyes. "You were right to call me, Boz." Whatever Dirk or his cohorts had in mind couldn't be good. At least he was confident that Ivy would never consent to this. "Keep a close eye on this development. And one more thing…"

"Yes, boss?"

"You were right to call. Once I clear my mind on the beach, I'll be able to think more clearly about these issues."

Bennett tapped off the call. Rolling his shoulders, he paced the width of the windows overlooking the San Francisco Bay. Staring at the suspension bridge, he recalled what an innovation it had been when it was built in the 1930s during the Great Depression. He'd studied the history of the Golden Gate Bridge in school. Many people had thought it impossible. The center spanned 3,000 feet, nearly twice the length of any similar bridge in existence. But that hadn't stopped the architect from finding a solution.

And whatever Dirk had in mind wouldn't stop Bennett and others in the community from fighting to maintain the small-town ambiance of Summer Beach.

This was their home.

And that was why he'd been elected. Not to line the pockets of a few but to protect the community they had all worked to create.

He couldn't imagine Summer Beach morphing into what Dirk envisioned. If only residents and Main Street businesses would hold firm to their vision of the community. He thought most would, but he was concerned about old Charlie and his buddies, who spent their time placing minor bets at Java Beach. Charlie owned a small building on Main Street with his sister that they rented to a local surf shop owner.

The building was close to the one Dirk had set his sights on.

Bennett knew Charlie lost a lot of his income at the horse races. The older man might be the weak link, and if Dirk spent any time at Java Beach, he'd know that.

9

"This collection of paintings is exquisite," Ivy said as she and Bennett trailed Meredith through the long, expansive room the other woman referred to as the gallery.

As they walked, Ivy held Bennett's hand, savoring the warmth of his touch. She stole a glance at him and smiled. She was still tingling from his kisses in their room. Even though they'd been detained on their trip, the renewed romance she hoped for on their honeymoon was blossoming. From his expression, she could tell he felt the same.

They would have plenty of time on Mallorca once they arrived. Ivy dragged her attention back to what Meredith was saying. She was interested in the artwork, too.

Bennett grinned and did the same. "It almost seems the house was designed around the art," he said.

"It's interesting you say that," Meredith said. "My aunt found a journal Amelia had kept before and during the construction. She worked with Julia Morgan to accommodate the paintings she had acquired throughout Europe."

Everything about the space was ideal for the artwork, from the ceiling height to the lighting. Ivy noticed discreet, thoughtful touches similar to those in her home. It was evident the same architect designed both houses, even though there were different styles.

"These are from some of the same artists we discovered at the inn." Ivy paused, admiring the artistry of a landscape. "Wassily Kandinsky, I believe. And Paul Klee." She turned to another painting. "And that looks like an early Marc Chagall. All were part of the Degenerate Art exhibition. She must have grouped these together to tell the story. At least, I would have."

Meredith's eyes brightened. "That's correct. Few realize that."

Bennett looked at her with admiration.

Recalling the thrill of uncovering those long-lost master-pieces, Ivy pressed a hand to her heart. "You can't imagine how exciting it was to discover those pieces. And to restore them to their place in history."

"I wish I could have been there for that," Meredith said. "Amelia was quite a woman." She turned to the opposite wall. "Amelia created themes in her presentations, though some-times they're not immediately apparent. See if you can figure out the connection here."

Ivy studied the collection, from which one was missing.

Bennett leaned in. "These are all museum quality. And the one that was here?"

"Aunt Viola lends pieces occasionally," Meredith replied, nodding at the blank space.

"I'm surprised these weren't sold separately from the house," Bennett said. "Collectors would love these paintings."

Meredith folded her arms and nodded. "My aunt wanted to keep the integrity of the home, so one of her conditions of purchase was that the artwork and furnishings would remain."

"That was admirable," Ivy said. And costly, she imagined.

"Viola has long been a fan of Beatrix Potter," Meredith continued. "She visited the house where the artist often worked in England and was impressed that artifacts from the artist's life were still intact in the home. Viola recognized this house as a living museum to Amelia's collection and promotion of certain artists."

"That's very forward-thinking of her," Ivy said.

She gazed at the opposite wall, where the paintings were of delicacy and restraint. They were lighter in tone with superb use of color. All the works featured women and children. In a flash, Ivy knew why they were arranged in this manner.

"This is the women's wall of honor." Ivy walked along, identifying the artist of each work she passed. "Berthe Morisot, Mary Cassatt, Rosa Bonheur. But this last one... whose is that?"

"It's by Virginie Demont-Breton," Meredith replied. "You have an excellent eye for art."

Ivy smiled at the compliment. "It's my passion, although I spend more time tidying guestrooms."

Meredith frowned. "With your talent, that seems a shame."

Ivy felt her face warm, not that she was embarrassed by her physical labor. Yet, she recognized the truth in Meredith's observation. There wasn't anything to be done about that, though. Ivy prided herself on being willing to put in the work.

Following behind her, Bennett reached for her hand. "Ivy really is quite talented. Guests always comment on her seascapes, and she has done several commissions."

Her husband spoke with such pride that Ivy was almost embarrassed. "I enjoy painting. The enclosed sunporch at the inn has the perfect light. I've made it my studio."

Bennett touched her shoulder. "You should spend more time there doing what you enjoy. You're talented, sweetheart. Amelia would have approved."

Meredith raised her brow with interest. "I'd like to see some of your work. I have a contemporary collection in my home."

Ivy appreciated Bennett's confidence in her, though she had to restrain the urge to automatically dismiss her ability as she once did. Instead, she accepted Bennett's compliment.

"My sister included some of my pieces online in one of her blog posts," Ivy said. "I've received a fair amount of interest."

"It's no surprise to me." Bennett beamed at her. "My wife gained a lot of fans at an art show she and her sister held on the grounds of the Seabreeze Inn."

"We've read about that," Meredith said. "Viola had been following events at the inn. I hope you don't think that's odd or forward, but she feels a kinship with you through Amelia and Julia. And your love of art. What a coincidence that you both enjoy art. I couldn't think of two better women to carry on Amelia's legacy."

Ivy glanced at Bennett with a good-natured warning. "Some people think Amelia's spirit is orchestrating these coincidences. But that's all they are, right?"

He nodded back. "Amelia was a forceful woman who took risks and spoke her mind. It wasn't only the artwork she rescued."

Meredith's eyes widened. "We also read about the rooms you discovered in the attic where she harbored important refugees from the war—artists, scientists, and physicians."

"That was Ivy and her sister Shelly who discovered those," Bennett said, squeezing Ivy's hand.

"It was quite by accident," Ivy said with a little laugh. "But we have continued finding clues all over the house and managed to piece them together. Pages from Amelia's journals, handwritten notes or thoughts, a family photograph album—even a small hand-sketched book detailing her trousseau with fabric swatches."

Meredith pressed a hand to her chest. "Oh, that sounds intriguing, and we would love to see all those. I've become quite caught up in their stories, too."

"You're welcome at the inn anytime as my guests," Ivy said.

"The inn has become quite popular this last year," Bennett added, the pride evident in his voice. "Best summer ever, right, sweetheart?"

Ivy turned her face to his and smiled. She appreciated his support of her efforts. "People love visiting Summer Beach."

Meredith smiled at their sweet exchange. "My aunt and I will plan a visit." She glanced at her watch. "It's time for tea. Aunt Viola has been looking forward to hearing your stories about Las Brisas del Mar."

Ivy could have stayed in the room for hours, but she also wanted to talk to Viola. With a last lingering look at the paintings, she followed Meredith.

As they walked through the rooms, Meredith continued her commentary on furnishings and important guests the Ericksons had hosted.

"Amelia was friends with Peggy Guggenheim—they shared their love of art—and Eleanor Roosevelt. So many others have graced these rooms, including the crème de la crème of San Francisco society. The Ericksons were well known for their elegant soirées. I sometimes imagine what it must have been like back then."

They passed a collection of framed black-and-white photos that Ivy assumed were casual shots of the Ericksons' family and friends. People were gathered by what looked like a country home, but she couldn't place the location. She paused to admire them, and then, curious about one of the men in the photograph, she stepped closer.

"Is that…?

A smile lifted Meredith's face. "Amelia with her friends, yes. Do you see anyone familiar?"

"I think so. Isn't that Pablo Picasso? And Joan Miró?"

"They were friends," Meredith replied. "I just love these. Amelia's personality really shines through. You can see how passionate she was about art. She was so supportive of artists. When I look at these, I love to imagine their conversations."

Ivy lingered a moment longer, relishing these rare photographs. Again, she wondered where and when they were taken. Spain, perhaps? Yet Picasso had not returned after the war.

Some photos were of the two artists alone, others were with friends or maybe family members. In one, Amelia appeared to have something dangling from her neck. Ivy leaned in for a better look but couldn't make it out.

"These are fascinating. Do you mind if I snap a few shots?" Ivy asked. "I wonder if some of these people are other artists."

"What an interesting thought." Meredith waved a hand. "Go ahead."

Walking through this home was even better than exploring a museum, Ivy thought. As immersed as she had become in Amelia's saga, this had become personal. Ivy walked in her footsteps every day.

She thought of what she could do for young artists. She could host them at the inn, showcase their pieces for sale, or plan another art show on the grounds and include them. But she couldn't do any of that if she accepted an offer to sell the property. The thought saddened her. Yet, then she would have time to volunteer in the Summer Beach schools' art department. She made a mental note to make that call when she returned.

They walked past a staircase, and Ivy noticed a carved wooden medallion on the sturdy newel post, like the one in her home. She touched the wooden piece for luck, but it shifted a little.

She whipped her hand back. "Oh, did I damage that?"

"It does that," Meredith said. She slipped the carved piece back into position, covering a gouged space.

When they entered the sunroom, Ivy noted several sculptures and cataloged those in her mind. A spectacular view of the Palace of Fine Arts loomed through a bank of windows.

Viola rose to greet them. "I trust my niece gave you a proper tour," she said, grasping Ivy's hands.

"Her tour was quite informative," Ivy said, greeting the older woman. "Meredith told us how you insisted on keeping the art and furnishings intact with the house."

"My home and family heirlooms might have gone up in flames," Viola said with a trace of sadness. "But that was replaced with an opportunity to share this home with the community and ensure Amelia Erickson's legacy is preserved. She did much for the city by raising money for public buildings and parks. She also helped establish a women's bank to lend money specifically to women for business startups and home mortgages—loans they couldn't get on their own in those days. Amelia deserves a museum of her own someday."

"That sounds like a noble effort." Ivy ached to ask Viola why she refused to talk to Megan, but she would wait until the opportunity presented itself.

Viola gestured to an antique settee. "Please sit down, and I'll tell you more about what I have planned." She nodded toward the tea service on a low table between them. "Oolong or Earl Grey tea?"

The aromas were so inviting it was hard for Ivy to choose. "Oolong, please."

Meredith leaned forward, "May I help you, Auntie?"

"I enjoy serving my guests." Though her hand wavered a little, Viola poured the tea with a practiced movement. Meredith served small tea sandwiches of cucumber, salmon, and chicken salad.

"What a lovely tea service," Ivy remarked. She lifted a delicate, gold-rimmed teacup to her lips. Although she had some lovely pieces from Amelia at home, the Ericksons had entertained in a far grander style here.

"These are part of Amelia's Meissen collection," Viola

said. "Some of her Sevres porcelain pieces are there." She nodded toward a glass-faced display cabinet. "The Ericksons had exquisite taste, and I enjoy sharing their treasures with others who appreciate them. I'm just a custodian who happened to be passing through."

"My aunt is being modest," Meredith said. "She's a dedicated preservationist."

Viola shrugged. "Maybe an amateur one, but I would like to have a proper historical preservationist continue the catalog I began. It's quite an undertaking."

"And what will you do with it all?" Ivy asked, still waiting for the right moment.

"Well, I won't live forever, so I've arranged to leave this house in a trust. In that way, it can be supported in perpetuity to benefit the community and serve as a museum."

"What an intriguing thought," Ivy said, ruminating on that.

Viola's voice gained strength as she spoke. "So many women's accomplishments have been lost to history. We only just discovered Amelia's involvement in the women's bank. And that has inspired me." With a glance at Meredith, she hesitated.

Her niece patted her arm. "Go on, Auntie."

"Meredith has her own life, so we would need someone, perhaps a team, who might take on such an overwhelming task. We're planning for the future."

Meredith nodded. "This is Viola's passion, but I'd rather spend my time in the garden."

"So would my sister," Ivy said. "Have you photographed the paintings and antiques yet?"

"I have some that were taken for appraisals and insurance purposes," Viola replied. "Occasionally, a university student visits to study and catalog items, but there is still so much more to unpack. There are crates in the cellar I haven't opened."

Ivy was intrigued at the thought. What else might be hidden away here?

"They were quite the collectors," Bennett said. "Are many people in the city interested in the Ericksons' history?"

"I believe so," Viola said, sipping her tea. "Their lives intersected many other notable people of the era."

"Wouldn't it be interesting if a documentary could be made," Ivy said, floating the idea. "So many more people could see a film. That could increase interest and support for a museum."

Viola grew quiet for a moment, and Meredith leaned forward. "Aunt Viola doesn't like to be filmed."

"It's not my story," Viola said, correcting her. "Why would anyone want to see me on the screen?" She shook her head.

Maybe Megan hadn't made that clear to her, Ivy thought. Then again, Megan might have mentioned that, thinking that would interest Viola. "I have a friend who is a documentary filmmaker. She has a keen interest in Amelia's story."

"Someone called a few months ago," Meredith said.

Viola pursed her lips. "I doubt we'll hear from that one again."

"You were a little short with her, Auntie," Meredith said.

Viola sighed and looked away. "Well, what's done is done."

"That wouldn't have been Megan Calloway, would it?" Ivy asked.

Viola looked up in surprise. "Why, yes. Do you know her?"

"Actually, I know her quite well," Ivy replied. "Megan has been researching Amelia's story behind the inn—the Las Brisas del Mar era, she calls it. If you would like, I could introduce you. She would understand your concern."

"She's passionate about her projects, but she's not what I would call a pushy Hollywood type," Bennett added. "She and her husband bought a home in Summer Beach because they like the slower pace of our little town."

Ivy tucked her hand into Bennett's in silent support.

Meredith touched her aunt's shoulder. "Perhaps we could meet Megan when we go to Summer Beach."

Viola ran a finger around the edge of a saucer in thought.

"Or she could visit you here," Ivy added as if the idea had only just occurred to her. She didn't want to seem too forward.

"Since you know her, I might reconsider," Viola said slowly.

Meredith gave Ivy the briefest of nods, then quickly changed the subject. "You said you've found some of Amelia's journals. Did she write anything interesting?"

Ivy picked up on that and swiftly steered the conversation. She and Meredith could talk later. Ivy told Viola and Meredith about the fragmented writings she and Shelly had discovered.

"By the time Amelia was in mostly full-time residence at Las Brisas del Mar, her memory was declining, so we've found many odd things tucked away in little places. They form a narrative to her life that we're beginning to understand."

Viola leaned forward with interest. "What kind of items?"

Ivy thought for a moment. It was difficult to choose because they'd found so many. "Here's an example. Of course, you've read about the masterpieces we discovered behind a concealed entry to the lower level, but we also found Amelia's construction supply receipts and lists. From those and corresponding historical events, we reconstructed what we believe to have been her motivation."

"That was the part I wondered about," Meredith said. "Why go to so much trouble?"

"That mystified us, too." Ivy put down her tea. "But you see, after the attack on Pearl Harbor, Japanese submarines were spotted off the coast of California. Within the month, Amelia bought supplies, stashed her valuables on the lower level, and used that construction material to conceal the entry to the lower level. After what she'd been through in Europe, it was natural for her to believe the California coast might be attacked."

"Fascinating," Viola said. "That line of reasoning certainly makes sense. She closed this house during that time, although later, she reopened it to give shelter to nurses and other women assisting the war effort in the Pacific. The hotels were full of young men and women reporting for duty and their loved ones seeing them off."

They chatted more, and Ivy enjoyed learning more about this phase of the Ericksons' lives in San Francisco. Viola reached for a thick padded album to share photos of events and fundraisers from that era. Ivy was fascinated with the details.

The conversation flowed until Viola called for a break before dinner. Realizing this was a great deal of activity and conversation for the older woman, Ivy and Bennett excused themselves.

After a stroll around the neighborhood, which filled Ivy with ideas for projects that she captured in photos, they returned to the house.

Bennett placed another call to Boz, and she checked in with Shelly and Poppy about the inn. She spoke to Sunny about her classes, which were going well. As much as Ivy loved her family, she hoped they could disengage with Summer Beach once they arrived in Spain. Unless it was an emergency, of course.

Immediately, she cast that thought from her mind. All would be well, she told herself.

While Bennett spoke with the city office, Ivy moved onto the balcony to wait. Bennett's continuing workload was concerning, but he had assured her that Boz and other council members had matters well in hand. They would have their honeymoon, he promised.

She had to trust him on that.

As the sun sank to the horizon, a golden, ethereal light

illuminated the iconic Golden Gate Bridge. She folded her arms and stood in awe, framing the view in her mind. The sounds of the city receded, and she imagined what this view was like so many decades ago. Just then, something in the garden below caught her eye. Peering down, she spied shadows shifting between the trees and shrubs, but it was only the breeze off the ocean rustling the leaves.

Ivy could understand how people might mistake those for wandering spirits. With a slight shiver, she turned back to the view and waited.

After concluding his conversation, Bennett followed her outside. He paused, lifting his phone to take a photo and showed it to her. "For your inspiration."

Bennett did that a lot for her. She looked at the shot. Her silhouette appeared dark against the fiery sky.

"If only I had time to paint more."

"You could, you know. Hire more help for the inn."

Ivy thought about the phone call she'd taken. What would her life be like if she had all day to paint scenes like this? The thought seeded in her mind. No guests, no plumbing problems, no peeling paint.

Quiet. Like this.

Bennett glanced at his watch. "We should join our hosts for dinner."

"I wish they would have let us take them out." Still, Ivy understood. Viola moved slowly, hiding what might be arthritic pain.

"Viola seems pleased to have us," Bennett said.

Indeed, Viola's face lit with interest over dinner as she listened to their stories of the house in Summer Beach. And when she shared her findings, she became animated.

At a break in the conversation, Bennett excused himself to use the facilities, and Ivy turned back to Viola and Meredith.

She was curious about this house and wondered if Amelia

had the same habits when she lived here as when she was in residence at Las Brisas del Mar.

"Have you found anything unusual in this house?" Ivy ventured.

"Nearly everything here is unusual," Viola said.

Ivy's eyes rested on a small box in her sightline. It sat on a shelf, illuminated with a soft light, as were other important works of art.

"That's an exquisite box," Ivy said. It was made of a highly grained wood with what looked like gold trim and semi-precious cabochon stones. "Is that decorated with real lapis and malachite?"

"Why, yes. And high-content gold fittings. It's interesting that you should ask about that. That is one of the oldest pieces of Amelia's here in the house. That was a gift from her parents before her wedding. Supposedly, that was part of her trousseau."

"Many young women today don't even know what the word *trousseau* means," Ivy said, recalling a conversation she'd once had with Shelly. "How did you learn about its history?"

"That's one of the items we found described in one of her early journals. Unfortunately, it's locked, so we've never opened it."

Ivy was intrigued. "Do you think there's anything in it?"

Meredith shook her head. "We gave it a good shake and couldn't hear anything rattling around—no jewels or gold coins, I'm afraid."

Viola leaned forward, resting her wrists on the edge of the table. "All this comes with a price of maintenance. Living in a large, old home has its challenges, especially one with such treasures. When my security system malfunctions, it gives me such a fright. And often, I see workmen more in a week than I see friends. How do you manage, dear?"

"My sister and I have learned basic repair skills, and my brother is a contractor, although he's quite busy on large commercial projects." Ivy let out a little sigh and lowered her voice so that Bennett wouldn't overhear her. "I love the old Las Brisas del Mar, but I've thought of selling the property because of the maintenance it needs. Roof, plumbing, electrical. Everything is so expensive."

Meredith's expression changed, her eyes widening in surprise. "But would you stay otherwise?"

"It's our home, so I would like to," Ivy replied. "I have the same sense of responsibility to preserve it that your aunt has."

"That's understandable, my dear," Viola said. "It's a calling, a mission to preserve the past to educate future generations."

"Why, yes," Ivy said. "I love sharing the history of Las Brisas del Mar with the community. We once hosted an art show on the grounds. A friend funds the music program at the school, and the children practice and perform at the inn. We enjoy offering the house for community events and fundraisers."

"It sounds like a real centerpiece of the community," Meredith said, glancing at her aunt.

"It is, but I must be practical," Ivy said softly. "It's always been a financial stretch for me, which is why my sister and I transformed it into an inn."

Usually, Ivy wouldn't share so much. Still, she was comfortable confiding in Viola and Meredith, much like strangers at the inn confided in her.

She looked between the two women. "I haven't told my husband yet, but an investment company is prepared to make a sizable offer. Perhaps selling would be the right thing to do before the property develops serious problems that I can't afford to repair."

Viola raised her brow in surprise. "That certainly requires serious consideration. But what a shame. You seem so well-suited to care for the property. And what a benefit to the community it is."

Meredith nodded in understanding. "Is this investment company planning on restoring it?"

"I honestly don't know," Ivy replied. "The man who called me didn't answer that directly. He only mentioned it would make a good luxury destination."

"I see." Viola pressed her lips together in a thin line.

Ivy interpreted the other woman's silence as disapproval, but she didn't have Viola's money. Ivy had to be pragmatic.

Bennett returned, ambling into the room. "What a beautiful home. You keep it up so well. I know that's a challenge."

"We were just discussing something along those lines," Viola said. "Do you enjoy living in such an old, historic home?"

"I grew up in Summer Beach," Bennett replied, his voice thick with emotion. "I've loved that property for years, though I never thought I'd live there." He reached out to stroke Ivy's hand.

"My late husband is the one who acquired it," Ivy explained. "Unbeknownst to me, that is. He bought it to tear down and build a new resort with his girlfriend."

"Oh, dear." Meredith pressed a hand to her chest. "You have been through a lot."

Ivy shook her head, making light of Meredith's sympathy. "It's true, those were difficult times, but I believe life works out for the best. I never would've connected with Bennett, and I never dreamed I would be an innkeeper, especially of such an incredible property." She shared the story with the two women.

When she was finished, Viola's eyes gleamed. "I knew you had gumption when I read the news story about your discovery. Not many people would return such artistic masterpieces to their rightful owners. You have a noble spirit, my dear."

Ivy dipped her head, feeling a little embarrassed that she might have overshared. "I just did what I had to do, that's all."

"You'd be surprised how many people don't," Meredith said.

Viola brightened as they were finishing dessert—a sublime Pavlova the chef had prepared. "Would you like to see the library next?"

"I'd love to," Ivy replied.

After dinner, the small party made their way to the wood-paneled library. Inside, leather and fabric-bound volumes filled shelves that soared to the ceiling. A tall, wheeled ladder provided access to the upper reaches.

"This is incredible," Ivy said, pausing in the doorway. "Have you read many of these books?"

"I've consulted many concerning the art collection." Viola motioned to a section that housed a collection of art tomes. "But there are many other topics. Their intellectual interests were broad."

"I see." Ivy perused the titles, feeling a kinship with the Ericksons across the years. "Painting, sculpture, antiquities."

"History and science are over here," Bennett said, motioning to another wall.

"Some of those are inscribed to Gustav," Viola said. "He must have had a great interest in such things. He compiled quite a collection of titles on the Roman Empire and astronomy."

"Here's a volume on the Hale Telescope," Bennett said, opening a book. "That's at the Palomar Observatory near San Diego. The facility took years to build, but it's still used today." He turned the pages with care. "It appears to have been written as it was being built."

"And here's a three-volume set of *Jane Eyre* by Charlotte Brontë." Ivy touched one of the leather-clad books with reverence. She recalled reading the Brontë sisters when she was younger.

"This room is full of literary treasures," Viola said. She gestured towards several red leather volumes festooned with gilt borders and lettering. They sat in a place of prominence on a book stand. "Look at these beauties by John James Audubon, *Birds of America*."

A shiver coursed through Ivy. Even without knowing anything about them, she knew books of that age and quality were exceedingly rare. To her, the room fairly vibrated with the treasures of history. She wondered if Amelia might have tucked away anything here.

"Amelia and Gustav had wide-ranging interests," Meredith said. "And they impacted so many lives in the aid they extended."

Viola nodded. "We walk in their footsteps, preserving their accomplishments. Many others build on what they supported in their time."

"Makes me question how we spend our time," Meredith said.

"You do quite a lot, my dear." Viola placed a hand on her niece's shoulder and said to Ivy, "Meredith volunteers at a hospital several days a week. And that one person you support and help to heal might go on to touch millions. We don't always know."

"That's so true." Ivy had been listening thoughtfully to the exchange. "One Christmas, a young man appeared at our inn. As it turned out, Nick's parents had been among those Amelia had given shelter to at her beach house. Now, he's committed his life to doing important work in the medical field."

"Amelia's actions came full circle," Bennett said, joining the conversation. "Nick gives back to humanity every day. A small pebble of assistance can ripple through the world in a positive manner. Or even in a small community."

Watching Bennett, Ivy understood the meaning behind his words. His work on behalf of residents had a more significant impact on those who lived in Summer Beach than one might imagine. Being a mayor wasn't just a job to him; it was his calling.

"I suppose you're right," Meredith said, smiling at the thought.

"My niece is too modest," Viola said. "She also helps me host nonprofit fundraising events here. It seemed silly to be rattling around this large home by myself. Why should these groups be paying exorbitant fees for event space when I can offer all this for free—and make sure more money goes where it's needed?"

"It sounds like you're carrying on Amelia's work," Ivy said, acknowledging the older woman.

Viola took another book from a shelf and handed it to Ivy. "Since your sister enjoys gardening, you might like to share this with her. I can send it to you to save carrying it on your trip."

"Oh, I couldn't take this." Ivy had told Viola how Shelly had renovated the surrounding gardens. "It's part of the collection."

Viola pursed her lips. "Please, it's a gift. Something to remember your unexpected trip by."

They spent a little more time in the library before Ivy noticed that Viola's eyelids were growing heavy.

"We have a long day tomorrow," Ivy said. "Bennett and I should rest, but we've really enjoyed your hospitality."

"I have a prior commitment tomorrow, but since your flight doesn't leave until the evening, you might enjoy visiting Sausalito," Viola said. "I would suggest the Palace of Fine Arts, but it will be closed."

"We'll have to return for that," Bennett said.

"Indeed," Viola said. "You've just missed Sausalito's marvelous art festival. However, you could visit some of the galleries. It's a charming town."

Ivy wondered if Bennett would be up for that. "At the art show we hosted at the inn, I met a couple who owns a gallery there." They had taken a couple of her seaside paintings and wanted more. Those had sold, yet she hadn't had time to do any more for them.

Bennett put his arm around her. "I remember. Let's do that."

Suddenly, Ivy wasn't so sure. She was slightly embarrassed that she had put other duties before her art. Just like when she'd been married before. Only this time, it wasn't her husband and daughters requiring her full attention. It was the inn and its guests.

10

The following day, Ivy rose early to watch the fog gather over the water. The rising sun was the conductor of the orchestra of birdsong that rose in the air.

Standing on the balcony, she tugged a terrycloth robe Viola provided against the mist. Although it was cooler here than in Southern California, she relished the brisk morning and the view across the San Francisco Bay to Marin County.

She heard Bennett behind her and turned.

He wrapped his arms around her and nuzzled her neck. "Good morning, my love. Sleep well?"

"Always with you." That was true. Knowing that he was resting beside her was calming. No matter what had happened during the day, his steady breathing was reassuring, and she usually fell asleep with her hand on his chest or shoulder.

"The Lyon Street Steps are nearby. Want to join me for a workout? It's downhill first."

Ivy's first inclination was to decline, but this was their honeymoon. She didn't need to prepare breakfast for guests or lead the morning beach walk. "As long as I can take it slow on the way back up."

Meredith had told them the steps were equal to about

eight flights of stairs with more than three hundred steps. One at a time shouldn't be too bad. And they both had shorts and T-shirts in their carry-on bags.

Bennett grinned. "Let's go."

Even downhill was taxing, but Ivy kept pace with Bennett, though she suspected he was taking his time with her. Nevertheless, she appreciated it. The landscaping surrounding the steps was lovely, too, with well-kept shrubs and trees.

"It's a good place to train," Bennett said, motioning toward groups of people climbing together.

"Now you tell me."

"We can take a taxi back if you want."

"No, I can do it. Slowly, that is." She led the way, single file, as others raced down beside them to get in their morning workouts. She was tempted but kept her pace. The view over the San Francisco Bay was astounding, and the grand old Victorian homes they passed were quaint reminders of the city's history.

At the bottom, on Vallejo Street, stood a large piece of public art—a golden heart with a bird in flight. The sight of it filled her heart with appreciation.

They continued to the Presidio, a park area filled with trees and trails once used by the Spaniards that dated back a few hundred years.

"I love all the history in San Francisco," she said, taking deep breaths as they continued their brisk walk. "This is a beautiful way to experience the city. But you can go ahead if you want. I'm slowing you down."

"You're doing great," Bennett said. "I don't have to run every morning, not that I have been. This is a good way to ease back into it."

They bought coffee from a vendor and took their time enjoying it before returning to the steps. Once they began the steep flight, they climbed methodically and rested as they went.

When they reached the top, Ivy turned to look down and catch her breath. "Wow. My heart is pounding. Just look at how far we've come."

"We have, haven't we?" Bennett said, embracing her. "I think about that almost every day."

"So do I," Ivy said, laughing while she kissed him. She was beginning to love these unexpected detours on their trip, which made them even more fun. Who needed a to-do list on a holiday?

"Life never ceases to amaze me," he said, his voice rich with emotion. "You were that cute girl on the beach, and I was just some guy with a guitar. We had a little crush, and then you were gone before we'd even got to know each other. Who knew we'd get a second chance after all those years?"

Ivy clasped her hands around his neck, enjoying this moment. "I'm glad we did. You were the last thing I expected to come into my life after Jeremy died. I had a lot of issues to work through, and I know it was tough on you, too. Thanks for being so patient with me."

"I wasn't going anywhere." He caught her hand, and they began to walk. "Nor do I have any plans to. I love our life, Ivy Bay."

"Even with guests traipsing through our lives every week?"

"It's what you love to do," Bennett said. "And we meet a lot of interesting people we wouldn't otherwise."

"Like the skinny-dipping sorority sisters?"

Bennett laughed. "And drunken actors you have to rescue from the pool."

"And then Rowan returned and nearly burned the place down at Christmas," Ivy said, relishing their memories of Rowan Zachary and his son's wedding at the inn. "But what if I weren't an innkeeper?"

Bennett wrinkled his brow. "I realize situations change. If that's what you wanted, I would support your choices."

"I didn't set out to run an inn," Ivy pointed out. "I fell into the role through sheer desperation. I had to make a living, and teaching art didn't pay the bills."

"You're an artist first," Bennett said, nodding. "I understand. And I might not always be the mayor of Summer Beach. Would you still love me then?"

"You know I would."

"Same difference then. I might not be elected for the next term."

Ivy looked up in alarm. "I can't imagine who would do a better job than you."

"If I've done my job training others, that should be a sizable number. Some might not think I'm progressive enough for Summer Beach. Or maybe the small-town feeling doesn't appeal to them."

"I like it the way it is. If people want something glitzy and loud, they can move."

He chuckled and kissed her cheek. "You seem to have something on your mind lately. Want to talk about it?"

She did, but not right now. The conversation with Milo about the offer on the inn could wait. Besides, she hadn't received it in writing. She assumed he would email or mail it to her.

"I can't think of anything more important than breakfast," she replied. "I'm starving."

"Meredith asked us to join them." He paused and hugged her. "But we should hurry. I think there's room for two in that shower. Imagine the time we can save."

Ivy lifted her chin. "You act like you're on a honeymoon or something."

Bennett grinned. "We've waited a long time for this trip."

"Then let's make it worthwhile," Ivy said, laughing.

AFTER HAVING breakfast with Meredith and Viola, Ivy and Bennett set off for Sausalito on a ferry across the San Francisco Bay. On the way, Ivy called the gallery and left a message that she would arrive soon.

Standing at the bow of the vessel, Ivy turned her face into the breeze. The sea spray cooled her face, and her hair whipped around her shoulders, but she didn't care. Bennett stood behind her with his arms wrapped around her.

"Want to start at the gallery?" he asked.

She hesitated before answering. As much as she dreaded facing the owners who'd sent numerous emails asking for more of her paintings, it would be better to get that awkward meeting out of the way. Her mother had already chastised her for not following up with them.

"Sure, why not?" Ivy tried to sound flippant, but from the way Bennett looked at her, he saw right through her.

"What's bothering you?"

Ivy sighed. "I haven't had time to do any more work for the gallery, although I'd like to. I feel like I've failed them."

"You mean, you've failed yourself."

"Hey," she cried, a little irritated that he knew her so well. "That hurt."

"I didn't mean it quite like that," Bennett said, smoothing a hand along her back. "The things that mean the most to us also bother when we don't produce as we'd like."

"That's a better way of putting it." She brushed her hair back and held it with her hand against the breeze. "I guess I have felt like I failed myself. I only want to do my best work."

"That's understandable."

Ivy leaned against the railing, enjoying the brisk sea spray. The morning clouds had parted, and the sun shimmered off the chilly ocean waves. Behind them, the glittering view of San Francisco was breathtaking. Ivy took a few photos to remember the view.

Soon, the ferry passed Angel Island before pulling alongside the Sausalito dock, where they disembarked.

Near the water's edge to one side, Ivy marveled at an inn

with guest rooms that jutted over the tides. They made their way toward the main street and Gallery Nicole.

Inside, a woman with silvery blond hair wore what looked like a handprinted silk tunic. She looked up from her desk. "Ivy Bay, what a wonderful surprise to see you. How are your parents?"

"Sailing around the world," Ivy replied.

Nicole's eyebrows shot up. "Seriously?"

"They crossed the Pacific and will soon depart from Sydney."

"Oh, my goodness," Nicole said with wonder. "I want to be them when I retire."

"Don't we all," Bennett said.

Ivy quickly introduced them, and they chatted while Nicole showed them some of the gallery's impressive new pieces.

"We still have room for your work," Nicole assured her. "We have a lot of requests for beach scenes, and yours capture a unique perspective. If you have anything ready, I have a client who has just bought a home here and would love your work."

A sickening feeling gathered in Ivy's chest. "I haven't had the time to paint much this past year. The inn keeps me so busy."

Nicole's expression fell. "What a shame, but I know that's also important to you"

"We're trying to find a solution," Bennett said quickly. "Painting is Ivy's first love."

Was it still? She'd almost forgotten how she could disappear into her work for hours, but she simply didn't have that sort of time anymore. An emergency often called her away, even if it was only a leaky faucet in a guest room. She lacked the focus she needed.

With Sunny in school and Shelly working fewer hours because of Daisy, Ivy and Poppy ran the day-to-day business.

Poppy still had marketing clients she visited in Los Angeles, so she wasn't always available.

"This is a rare trip for us," Ivy said, smiling at Bennett. "Actually, it's our honeymoon."

"Congratulations." Nicole clasped her hands. "Thank goodness you found time for that."

Ivy felt her face color. "Actually, it's a little more than a year overdue." She told Nicole about their change of travel plans. "I almost didn't call you because I felt bad about not delivering anything new."

Nicole waved her hand. "No worries; I'm used to dealing with artists. The muse can be a fickle creature."

Ivy shook her head. "The only thing I need my muse to do is change the bed linens."

"I'd like that, too," Nicole said, laughing. Just then, the front door opened, and a couple strolled in. "There's my next appointment," she said, nodding toward them. "But whenever you have more pieces for the gallery, give me a call."

After Nicole left them, Ivy turned to Bennett. "That wasn't as bad as I'd thought."

Bennett put his arm around her. "Often, we blow things out of proportion in our minds. Feel better?"

"I do, but I should get back to painting."

"You will."

"I don't know when I'll find the time. Or rather, the uninterrupted time." She took a breath, but this wasn't the place to tell him about the offer.

"We'll figure it out," Bennett said.

"I know we will." And he'd promised to support her decision. Still, if she sold the property, there would be no going back. When she and Bennett talked about the inn earlier, she realized how much she loved it, too. It was a dichotomy in her mind.

With a curious look, Bennett clasped her hand. "Hey, there. If you're still with me, are you ready for lunch?"

Ivy shook herself back to the present. "Sure. What did you have in mind?"

"I know of a great fresh seafood restaurant a few doors down." Bennett edged toward the door. "And, until we're reunited with our luggage, we'll need at least another shirt for the trip. There's a clothing shop next door."

Following, Ivy glanced back, taking in the work of other artists who undoubtedly had busy lives as well. Torn between two loves, she left the gallery with some reluctance.

She recalled her mother telling her that distance often provided perspective on problems. Maybe she would find her solution on Mallorca.

*a*fter returning in the afternoon on the ferry to San Francisco, Bennett called to arrange a car to the airport. He didn't want anything to deter them from this flight.

In Sausalito, Bennett had bought a knit shirt, and Ivy had chosen a casual knit dress she could travel in. Barring any other unforeseen calamities, they would spend the night on the flight, arrive in Frankfurt in the morning, and reach Mallorca in the afternoon.

And then, he could breathe easier. Unless he received another call from Boz.

"We'll have a light supper on the terrace," Meredith had suggested when they returned. "You'll need a good meal before your flight. I understand the airline food has become nearly inedible."

Bennett had to agree, yet he didn't want to inconvenience them. Still, Viola insisted.

Now, they sat on the terrace overlooking the San Francisco Bay, talking about their day trip to Sausalito. Viola had arranged for a selection of local foods her chef had prepared, and they were enjoying a leisurely meal of Dungeness crab with cioppino and seasonal vegetables.

"When you return," Viola began, "you'll have to allow more time to explore San Francisco and the surrounding area. Then, you could continue to Sonoma and Napa Valley."

Bennett glanced at Ivy, who had a faraway look in her eyes. Something was on her mind. He could only surmise that she didn't want to talk about it yet. He clasped her hand at the table. "Someday, we'd like that, wouldn't we, Ivy?"

Jolted from her thoughts, Ivy replied, "Oh, yes. Yes, of course."

"And we hope to see you in Summer Beach soon," Bennett added to Viola and Meredith.

Viola shook her head. "I don't know. Traveling is so difficult these days. Not like it used to be. Why, we used to dress in our finest outfits to fly. Today—"

"I'll make sure of it," Meredith interjected. "I could drive, or we could take the train."

"Or my friend Betsy can come with us," Viola said, brightening. "She and her husband have their own plane. There, it's settled. I'll call her this week, and we'll make arrangements."

Meredith laughed. "Oh, Auntie. You're so spoiled."

"Yes, and I've earned that right," Viola said. "When I was young, I wielded a hammer alongside your father and my husband." She turned back to Bennett and Ivy. "The next time we meet, I'll tell you how my grandmother came to San Francisco as a servant and worked her way up through society."

"We look forward to hearing that." Bennett smiled, and he knew it would be another memorable story.

"We'll welcome you to the inn," Ivy said. "And I'll arrange for you to meet Megan Calloway. She'll be thrilled to talk to you."

"I'm quite looking forward to it now," Viola said.

Looking to Ivy and Bennett, Meredith smiled. "You've

given my aunt something new to look forward to. I'm so glad you stayed with us."

"We apologize for the short notice," Bennett said.

Viola waved her hand. "Think nothing of it, really. What's the use of having a home this size unless you can fill it with friends? Why, that would be a lonely existence, indeed. After Gustav passed away, I understand why Amelia didn't want to remain. There are so many reminders of him here."

They continued the conversation until it was time for Bennett and Ivy to leave for their flight.

Viola kissed Ivy on the cheek. "We are united through our shared history of the Ericksons, especially Amelia. I believe there is a reason each of us ended up with one of her beloved homes and possessions. We're stewards of history."

"And you're both so generous of spirit," Meredith added. "I can hardly wait to visit Las Brisas del Mar. I mean, your Seabreeze Inn."

"And we look forward to having you," Ivy said, giving them each a hug before they left.

If Bennett didn't know Ivy so well, he wouldn't have noticed the trace of discomfort in her expression or the way she blinked back her emotion.

AFTER ARRIVING at the San Francisco airport, they were just about to enter the terminal when Bennett's phone rang. He started to turn it off, and then he saw the number of City Hall light up the screen.

"Sorry," Bennett said, shaking his head. "I have to take this."

"I understand," Ivy replied, although she drew her brow in concern.

He dropped his carry-on bag on the ground and tapped his phone. "Bennett here."

Nan's voice floated through the phone line. "Oh, Mr.

Mayor, I'm so glad I caught you. We have a situation here, and it's gotten out of control. Boz didn't want to disturb you, but I knew you'd want to know about this new development."

"You're all working late?" Bennett pinched the bridge of his nose.

Nan hesitated. "We're working through solutions, so I thought I'd call you."

"Is it the lawsuit?"

"Oh, no. It's much worse. That horrible Dirk made an announcement. The council had to call an emergency meeting."

Before he could answer, Ivy's phone buzzed.

"Hi, Poppy. What's up?"

Bennett saw the expression on Ivy's face change. "No, I hadn't heard," she said. "*Every* room is booked?"

Passing a hand over his forehead, Bennett asked, "Nan, what's going on?"

"Dirk announced a new spring break blowout in Summer Beach with a large tequila sponsor." Nan sounded hysterical, and her words tumbled out in a harried avalanche.

Bennett gripped the phone. "He did *what?*"

"He arranged to have it announced on social media by some influencers—whoever they are," she said, her voice wavering. "Calls are pouring in with young people trying to reserve rooms and secure lodging. They're mostly college students. All the inns and seasonal rentals are booked up. Summer Beach doesn't have that many rooms, so we're flooded with calls from people complaining that they can't find lodging. I can't keep up with the phones."

"Slow down and take a breath." He'd never heard Nan this rattled and was concerned about her. In the background, other phones were ringing.

"I'm trying," she said. "The council is alarmed because Dirk is projecting upwards of fifty thousand kids pouring into Summer Beach. We don't have the police, fire, or medical facilities to handle them. This is a disaster in the making."

"He had no right to do this. He needs to apply for a permit like anyone else, and we have a limit on attendees." Or they should, he thought. To his knowledge, no one had ever had an event of this size.

Bennett suspected Dirk planned this announcement for when he would be out of town. It was a strategy to pressure the city for approval. If they denied his request, he would claim damages.

"The council members need to talk to you right away. They want to issue a statement first thing in the morning."

"Can you put me through to Maeve?" He needed to run this past the city attorney.

"She's on her way here and on the phone. I'll have her call you right away. And the television stations are calling to ask what we think of all this." Nan's voice caught. "Oh, I wish you were here. This is such a disaster."

Bennett rubbed his jaw. There was still time to turn around and go back to Summer Beach. He glanced at Ivy, whose eyes were round as she listened on her phone.

Nan sounded like she was near a breakdown. "We can't let this happen, can we?"

"Listen to me, Nan. You don't have to answer every call. It's after business hours, so let them go to voice mail. Tomorrow, get some help if you can. See if Boz can spare someone to help answer phones."

"I can't imagine that many people in the town and on the beach," Nan said. "I've seen those crowded spring break videos. They'll destroy the beach, trample people's property, and drive away other visitors. Some businesses would benefit, but I don't think it will be worth it to the city. The kids certainly won't be pouring into Antique Times."

Bennett wasn't sure what they could do until he spoke to Maeve. This was a situation he'd never had to face before.

"Nan, this is months away. We'll handle this."

"But the calls…"

"Just let them go to voice mail and try not to worry about it," he said, his anger against Dirk rising. "Have Maeve call me right away."

Bennett hung up and blew out a frustrated breath. "What a jerk." He wanted to call Dirk and give him a piece of his mind, but he had to handle this properly. Dirk was playing them. He'd set this up to create the most chaos possible.

Ivy hung up and turned to him. "Poppy just filled me in. People are trying to book rooms for eight or ten people. They're willing to sleep on the floor. It sounds like a disaster, especially for our plumbing. Is this really going to happen?"

"We'll do everything we can to stop it." He had a sinking feeling as he glanced at an electronic board where flights and boarding gates were flashing. Mallorca seemed to be growing farther and farther away.

Ivy followed his gaze. "We're not going to make it onto the flight, are we?"

"We will try." Seething, Bennett clenched his teeth.

"I know you have to deal with this. If we need to go home…"

Bennett wrapped his arms around her. "You're my wife, and I promised you this trip a long time ago. I'm waiting for a call, and we will do the best we can."

"If only we didn't have so many outside pressures," Ivy said. "It seems we take one step forward and two steps back."

"This is part of the job, sweetheart."

"Can't we just run away somewhere?"

Bennett quirked up a corner of his mouth. "We're trying, aren't we?"

"I suppose we are." Ivy sighed and shook her head.

As other travelers rushed past them, Bennett glanced at the time. "We have ten minutes before we have to go through security…" He hated to finish that thought.

"Or not, right?"

Bennett's gut churned with anger, but not at Ivy. "I'm afraid so."

Ivy motioned to the bench. "Let's sit down and wait. Ten minutes."

With a longing glance toward the airport's sliding doors, Bennett picked up his bag and joined her. He leaned his elbows on his knees, thinking of what his team at the city could do and whether he should return.

Ivy placed her hand on his shoulder. "You didn't see this coming?"

"Not this specifically, although I knew he'd try something underhanded. Dirk smells opportunity in Summer Beach, and he's not letting up. This is a serious threat to the community."

"What can we do?"

"Continue the fight. I've spent years protecting Summer Beach, promoting its way of life, and creating opportunities for those who call it home. Maybe it's not the most progressive community, but that's not what most residents want. We've fought before to maintain our unique ambiance and protect our business owners."

Bennett had led the city in conflicts against major big box stores, fast food chains, and discount mall developers, including a lawsuit with Ivy's late husband over the historic inn property. The way he saw it, this was more of the same— people wanting to profit off Summer Beach at the town's expense.

Ivy smoothed her hand across his shoulders. "I agree with you. A downtown full of bars blasting music and alcohol-sponsored blowouts on the beach will not go over well. For all those who live nearby, their quality of life would be destroyed." She kissed his cheek. "I can't say I won't be disappointed if we don't get on that plane, but I'll understand if we have to turn back."

"Thanks for that." Bennett took her hand and kissed it. He treasured this woman.

For too long, he'd fought these encroaching concerns alone. While he had a capable team at the city, he hadn't had anyone he could truly confide in. He'd been on his own after Jackie died, so Summer Beach had become his reason for living.

But his continued leadership was also up to the voters.

"Win or lose on this issue, some residents will be upset," he said.

"You can't make everyone happy. But you do a good job for most." Ivy bumped his shoulder and grinned. "Especially for me. Speaking as a constituent, of course."

Bennett put his arm around her. "Changing the zoning to allow the inn was best for the community."

As if considering that, Ivy didn't say anything for a moment. Then she poked him and said, "You just wanted a place to stay after the fire."

Despite his worries, Bennett chuckled. "That had nothing to do with it."

"You're telling me you just happened to end up in the room next to mine?"

"Call it executive privilege." He brushed a strand of hair from her endless green eyes and thought again how lucky he was.

"How much longer?"

Bennett glanced at his phone. "Three minutes."

$\mathcal{E}$ ven though Ivy had been expecting the call, when Bennett's phone rang, she jerked to attention on the bench at the entry to the San Francisco airport. Other travelers flowed around them like a river, but her entire focus was on Bennett.

He leaned forward and answered his phone. "Bennett here."

The conference call was with Maeve, Boz, and city council members. Bennett listened with a grim look.

As much as Ivy yearned for this private time just for themselves, preserving their way of life in Summer Beach was more important than their trip. She'd been through enough to understand the value of looking beyond today.

If Ivy had learned nothing else these past few years, it was to have the courage and creativity to change what she could and the grace to accept what she couldn't, like this situation.

Of course, that was usually easier said than done.

While she waited for Bennett to conclude his call, she scanned through the email on her phone. She stopped at one that had just come in from Redstone Investments. She tapped it, and her heart leapt.

Letter of Intent to Purchase.

She enlarged it and began to read. The figure Milo quoted loomed on the screen. The choice before her now could change their lives.

Ivy chewed on her lip as she waited for Bennett. She didn't want to burden him right now. Let him handle one issue at a time, she decided. Still, the offer stuck like a barnacle in her mind.

After the longest few minutes, Bennett finally spoke. "That sounds like a solid plan, Boz. And good advice, Maeve. I trust you all to implement it. You know where I'll be if you need me."

Ivy heard Maeve's strong, clear voice over the phone. "I doubt we will. You've already laid the groundwork for this strategy, and the council and Boz know what to do. Go enjoy your honeymoon."

Grinning, Bennett replied, "We sure will."

"And tell Ivy those reservations might not stick," Maeve added. "She'll probably want to have a waiting list for reservations for that time period."

Ivy understood. She would have to tell Shelly and Poppy, but that could wait a little while. Or she could text them.

Bennett hung up and wrapped his arms around her. "We're free, sweetheart. At least for a week. Let's get on that plane before someone else calls."

Relief washed over her. "Tell me what happened."

"We need to get through the security line and find our gate, but essentially, Dirk is signing agreements and making promises regarding rights he hasn't secured. And won't, according to Maeve. It's complicated, but I'll explain once we're airborne." He grinned and picked up their bags. "We are not missing that flight. Let's go."

They joined a long line of what looked like hundreds of people queuing up for security. The line snaked back and forth.

The security agent at the entry to the line checked their tickets. "Sorry, but you folks are in the wrong place."

Ivy's heart dropped, but then the woman pointed to a shorter line. "Fortunately, you're supposed to be over there. Have a good trip."

After glancing at the tickets Teresa emailed, Ivy saw her mistake. "My goodness, would you look at this? Teresa upgraded the new tickets. How incredibly thoughtful of her." Maybe they would make it after all.

"That's a welcome surprise. This way, sweetheart." Bennett took her hand and grinned. "Have your passport ready. Nothing is going to stop us this time."

By the time Ivy and Bennett settled into their relatively comfortable business-class seats, the sun had dipped beneath the horizon. She gazed from the airplane portal window into the star-speckled sky, willing this flight to be smooth and uneventful. If anyone needed a respite, it was Bennett.

As they lifted off, a hush swept through the cabin, and she clasped Bennett's hand. The city glittered below, and the moon illuminated the ocean's breaking waves. After a few minutes, the scene below dimmed in the distance.

She eased back in her seat and let out a sigh of relief. Just the two of them, enveloped in a cocoon and soaring into the sky. It was magical. Feeling grateful, she exhaled the stress she'd been carrying and threaded her fingers with Bennett's. This would be a trip to remember.

After watching a movie together and sleeping for several hours, Ivy awoke to the sound of a food service cart trundling down the aisle. But it was too early for her to eat.

They touched down in Frankfurt shortly afterward, had time for croissants and fresh, rich espresso, and connected to Mallorca without incident.

Once on board their last flight, Bennett tucked her hand in his.

"We made it," Ivy said, fastening her seatbelt with a firm click.

Bennett chuckled. "Don't jinx it just yet. Remember what happened in Palm Springs?"

"Shelly isn't having a baby this time," Ivy replied with a smile. "But try not to check your phone."

Around them, Ivy caught snippets of conversations in Spanish, Catalan, German, and English. Wherever she went, people had similar concerns about family and work. However, on this flight, most seemed happy to be on their way to Mallorca, a popular holiday destination.

To her, traveling was exciting; the exposure to new customs and cultures she found fascinating and invigorating. She could hardly wait to explore the island, try different dishes, and learn more about the history of Mallorca.

A little while later, the turquoise waters of the Mediterranean Sea stretched beneath them, sparkling in the sunlight.

Ivy gazed from the window, her hand in Bennett's, recalling the memorable times they'd had so far. "Look at that. What a gorgeous color."

"We're almost there," Bennett said. "We've survived a lot to get this far. Lawsuits and floods, for starters."

"Don't forget fire and earthquake."

"Pestilence could be next," Bennett said, grinning. "Have I told you about our tarantulas in Summer Beach?"

She'd heard about those but had never seen them. Ivy swatted his hand. "Shh, don't bring that on."

"We've done a lot in a short time, though. Blended our families, made a home for ourselves, and did a lot of good for the community. We've earned this, sweetheart."

"It has been a whirlwind." Ivy brought his hand to her lips and kissed it.

They had also forged strong bonds. At only a year into their marriage, they were still at the threshold of their lives together. She couldn't help but wonder what lay ahead for them.

"There's the island," Ivy said, excitement coursing through her. She watched from the window as they flew over green, mountainous peaks and crescent-shaped bays toward the capital city of Palma, where they would land.

Bennett leaned over her to look. "Before we left, I read up on the Balearic Islands and Mallorca's history and culture. There's a lot to see here. You won't want to miss the cathedral in Palma that Meredith mentioned."

Ivy had also read that the island had been part of the Roman Empire and remained a prize throughout history. "I'd love to explore some museums and art galleries. Will you be up for some of that?"

"Sure," Bennett replied. "There's a good golf course and spa at the hotel, too. And some caves. We'll fit it all in. Along with plenty of time for just the two of us," he added, kissing her cheek.

"I like the sound of that," Ivy said.

Languishing with him in bed without the thought of having to check on guests was a delicious, decadent thought.

As if reading her mind, Bennett said, "We needed this. Just us. I'm sorry if I put it off too long."

Ivy stroked his face and smiled. "That makes two of us. Now, no more apologies. We did what we had to, and now we're here."

After the flight landed, they wound their way through the airport terminal toward the baggage carousel. Ivy was pleasantly surprised at the large, modern facility with plenty of international shops. After collecting their bags, they emerged into bright sunshine.

Teresa had arranged a car for them. On their way, they passed stretches of land dotted with old, long-stilled windmills. Soon, they arrived at Palma, a modern city by the sea with plenty of quaint sections and history.

"What a beautiful area," Ivy said, taking in the outdoor cafes surrounded by trees, flowers, and foliage. People strolling along the street wore relaxed, casual styles in vibrant shades.

To her, the colors looked different here. The sea was a vivid shade of turquoise blue, and the mountains that rose in the distance were covered with trees in variegated hues of green. Palm trees swayed overhead, and bougainvillea in brilliant pops of fuchsia, magenta, and crimson spilled across white stucco walls and terra cotta tiled rooftops. Although she had never been here, the architecture and plantings were familiar.

"This reminds me a lot of home," she said as they passed through the town. Umbrellas covered cafe tables where people lingered over plates of fresh food and drinks.

"That makes sense," Bennett said. "California was once part of Spain."

"My mother once said she had a distant cousin who lived here. I believe her name was Clara." She would have to ask her mother about that.

"Did she leave any family?"

Ivy shook her head. "Not that I know of." Yet, she couldn't help feeling a sense of *déjà vu*, although that was impossible. She shimmied her shoulders to rid herself of the odd sensation.

"What was that about?" Bennett asked.

"I have a strange feeling about this place," she said. "It's almost as if I've been here before, even once belonged here. Wouldn't it be interesting if places could be imprinted in your ancestral memory?"

"It might be possible," Bennett replied, looking at her with interest. "There's still so much we don't know about the brain."

The quiet car wound through Palma and continued up an incline until it reached the hotel's elaborately scrolled entry gates, which swung open for them.

When they arrived at the entry to the Castillo Hotel Son Vida, Ivy happily took it all in. A turret, indeed worthy of a castle, rose above the hotel on one side. On the other, shimmering pools and an undulating golf course gave way to a panoramic view of the Bay of Palma beyond. Palm trees swayed gently in the breeze.

"Teresa told me that this once was a large family villa," Ivy said. "And it was built on the site of an old castle. The property had been in the family for generations."

"You're certainly the queen of my castle," Bennett said.

Playing with him, Ivy raised her eyebrows. "Excuse me?"

"I suppose the inn is *your* castle," Bennett said, quickly rephrasing. "But mine is still on the ridgetop waiting for us."

Even the driver grinned at that. "Every *señora* is the queen of her castle," he said. "It's a wise man who understands that."

"You've got that right," Bennett said as he hugged Ivy to his side. "This week, we have a real castle to explore."

Again, Ivy wondered if Bennett was happy living at the inn. Despite what he said, she wouldn't make the mistake she had in her first marriage of assuming their lives were fine. While living in the converted chauffeur's quarters at the inn might have seemed like a lark at first, she could understand how it might grow old for a man accustomed to having his own home and privacy.

Although she didn't want to ruin their long-awaited holiday, these were some of the discussions they needed to have. At home, one day bled into another, often with little time for reflection, especially during the busy summer season.

"Welcome," the uniformed doorman said as he assisted their arrival.

After taking their names, their bags were whisked away, and they were greeted by several staff with such grace. It was as if they were arriving at a private country home.

This was a level of service Ivy wished she could provide to

her patrons, though she and Shelly and Poppy still did their best to make their guests feel welcome.

"I'm feeling awfully spoiled already," Ivy whispered to Bennett.

He took her hand, and they climbed the front steps. "I'll make sure you're completely pampered."

"And I'll do the same for you, darling," she said.

Ivy paused in the doorway, taking in the artistry and ambiance of the space that stretched before her. Rather than cavernous, the entry was well-proportioned and inviting.

Beyond the white marbled entryway glittered a chandelier. It was suspended over a descending curved staircase lined with wrought iron scrollwork. On the far stone walls hung two full-body portraits of a woman and a man in fine period attire, but it was the glimpse of a detailed pastoral scene in a dining room beyond that piqued her interest.

As she'd promised Teresa, she would take plenty of photos later.

Far from being ostentatious, the welcoming, gracious interior was one of unfettered ease and quiet elegance.

Ivy slipped her hand into the crook of Bennet's elbow. "I think we've landed in paradise."

A smartly uniformed host at the discreetly situated front desk nodded to them. "Welcome, Señor Dylan. Señora."

The staff was cordial, hospitable, efficient, and friendly. Next to Ivy, a German couple checked in, and she heard another front desk clerk glide effortlessly between languages.

"The Seabreeze Inn has a lot to aspire to," she said with a small sigh.

Bennett kissed her cheek. "Your inn is perfect for what it is —a beach house respite."

The front desk clerk overhead them and raised his head. "You're in hospitality as well?"

Ivy nodded, smiling. "However, my inn is nothing as grand

as this. It's in Summer Beach, a small town in Southern California."

They chatted, and the clerk read a note on his screen that Teresa had added to their reservation. "I see that this is a special occasion. Your honeymoon?"

Ivy and Bennett looked at each other and smiled. "It is," he said. "We're lucky to have found each other again."

"One moment," the clerk said, raising a finger before he disappeared into an office.

"Maybe they don't allow the competition," Ivy said.

Bennett encircled her in his arms. "I don't think it matters. We're thousands of miles away."

"Thank goodness."

A few moments later, the man reappeared. "We have a special room for you. Please enjoy your stay with us."

"I'm sure we will," Ivy said.

They made their way to their room. When Bennett swung open the door to a suite, her heart leapt.

"This calls for the grand gesture," Bennett said, sweeping her into his arms and off her feet. "The least I can do is carry my queen across the threshold."

Ivy cried out in mock protest, although she loved being in his strong arms.

After kissing her, he placed her on her feet and twirled her around. "This is incredible. We'll have to do something special for Teresa."

"A weekend at the inn pales compared to this." Ivy turned to take in the large bedroom and sitting area decorated in serene shades of silvery gray and muted blue.

She took Bennett's hand and led him into the bathroom. The luxurious marbled space had a deep tub and separate shower, both large enough for two.

"Fancy a bath after that long flight?" Without hesitating, Bennett peeled off his shirt and tossed it to one side. "And maybe a nap?" he asked, nuzzling her neck.

"That sounds perfect," Ivy replied, sliding her hand along his chest.

She ran water into the tub and poured a generous dollop of bath oil. *Hierbas de Mallorca*, she read on the label. The fresh scent of citrus and herbs filled the air. Breathing in, she detected lemon, lavender, and rosemary.

When she turned, Bennett had slipped into a white terrycloth bathrobe, and now he held one out to her.

This would be a honeymoon to remember. With their travel troubles behind them, she looked forward to a week's respite.

Just as Ivy was about to disrobe, her phone buzzed.

"Ignore that," Bennett said, grinning.

Ivy intended to, but her daughter's name flashed on the screen. "It's Sunny." She bit her lip, weighing her responsibility against her desire to relax with Bennett.

"Answer it," he said, folding her robe over his arm. "If she's calling you here, she needs you."

13

"*O*h, Mom, I'm so glad you picked up," Sunny said over the phone. "I'm sorry to bother you, and I know I shouldn't have, but I really need help."

Her daughter's voice sounded tight, as if her emotions were dammed but destined to burst forth. Ivy mentally braced herself. "What's wrong, honey?"

"It's about Cooper," Sunny began.

Cooper. Tall, good-looking, extremely self-assured. She recalled meeting him last summer but didn't think they were serious. "And you broke up?"

"Worse. I don't know how to tell you this."

Oh, dear heavens, she's pregnant. Ivy sank onto the edge of the tub, aching for her daughter. Thoughts raced through her mind, but she tried to remain calm. Sunny could barely manage her own life, let alone take care of a baby.

"There isn't much I haven't heard before, sweetie. No matter what, you know I love you."

His brow drawn, Bennett sat beside Ivy and put her arm around her.

She appreciated his support more than he could imagine.

Jeremy would have been throwing a fit, and she'd have two hysterical people on her hands.

Sunny was crying now, unable to speak. Ivy's heart lurched for her daughter, but she gave her some time. Finally, Ivy asked, "Does Cooper know about this?"

"Know? Well, duh. He did it, didn't he?"

"Well, yes, but if you were taking precautions—"

Sunny emitted a horrified, strangled cry. "Mom! Oh, my gosh, what are you talking about?"

"If you're…" Ivy waited, but Sunny still didn't fill in the blanks for her. "Pregnant?"

"Noooo," Sunny wailed. "You're not listening to me."

"I'm trying to." Ivy let out a guarded breath. *Not pregnant.* That was good, but what else could it be?

"I was helping Cooper in a class he's failing."

"Sweetheart, I am here for you, but I'm not following you. Can you explain a little more?"

Vacillating between hurt and anger, Sunny spat out her words. "I'm going to be expelled, okay?"

Ivy pressed a hand to her forehead, partly relieved because she had imagined so many dreadful scenarios. She looked up at Bennett and mouthed, *school and boyfriend problems.*

On the surface, this didn't seem so bad. Sunny wasn't pregnant, and she hadn't been in an accident. She would be expelled for what, a few days? Not good, but not devastating. Still, her daughter had left out the details.

"We can deal with this, honey. Can you tell me what happened?"

"Cooper is failing a class, so I was helping him with his paper. Somehow, he got a copy of mine off my computer and turned it in as his own. When I turned mine in, the professor said I cheated and plagiarized him, so I'm in big trouble." Sunny let out a moan.

"Can you be more specific, honey?"

"I won't get credit for the class. Something about zero

tolerance. There will be a meeting, and then I'll be expelled from the university for good."

Ivy ran a hand over her face. Sunny's degree was in jeopardy, and she was so close to finally graduating. With Jamir's study tips, she'd actually been putting in the work this semester.

"Sunny, you can probably disprove this charge. What about Cooper?"

"They didn't do anything to him."

Now Ivy's anger rose. "How could that be?"

"His dad is a major supporter. Everyone at the university knows him. That's another reason I was helping him. But I didn't let him copy anything of mine. He probably grabbed the file when I went to the bathroom or took a call. That's all I can figure."

"We'll figure it out when I return."

"I can't wait that long. I'll get behind."

"Not if they made a mistake. They'll have to let you catch up. Can you keep working on assignments until we get this sorted out?"

"Mom, this is my life. If I don't get my degree…"

Ivy felt the hopelessness in Sunny's voice. "You'll get it. When is the meeting?"

"In two weeks."

"Then take that time to compile all your research material and other prior versions of files with time and date stamps. Anything you can think of that can prove this paper is your work. Don't let Cooper rob you. He's not worth it."

Sunny sniffed. "I wish you weren't so far away," she added in a small voice. "When are you coming back?"

"I told you, honey. Next week."

"You can't come back sooner to deal with this for me?"

Ivy closed her eyes. Sunny knew how much this trip meant to her and Bennett, so she wouldn't ask if she weren't feeling desperate.

On the other hand, Jeremy's indulgence of Sunny was partly why she felt she couldn't solve problems on her own.

Ivy gripped the phone and prayed she was doing the right thing. "Sunny, I will help you come up with a plan when I return. You will need to make a list of all your evidence—"

"Mom, no. You're the one who makes lists. And what good would that do?"

"If you'll listen—"

"You're not hearing me."

"Sunny, please let me speak. Make a list of your documents—the files and research materials. Any phone calls you might have made or emails you sent. Then, list your options and the actions you think you could take. Think of it as a strategy, like the games you've played."

"That's why I called you," Sunny pleaded. "You're good at that."

"I had to learn, too, honey." Ivy had faith in her daughter. "Write down exactly what you think happened. Include dates and anyone else who might have been there and seen something. I'll contact the school to confirm what you need to do, if they'll respond to me, but you must be prepared to help yourself. And if there was anything that you might have done for Cooper out of the goodness of your heart, you must be prepared to confess to that."

"No, I swear, it was all him." Sunny sniffed. "But I don't want to hurt him. I can't do this."

"I know you can, Sunny. You must make an effort to save your degree. Cooper has to pay for his mistakes and what he's putting you through."

"He stopped taking my calls."

"Well, there's your answer about him. I'm sorry for you." Ivy knew how that must feel. "The school should have given you some paperwork or instructions for a hearing or an appeal process."

"Yeah. But I don't understand any of it."

"Read it. Ask Poppy, one of your uncles, or Imani to help you if you don't understand. And have your list of materials ready when I return."

"I've never had to do anything like this. I don't know what you mean by evidence. Why can't you help me now?"

Ivy bit back a sharp remark. Instead, she said, "Evidence is simply your research, notes, and files you used to write your paper. Like I mentioned. You can do this, Sunny."

"Mom, please."

"You'll have to handle things like this as an adult. I won't always be around to fight your battles for you."

Even so, if what her daughter said was true, she would make sure Sunny appealed and returned to school. Cooper would not get away with this. But she wanted Sunny to practice standing up for herself.

After Ivy hung up, Bennett pulled her close. "I'm sorry to hear about all that."

Ivy blew out a breath. "She wants me to return."

"Do you think it would help?"

"It sounds like she has a couple of weeks. I think she'll need help getting back into school, but I also want her to think about how she can solve the problem. Sunny lacks the confidence to believe she can do that on her own."

"Sounds like a big deal, though. Are you sure?"

"I'll make a couple of calls, but I'm not certain that Sunny is telling me the entire truth. She's been known to conceal parts of a story that might implicate her."

"You don't believe her?"

Ivy hoped she was wrong, but she also had to be realistic. "I want to, but there might be more to it. That's all I'm saying. You heard what I told her."

Bennett nodded thoughtfully. "I don't mean to get in the middle of anything with you and your kids, but Sunny seems like she's been trying hard since I've known her. How long ago were these other issues?"

"Aside from when she used my credit card for a first-class ticket from Europe?" Ivy pressed her lips into a thin line. "Do you think I'm not giving her a fair chance?"

Bennett held up a hand. "I'm just saying I haven't seen any behavior that would make me distrust her. Besides the airline ticket incident. That's been a couple of years now, Ivy."

"Well, I've known her longer than you have." She stood and turned away from him.

Bennett was quiet for a few moments. "Still want that bath?"

Ivy shook her head. The moment had passed, and her heart was no longer in it.

"How about a massage at the spa?"

She shouldn't take this out on Bennett. "That would help. I'm so sorry—"

Bennett pressed a finger to her lips and kissed her. "No apologizing for your family. This is our life. Things happen outside our control, but let's keep what we have special. I think you handled that well."

"Then you changed your mind?"

Bennett rose and placed his hands on her shoulders. "The Ivy I met a few years ago would have flown back to Sunny's rescue, but now you're treating her more like an adult. She needs that, even if it is painful."

She appreciated hearing that from Bennett. "Her university degree is at risk, so I can't abandon her or let her jeopardize that. I want her to put in the work and understand the process, but I'll still make sure this is sorted out."

"I know you will. This is a taking-responsibility moment for her."

"That's what I'm hoping." In Bennett's eyes, she saw his love and compassion for her and her children. This was their time—maybe their only time together. Checking with the university could wait until tomorrow.

"Thank you for understanding."

"That works both ways."

She lifted her chin and smiled. "Have a massage at the spa with me. And after that, maybe some other honeymoon delights?"

Bennett kissed her. "I like the sound of that."

While Bennett changed, Ivy thought about how, for a split second, she'd thought of returning, then felt guilty when she told Sunny she couldn't. Did all mothers feel that way when trying to let their children fly on their own? She wished she could reach her own mother, but Carlotta was somewhere on the high seas, living her best life, doing what she loved while she still could.

As Ivy needed to do as well.

She stepped out onto the balcony overlooking the crescent-shaped cove in the distance. Here she was on her long-awaited honeymoon, the quiet time she'd yearned for with her husband. Yet, it was difficult to leave everything behind.

She exhaled her stress.

Maybe some people could compartmentalize their feelings. As a mother, she was used to multi-tasking and solving problems. Not that her oldest daughter required much of that anymore. After Misty had moved out, Ivy rarely heard from her about problems. Misty might call for advice, but she had never asked Ivy to rescue her.

Bennett appeared behind her and wrapped his arms around her waist. "Are you ready, my love?"

Ivy leaned into him, resting her head against his chest and the white cotton shirt he'd put on. "That was a long flight. I think we both need this. And maybe that long bath afterward?"

He reached down to kiss her. "That's the best plan I've heard in a long time. Let's not forget the honeymoon delights. Then maybe a nap, dinner, and a walk around this beautiful place."

"Best plan ever." Smiling, Ivy threaded her arms around

his neck. She was determined to find a compartment for Sunny's problems so she could enjoy a few hours of bliss with her husband. They both deserved it.

She ran her hands through his hair and kissed him back. Tomorrow would be soon enough for the rest of the world's problems.

14

"Feeling better now?" Bennett asked, taking Ivy's hand across the small dining table.

Ivy rubbed her hand over his and smiled. "Absolutely. I don't know what was more relaxing…" Others were dining nearby in the outdoor restaurant under the stars, so she didn't finish the sentence. She felt herself blushing at the memory.

What a wonderful afternoon and evening it had been. She and Bennet had soothing massages and returned to the room for the bubble bath they had delayed earlier, then spent several lazy, romantic hours together.

Afterward, they'd taken their time getting ready for dinner. This was Mallorca, and like the rest of Spain, the evening meal usually didn't begin until later. When they arrived at the restaurant, others were also just arriving. They were seated at a table with a view and served.

On this balmy evening, they were enjoying a sparkling rosé cava with freshly baked bread and light tapas—burrata with a creamy *aubergine* sauce, and Spanish almonds with olive oil, garlic, and cherries. A seasonal salad of berries and pine nuts in a sweet mustard vinaigrette was also delicious.

Ivy touched her glass to Bennett's before taking a sip. "This is such a romantic place."

Soft lanterns overhead illuminated the patio, and lights in the Bay of Palma twinkled beneath their lofty perch in the Castillo Son Vida restaurant.

Bennett kissed her hand. "You look beautiful tonight. That dress is gorgeous on you."

"That was so thoughtful of you," she said, smoothing the light silk that felt so soft against her skin. "I would never have bought this for myself."

"That's why it gave me so much pleasure," Bennett said, tearing a piece of bread for her.

Ivy delighted in her thrift shop finds, and before her parents left on their voyage, Carlotta had given her a lot of casual beach wear.

Yet, on their way to the spa, she'd admired a flowing silk dress in watercolor shades of aquamarine in the window of a hotel shop. When they returned to the room, it was in her closet. Bennett had arranged for it to be delivered while they'd had their massages. He was so pleased that she loved it.

She smiled at him across the candlelight. "Are you trying to spoil me?"

"We spoil each other," he replied, returning her smile. "I wish I could do more for you."

"You do plenty for me at the inn."

That was true. If Ivy or Shelly couldn't repair something, Bennett was the next one they called. And he supported her at all the events she held there.

"About that," Ivy began, seizing on the opportunity. Now that she had received Milo's letter of intent, she had to talk to Bennett. Even though she knew he would support whatever decision she made, it weighed on her mind.

Just then, a server approached them with the next course. "Tagliatelle with crispy Parmesan cheese."

"Right here." Bennett's face was wreathed with pleasure. "I'm starving."

Their last good meal had been with Viola and Meredith before they left San Francisco, so they had both been hungry after a day of travel, especially Bennett.

"What a presentation," Bennett said. "And it smells delicious. Are you sure you won't have some?" he asked Ivy.

"Just a bite. The burrata and salad were enough for me."

As he passed a forkful to her, he asked, "Now, what were you going to say about the inn?"

"Just that it's good to get away from it with you," she replied. "Mmm, that's yummy."

Bennett looked so happy. Ivy didn't have the heart to disturb his blissful meal, especially when she wasn't sure how he'd receive her news.

Part of her imagined he'd be thrilled about a sale. When she'd just arrived in Summer Beach, and he'd inherited the real estate listing from his business partner, they'd both been motivated to sell the house. But there hadn't been any buyers for a large old home in need of repairs, especially one with a restrictive historic designation.

She should be excited, although what she felt was more akin to relief. Or maybe she'd just been tired when that call came in. Either way, a sale would solve a lot of issues. It would be the practical move for everyone.

As Bennett ate, she thought about her youngest daughter. Sunny would want a place of her own when she graduated. Bennett's house on the ridgetop might be too small for Sunny's large presence, though Ivy would always want her daughters to feel welcome.

Still, Ivy had a nagging feeling about the offer she couldn't quite explain. As she thought about their options, a knot formed in her chest. Absently, she rubbed a spot just below her collarbone.

Bennett looked up at her. "Are you okay?"

"It's just an odd sensation that comes and goes." Quickly, she removed her hand.

"That could be stress related," Bennett said, furrowing his brow. "You should see your doctor when we return."

"Really, it's nothing."

Bennett rested his fork. "Ivy, I don't know what I'd do if anything ever happened to you."

"Relax. I'm sure it's not serious." She sensed he was thinking about his first wife. "But I'll see my doctor if it makes you happy."

"It will, very much." He reached for her hand and kissed it. "Thank you."

After dinner, they relaxed on the hotel's upper terrace for a while, enjoying being together. The lights were low, and people were nestled in small groups. A soft wind carried scents of sun-warmed island trees and the Mediterranean Sea.

Ivy inhaled deeply, casting off the stress of the day.

Seated beside her, Bennett wrapped his arm around her shoulders. "What a way to clear our minds."

"Today was a wonderful start." She leaned into him, relishing his protective, loving embrace.

"Still thinking about Sunny?" Bennett stroked her shoulder with a slow, circular motion.

His touch sent shivers through her. "I worry that this situation could derail her life."

"A lot of kids go through things that make them grow up fast," Bennett said thoughtfully. "I think she'll be fine."

"What if she isn't?"

Bennett was quiet for a moment before speaking. "Look at Mitch," he said slowly. "Even with his poor decision as a teenager and a short prison sentence, he still managed to turn his life around. In fact, he has probably done even better. That incident instilled strong motivation in Mitch to succeed. Real motivation comes from within, and unfortunate circumstances can provide the fuel. I'm not saying adversity is good, but it can be put to good use."

Her sister's husband had certainly proven himself with Java Beach and his chartered boat tours. "But Sunny is different."

"Is she? I think she needs to prove herself as well. You've said her father often bailed her out of problems. Let her do that for herself this time."

Ivy nodded. "I agree with you, but it's a fine line. I want her to graduate and experience that accomplishment."

"The fact that you're considering all this proves you're a good mother."

"Thanks for that," Ivy said. "And you're right about clearing our minds. This is long overdue."

"You juggle a lot, sweetheart. I admire that, but even a superhero like you needs a break." He brought her hand to his lips and kissed her fingers.

She smiled. "You're right. My superhero cape is a little frayed."

"Not long ago, you reminded me to step away. Now, it's my turn. The world, and even those we love, will manage without us for a few days. Think we can do that?"

Ivy nodded thoughtfully. "And we'll help each other find our balance."

"That's part of what marriage is about." In the quiet darkness, he trailed his finger along her arm. "Helping each other be the best they can be. I love seeing you succeed with the inn and your artwork. Honestly, that makes you very interesting. Sexy, even."

Ivy laughed. "You think changing sheets and juggling reservations is sexy?"

"You're a woman who doesn't shirk responsibility," Bennett said. "You're strong, capable, and creative. I find that very seductive."

Ivy looked up into his hazel eyes and saw that he meant

every word. "I feel the same way about you, Mr. Mayor. You never back down, and you lead with integrity. People love you for that. Especially me."

He gazed at her with a slight frown. "And what if someday I'm no longer the mayor? If I make an unpopular decision, someone else could win the vote. Even if I do what I think is best for the community."

"I'll love you no matter what." Ivy paused for a moment. "And what about the inn?"

"I love that part of our life," he replied. "How dull it would be without all the characters passing through. And you've provided employment for your family.

Before Ivy could speak, a server approached the table. "Last call for a warm-up on your tea," she said.

They declined and started back to their room. As they strolled through the wide halls, Ivy stopped in front of a large, realistic landscape painting. "This is a stunning work."

Bennett leaned in to read the caption card posted beside it. "It's by Antoni Ribas and depicts the landing of the Catalan-Aragonese army in 1229."

"That's a long view of history," Ivy remarked, stepping back to appreciate it. "When does it say it was painted?"

Bennett shrugged. "This says it won a gold medal in 1866 at an exhibition. Looks like it belongs in a museum."

Ivy squinted at the label. "The Academia de Bellas Artes in Barcelona. Impressive, but I'm not familiar with his work."

"If I may assist?" A hotel staff member paused beside them, and Ivy nodded. The young man began, "Ribas was just twenty-one at the time."

"But there's such maturity in his work," Ivy said.

"And originality," the young staffer agreed. "Ribas wanted to stay in Palma, so he designed sets at a local theater and taught at the Academia de Bellas Artes. He influenced many other artists. Would you like to know about the other works of art?"

"I would," Ivy said. She turned to Bennett. "If you're not too tired."

"I find it fascinating, too," he replied.

"My name is also Antoni," the younger man said, inclining his head.

Surrounded by the quiet of the hotel, Antoni led them through the hallways and paused by a landscape. "Besides Ribas, we have Fausto Morell with another historical scene that took place on Mallorca in 1329."

From that vigorous depiction, they moved on to two full-length portraits. "And these?" Ivy asked.

"Archduke Karl of Austria and his consort, Elisabeth Christine. The Archduke lost the fight for the Spanish throne but was later crowned Emperor Karl VI."

"In Austria, I believe," Bennett said. "If my European history is correct."

Antoni smiled. "It is."

As they approached the dining room, Ivy's heart quickened. "May we see inside this room? When we checked in, I spied some murals that looked amazing."

"Of course." Antoni opened the door. "These are among the most prized artworks here. Anckermann completed these just after the turn of the 20th century. It took him four years to complete these paintings, which are mounted on separate canvases."

The paintings were of casual, pastoral pastimes. "These are such natural portrayals," Ivy said, inspecting them.

Antoni gestured to the works. "These are depictions of a royal hunting expedition. Ferran Truyols, the Marqués de la Torre and owner of Son Vida, asked Anckermann to decorate the dining room. This was among the artist's last major accomplishments."

"My wife has a great appreciation of art," Bennett added. "She is also an artist."

"And where are you visiting us from?"

"Summer Beach, California," Ivy replied.

"Where she is the proprietor of the Seabreeze Inn," Bennett added with pride.

Ivy laughed. "It's not quite as grand as this. My travel agent told me you've had many important visitors over the years, including Maria Callas and the Spanish Royal family."

"Ah, yes," Antoni said. "Forgive me, but did you say Summer Beach? Where the incredible World War II collection of stolen paintings was found?"

"Why, yes," Ivy replied. "You heard of that?"

"That was major news in the art world, and it was reported here, too." Antoni shook his head in amazement. "And you gave them back to their owners?"

Ivy was accustomed to this comment. "They weren't mine to keep."

Antoni drew a hand over his jaw. "The hotel had a connection with the story. The woman who owned the house...her name was...?"

"Amelia Erickson?" Ivy was growing intrigued.

Antoni snapped his fingers. "Yes, that's right. She often dined here."

Bennett looked at Ivy with a small smile. "This can't be another coincidence."

"I don't believe in any of that," Ivy said.

"Pardon me?" Antoni looked slightly perplexed.

"It's a private joke," Ivy said, although a little shiver coursed through her.

"Maybe, but I believe there are few coincidences in life," Antoni said. "Perhaps a hand far greater than us guides our lives."

Ivy shivered again. It was too late for her to think about any of that, or she'd lay awake all night.

15

*I*vy blinked against the morning light and groaned. "Do you have to get up so early?"

Bennett laughed and joined her in bed. "Hey, gorgeous. It's not that early."

She turned to the clock by the bed and realized she had slept in. Throwing her arms over her head, she said, "The time difference must be affecting me."

"You needed your rest." He grinned and swept her messy hair to one side. "You sure were talkative in your sleep last night."

"What did I say?"

"Something about Sunny, then a conversation with Amelia, then negotiating with someone to sell the inn. Sounded like pretty crazy dreams."

"Wow, that's wild." Ivy sat up and leaned against the headboard, smoothing the ivory silk nightgown she'd bought especially for the trip. She wondered what she'd said about the inn.

"Do you need to check in with Sunny today?"

"She'll still be asleep at home," she replied, glad he didn't ask any more questions. It was too early to have that conversation with him, especially after what he'd said last night. "Have you been up for a while?"

"I have. I spoke to Boz before he turned in. We're nine hours ahead."

"And how are things at City Hall?"

"They'll handle the situation just fine."

"Is there trouble?"

"Nothing that concerns us this week." He leaned over and kissed her. "Let's have a great day. Want to see the island by train or boat?"

"Both, please."

"That can be arranged," he said with a grin. "I also spoke with the concierge and learned that we can take a train and then a tram to Port de Sóller," he explained, pronouncing the silent double *ll* as a *y* in Spanish.

She stretched languorously. "Is it one of those high-speed trains?"

"Not at all. It's a vintage train that dates from 1912 and passes through more than a dozen mountain tunnels; it's supposed to be an incredibly scenic journey. Once we reach the port, there are plenty of excursions from that point. Or we could make a day of it and sail from Palma another day."

Ivy loved the idea of a leisurely train excursion. "Why rush? The train sounds charming. We can venture out on the water another day."

"That's what I thought you'd say," Bennett said, kissing her again.

They dressed casually for the trip. Ivy wore a soft yellow batik print skirt and soft-soled shoes for walking. Bennett wore a knit top with casual trousers and deck shoes.

They had a light breakfast in Palma before boarding the vintage train at the quaint station. The train had been refurbished, but it still had the charm of yesteryear with its lacquered mahogany paneling, polished brass fittings, and gilded sconces.

They found seats on a leather sofa-like bench. Sash windows were slid open, letting in fresh air from the ocean. Other passengers joined them, though Ivy and Bennett still had plenty of room.

Soon after departure, the train began to gain altitude. The temperature became cooler, while palm trees gave way to olive groves and forests thick with pine and oak trees. The train stopped at small stations, then continued clacking through the countryside. On either side, lemon and orange groves thrived in the sunshine.

Trundling through the expansive Serra de Tramuntana region, Bennett pointed out rock-terraced hillsides where gnarled olive trees grew. "The concierge told me that many of those trees are more than a century old. And still producing."

"Shelly would love to see this area," Ivy said, shaking her hair in the fresh breeze that swept through the coach. "I could just imagine her in an old cottage surrounded by plenty of land to plant her gardens."

"Mitch would have a longer commute to surf," Bennett said. "But they'd be surrounded by coastlines. I wonder if they would ever consider that. Maybe we'd all gather here."

Ivy twisted her windblown hair into a knot at the nape of her neck. "It's fun thinking about alternate lives, even if it's only a dream."

"Hang on, there." Bennett smiled and bumped her shoulder. "That's not necessarily a dream, sweetheart."

Ivy arched an eyebrow in disbelief. "You would move from Summer Beach?"

"Don't act so shocked," Bennett replied. "Let's be open to possibilities. Maybe we could buy a little place here and escape during the off-season."

She turned toward him to see if he was serious. "Are you really planning for your retirement?" When he nodded, she folded her arms. "I didn't think we were ready for that yet."

"It's not as far away as you think, but we'll never retire

from life. Look at your parents. They're living their dreams and planning for even more adventures."

Ivy couldn't argue with that. "I suppose those who don't look ahead get stuck looking back."

"That's not who you are. Or me." Bennett put his arm around her and drew her to his side on the leather sofa. "Our world can be whatever we choose."

For so many years, she had lived her life by lists of things to do for other people—those she loved, of course, but still, it was a list of should-do's. Yet, she loved her life. Most of it, that is.

She could do without faulty plumbing, flickering lights, and leaky windows.

As she thought about those shortcomings, her chest tightened. Milo's phone call and email nagged her, and she had yet to tell Bennett. The reality of making such a final decision weighed heavily on her. Before doing anything, she would need professional advice on the property's value. She couldn't afford to make mistakes at this stage in her life.

"It's beautiful here, but what if we want our world to be Summer Beach?" she asked, thinking about what he'd said.

"Then that's an active choice, not one made by default."

She gazed at him with curiosity. But now was not the time to talk about the offer she'd received for the inn, not in a train car full of strangers.

Tomorrow, she decided.

When the train reached a high point on a slope, the conductor slowed to a stop. By the track, a wooden sign with hand-scrolled lettering read *Mirador des Pujol d'En Banya*. Most people disembarked to look at the expansive views and take photos. Ivy and Bennett followed.

"This view is astounding," Ivy said, standing at the railing. "And the fact that they stop the train so that everyone can take in the scenic view is amazing. Can you imagine the trains doing that in Southern California?"

"Maybe they should," he replied, standing close to her. "Let's enjoy the moment."

"That's why we're here." She ruffled his short hair, then turned back to the magical panorama, thankful they had made this trip.

They'd been so close to deciding against a honeymoon. Yet even in the short time that they'd been away, she could feel a deepening intimacy between them.

Ivy was beginning to understand why this was an essential journey for them.

She craned her neck, taking in the full view that surrounded them.

Majestic mountains rose from the valleys, with houses and villages nestled between peaks. Rows of crops and trees blanketed the hillsides—almond and carob trees, they were told. The sound of children's laughter echoed around them.

"Seriously, what would you think about living here someday?" Bennett asked.

"Is that an invitation?"

"Just curious if it might appeal to you. It's so serene and beautiful, which is important for artists."

Ivy glanced at him, wondering what brought this on. "You really are planning for your post-mayoral retirement."

He chuckled. "Maybe. Although not for a long time, I hope. This could be a good place for you to paint."

Ivy thought about the changes her parents had made in their retirement. Why not explore the world if you could and had a desire to? She'd been so focused on her daughters, dealing with Jeremy's death and infidelities, and setting up the inn that she'd never thought that far ahead.

Bennett gazed at her. "So, what do you think?"

His question sounded serious. "Maybe for part of the year. Mallorca has a warm climate and easy access to the rest of Europe. I'd miss my family, though."

"I'll bet they'd visit in a heartbeat." He looked out over the expansive view. "This really speaks to my soul."

"I've never heard you say that," Ivy said, surprised at his words. "I know how much you love Summer Beach."

"That I do. But we go through phases in life. And I'd love to travel more with you. Imagine painting this scene and doing it here. Maybe from the window of that house over there. Or outside. What's that called when you paint outside?"

"*Plein-air.*" She smiled at his enthusiasm. "It would be a departure from my seascapes, for sure." Scanning the vista that swept before her, she took photos to remember this setting. In her mind's eye, she framed the views, imagining how she would sketch them and the colors she would use. It would be a different palette from what she usually used.

A change might do them good.

The whistle blew, and passengers returned to board the train. Ivy and Bennett followed and took their seats.

After their conversation, Ivy felt lighter, as if a new world of possibilities was opening to them. The responsibilities they'd left in Summer Beach were receding, although she would check in with Sunny.

The train continued, passing through several narrow, darkened tunnels bored through the mountains. Lamplight illuminated the old coaches, which rumbled through the burrowed passageways as they had for more than a century. Ivy breathed in. Outside the open windows, moss-covered dank stone walls, while whistling winds cooled her face and filled the coach with a sweet, earthy scent.

When they reached the small town of Sóller, they disembarked at a charming old station. They had time to wander the streets and shops before transferring to a vintage tram that would take them to the port.

A flash of color caught her eye, and she turned. Across the tracks stood a large work of art comprised of painted tiles. Instantly, she recognized the distinctive shapes of the artist's signature red, blue, green, and yellow shades against strong black strokes. The abstract, surrealist composition was breathtaking.

Ivy pressed a hand to her chest in surprise. "That looks like a real Miró."

Beside her, an attractive woman about Ivy's age smiled. "Joan Miró lived on Mallorca, though he was from Catalonia. We adopted him because his grandfather was from Sóller, and he visited often. If you have time, you should see the exhibition of his work downstairs in the Fundació Tren de l'Art."

Ivy thanked her and turned to Bennett. "Did you know about an exhibit at the station?"

Bennett shook his head, looking as surprised as she was. "I would've said something about that. Wasn't there a Miró among the masterpieces you found in the lower level at the inn?"

"There was. Shelly really wanted me to keep that one. But it had belonged to a family with personal connections to the artist. I knew they would want it returned."

The woman glanced back at them with curiosity before continuing ahead of them.

Ivy paused at the top of the stairway, her heart quickening at the memory. Even today, it hardly seemed possible that those paintings had languished for so many decades in the old house.

"What a coincidence to discover Miró's work here."

Bennett raised an eyebrow. "You know what Shelly would say about that."

"I don't believe in any of my sister's woo-woo magical thinking. There are such things as happy accidents."

A smile curved Bennett's lips. "Like staying at Amelia Erickson's home in San Francisco?"

"Exactly," Ivy said. "We showed up, and Viola kindly hosted us. I refuse to believe some nonexistent spirit is waving a magic wand in my life."

Bennett slid a glance at her and chuckled. "No, of course not."

With a couple of hours until the tram departed from Sóller for the short trip to the port, they made their way downstairs in the charming old train station. A long, sketched sailcloth stretched to each side.

"These must be Miró pieces as well," Ivy said, awestruck that they had stumbled across such artistry.

The woman they'd met was ahead of them. She turned and acknowledged them again with a little wave and started off.

"She was helpful," Bennett said. "Many people here are like that. Almost like Summer Beach."

"I've noticed that," Ivy said.

Downstairs in the airy building were benches, potted plants, and casual photos on the walls of artists Joan Miró and Pablo Picasso. Ivy leaned in for a closer look.

"Oh, my goodness," she said. In the old black-and-white photographs, the two men appeared to be talking about their work and posing with others. "These are like the photos we saw at Viola's home."

Ivy leaned in. An awful lot like those, in fact. A strange feeling coursed through her, and she lifted her phone to snap photos of them.

In the last one, she saw the side of a woman, but she couldn't see her face. "Bennett, look at this one. Is that Amelia?"

"I can't tell."

"See that dress she has on? I can't remember if Amelia was wearing that in those other photos." She stared at the photographs. "I'll have to compare them later."

"I swear that woman is following us." Bennett grinned and gestured toward a doorway. "Let's go inside."

They walked around the space, admiring Miró's vivid paintings and Picasso's ceramic art. To have stumbled across this precious gem in the beautiful countryside of Mallorca was an unexpected pleasure. It was yet another surprise that Ivy never imagined their honeymoon might hold.

Afterward, they strolled onto the cobbled street and toward the center of the small town. They chose a table outdoors and sat under an umbrella, and a server brought them menus. They ordered the local specialty, a sweet *ensaïmada* pastry to share, along with hot chocolate.

"This leisurely day seems so decadent," Ivy said, cupping her chin in her hand as she leaned on the table. "I can only imagine what's going on at home. What if they've had another flood?"

"Then Shelly and Poppy will handle that—without needing to call you." Bennett was studying the menu with interest. He looked up and smiled at her. "Isn't that a good feeling?"

"I suppose so," she replied, still concerned. "But I'm especially worried about Sunny. She might have issues, but I do believe her. I don't think she was cheating."

Bennett brushed a strand of hair from her face. "Neither do I. But I think you're right to encourage her to handle it first. She won't learn any other way."

"I'm feeling guilty about that. What if I let Sunny down when she really needs me? This isn't a flat tire or something minor; this is her university education and a degree she'll need."

"That also means it's worth fighting for. Let her try. She might surprise you. Imagine how good she'll feel if she sorts this out."

"I hope so. It's a risk."

Their food order arrived, and it smelled delicious.

"And this is only a week. Our week," Bennett added. "That's what you've been telling me."

She kissed him on the cheek. "You have been listening to me."

"Every word. We haven't been married long enough for me to stop," he added with a playful glint in his eyes. When Ivy looked shocked, he pulled off a piece of the pastry as an offering. "I'm only kidding. I love listening to you."

"You'd better," she said, biting into the sweet treat.

Ivy sipped her hot chocolate and broke off another piece of the *ensaïmada*. The flaky, coiled pastry was delicious. She brushed powdered sugar from her fingers before savoring more of her chocolate drink, a tradition on Mallorca.

"That's pretty tasty," Bennett said, pulling apart the pastry with gusto.

Ivy watched him relish the food. "The rest is yours."

They strolled around the small town, visiting a lovely old parish church from the thirteenth century named for Sant Bartomeu de Sóller. Ivy took it all in, admiring the original elements of its Romanesque-Gothic style and later renovations in Baroque and Gaudi styles.

As they sauntered along the narrow streets, Ivy spied a shop that sold traditional handwoven Ikat-dyed household linens.

"These remind me of some my mother once had," Ivy said.

Bennett held the door for her. "Let's go inside."

She browsed the small shop before deciding on a blue-and-white runner with vivid Ikat flames. "This will be nice for our table on the balcony at home."

They listened as the older woman who owned the shop explained the traditional process of wrapping and dying the yarn before weaving it to produce a pattern visible on both sides of the cloth. It was a labor-intensive process that yielded beautiful results.

"This makes me feel good," Ivy said as they left the shop. "I love supporting other artists."

"That's another thing I love about you," Bennett said, kissing her again.

After stopping for mango gelato at a small shop near the tram station, they waited with others to board the wooden tram that would take them to Port de Sóller.

Just before departure, the woman from the train station who had directed them toward the art exhibit slid into a seat across from them. She wore a lightweight linen dress and espadrilles, and her dark hair was clipped back. She smiled genially at them.

"Well, hello again," she said. "Did you enjoy your visit to Sóller?"

"We did," Ivy said as the small tram departed, chugging toward the port on its narrow track. "It was charming, and I bought a few things in the village." She showed the woman her treasures.

"My sister has a shop there, so I visit often. I'm Raquel."

Ivy introduced themselves. "Where would you suggest we eat in the port?"

"You might enjoy Villa Luisa with its views, or if you're staying for dinner, Randemar is exquisite." She named a few other restaurants they might like. "You'll find a lot of shops and a marina there. And the views of the port and the mountains are lovely."

"Sounds like our sort of place," Bennett said.

Raquel glanced between them. "I couldn't help overhearing your conversation at the train station. I share your love of art, too. That's why I was surprised to read about a discovery of art lost during the war. Our local paper carried the story because of our connection with some of the artists. When I heard you mention finding a Miró at an inn... Well, forgive me for being forward, but are you the people from California who found the Erickson collection?"

"My sister and I did," Ivy replied, amazed that the story had touched so many people. "My sister still chastises me for returning the paintings."

"I can imagine." Leaning forward slightly, Raquel hesitated again. "My grandfather was especially interested in the story."

Maybe it was the tone of the woman's voice, but the fine hairs on the back of Ivy's neck bristled. She could have left it at that and changed the subject. Instead, she glanced at Bennett. If her hunch was right, he would say this was more than a coincidence. She turned to Raquel.

"Did your grandfather ever meet the Ericksons?"

Raquel slid her gaze to one side and lowered her voice. "Much more than that. Would you like to walk around the port when we arrive? We're almost there."

16

"*H*ere comes an interesting couple up the front walk," Shelly said, standing beside the front desk with Daisy on her hip.

The man looked about thirty-five and wore ripped jeans, a designer shirt, and expensive sunglasses. The woman looked a lot younger and was far overdressed for Summer Beach in a tight red dress and high heels.

"My guess is Los Angeles," Shelly said. "She stands out like a stop light."

If Shelly were in the city, she'd feel underdressed, but this was Summer Beach. Any sort of sundress, or jeans and a T-shirt—like she had on now—was fine here. And no matter what cute outfit she put on Daisy, that kid was a mess waiting to happen.

Shelly could hardly remember the last time she'd worn her clothes from New York.

Poppy looked up. "Stilettos and a shiny halter dress—where did she think she was going? Put me down for New York."

"No way, but you've got a deal. The usual?"

"Double it. I'm sure this time." Poppy slid two pennies

from two cups in the drawer and put them to one side. "If we're wrong, we let it ride. Hey, look. My penny cup is a lot fuller than yours."

Shelly quirked a grin. "Bet you've been sneaking pennies in there."

"I would never do that. You're just jealous of my incredible deductive reasoning."

"Okay, Sherlock," Shelly said, laughing.

They shook hands as the front door creaked open. That reminded Shelly she'd promised Ivy to oil the hinges.

The couple stepped into the sunlit foyer. "Hey, there," the man said, lifting his fashionably stubbled chin.

He had an attitude—as if he'd just stepped off a Hollywood sound stage.

Shelly nudged Poppy under the desk. "Welcome to the Seabreeze Inn. Are you checking in?"

"Looking around." He snapped a business card to Shelly, exuding confidence that edged on arrogance. "I'm Milo Rivers with Redstone Investments. I spoke to Ivy Dylan, and she said to come by while I'm in town."

Shelly cast a quick look toward Poppy. No one called her sister by Bennett's last name unless they knew her through him. She'd reclaimed her maiden name of Bay after learning of Jeremy's adultery.

"I'm Shelly, her sister." She glanced at the card he'd given her that touted several glamorous locations. "London, Las Vegas, and South Beach in Miami? Ivy didn't mention you'd be visiting, but they were awfully busy before they left."

"Oh, yeah," Milo replied. "Shirley. She mentioned you."

"Did she now?" Shelly was wise to that old trick, and he wasn't a very good listener. "Nice to meet you, Ralph. Is there something I can help you with?"

Beside her, Poppy coughed. She tossed the pennies into another cup.

Ignoring Shelly's comment, Milo lowered his sunglasses,

revealing piercing dark eyes beneath a slash of dark eyebrows. "She might not have told you yet. See, Ivy has agreed to sell the inn."

"To, to you?" Shelly stammered, her heartbeat quickening. She wasn't aware of this, but Ivy had been feeling over-whelmed.

Still, this guy might be working some kind of angle. Shelly narrowed her eyes, sizing him up. Everything about Milo spelled new money, from his expensive Italian loafers to his dark, blond-tipped hair.

"I just spoke to her and Bennett on Mallorca," he said. "Ivy can explain it to you after they return from their honey-moon. As long as we're here, do you mind giving me a tour?"

The woman beside him bent her head as if to check her phone.

Caught off guard but with no reason to refuse if he'd really spoken to Ivy, Shelly shrugged, still feeling uneasy. "Sure, I suppose."

"Only through the common areas," Poppy quickly added. "We have a lot of guests."

"That's right," Shelly said.

They weren't full, but she appreciated Poppy's quick think-ing. No way did she want to get locked in a room with this pair. "This is Poppy, our niece. She handles marketing and a whole lot more."

Poppy stepped out from behind the desk. "I'll come along in case you have questions."

Milo nudged the woman with him, who swiftly lifted her phone and began taking photos.

"This is Charmaine, my assistant," Milo said when he noticed Poppy looking skeptical. He glanced around. "This is what we do in acquisitions. Nice place, but it's on the small side for us."

As though trained, Charmaine nodded in confirmation.

"This way, then." Shelly shifted Daisy to her other hip and

hoped she'd behave for a few minutes. This would be a quick tour.

She led the pair through the parlor and reception areas before entering the grand ballroom. "This is the centerpiece of the inn. We host a lot of parties, weddings, and holiday events here."

"Even Carol Reston has performed here," Poppy added.

Milo smirked. "Is she still alive?"

"She lives on the ridgetop," Poppy said with a defensive edge. "Everyone in town loves her."

Shelly watched their visitors, sizing them up as she had when she lived in New York. Milo was flashy, ruthless, and shrewd. She knew his type, and she didn't like it. She'd have to warn Ivy.

Milo looked up, and his eyes gleamed. He was probably tallying the value of the chandeliers.

"Excellent space," he said to Charmaine, who teetered around the room on her heels, tugging her low-cut neckline to keep from spilling from the dress.

Shelly almost felt sorry for her, but Milo was just so obvious. Charmaine had to have known what she was getting into. But maybe she really needed the money.

The pair walked away from them, inspecting the room's elements. The fireplace, the fittings, the furnishings.

"Do you think those two are for real?" Poppy whispered.

"No one except some locals knew that Ivy and Bennett were going to Mallorca."

"Should we call them?"

Shelly shook her head. "At this time, they're probably out to dinner. I don't want to bother them there. If Ivy decided to sell the place, that's her business. Nothing will happen until she returns."

Not that Shelly liked it, but she had no say in it. It was Ivy's inheritance, or what Jeremy had tried to steal. He'd emptied their retirement account for this and his new girlfriend. Maybe that's why Ivy wanted to get rid of it. She could understand her sister wanting to make a clean start, especially now that she was married.

But Shelly sure would miss this place. She let out a sigh and turned back to the pair.

"Want to see the rest of it?" Shelly called out. She didn't want to spend any more time with them than necessary.

"Are you taking notes?" Milo said to Charmaine.

She nodded. "And a lot of photos."

"Bathrooms, too. We'll have to enlarge them."

"Look at all the doors that open to the ocean view," Charmaine said, tapping her phone. "Reminds me of the club in South Beach. And it already has a great dance floor."

"That's what I figured," Milo replied, looking at the polished parquet wooden floors. "We'll tear out that wall and enlarge it. Got to make room for the crowds."

"A club?" Shelly blurted out, incredulous. "You can't do that. It's not zoned for it. Besides, this is a historic building."

"Relax, I know my way around permits," Milo said with a derisive laugh. "History can be reinvented."

Shelly felt uncomfortable, and she could tell Poppy did, too. Even Daisy was fussy. "Shh, little one. Let Mommy work a little longer."

After Milo and Charmaine had taken photos of the ballroom, Shelly and Poppy led them through the butler's pantry and into the spacious, old-fashioned kitchen.

"Nothing fancy here," Milo said. "But it will do. Let's see the property in the back."

They stepped outside, and Shelly led them to the pool.

"Wow," Charmaine said. "I feel like I've seen this before."

"It's a smaller version of the one at Hearst Castle," Poppy said. "Same architect."

Milo perked up. "Yeah? What's his name?"

Shelly folded her arms. "Julia Morgan." *You jerk*, she added under her breath.

Charmaine quickly hid a smile.

At least the blond had some backbone, Shelly thought. As she led them past her garden, Milo carelessly stepped on a squash plant.

"Hey, watch it," Shelly said. "That's part of our fall harvest."

He glanced down and wiped his loafers on the grass, unapologetic and cursing under his breath. "We'll pave this over anyway."

"And there's the beach," Poppy said, taking matters into her own hands. "You can see all that on your own. We need to get back to our guests now, so if you'll excuse us, we'll let Ivy know you came."

"You do that," Milo said. He started down the beach, while Charmaine stumbled and sank into the sand behind him.

Just then, Jamir pulled into the car court, and Sunny got out of his car, her strawberry blond hair glinting in the sunlight. "Thanks for the lift."

"You bet," Jamir said, giving her a fist bump. "Should I pick you up tomorrow?"

Sunny looked dejected. "I guess so."

"See you early then. You got this, sunshine." Jamir backed out and left.

Lifting her hand, Shelly waved to Jamir. "Did you go to school with him?"

Sunny slung a worn backpack over one shoulder of the sweatshirt she wore over shorts. "I'm still trying to get in to see the dean. Maybe tomorrow."

"Good luck with that," Poppy said. "Has Cooper confessed to anything yet?"

"He's not budging," Sunny replied. "I still can't believe he did this to me. Jamir thinks he was dating me just for help in the class."

"Surely you can prove what he did," Poppy said. "Do you have any notes you made or research?"

"Mom asked me the same thing," Sunny replied. "She gave me a whole list of evidence to gather."

"Your mom is smart," Shelly said. "She'll help you when she gets back."

Sunny chewed on a corner of her mouth. "We talked about that. Maybe I can figure this out before she returns."

Surprised, Shelly slid a look at Poppy.

"You probably can," Poppy said, nodding. "What Cooper did was so mean. And sloppy. He didn't deserve you." She let out an indignant little puff of air. "Just open your laptop. You can prove that was your work in ten minutes. Jamir was right. You've got this."

Sunny lifted her chin. "Cooper turned out to be such a jerk. Probably thinks I'm stupid enough to just slink off."

"Not you," Shelly said, bumping her fist. "Cooper doesn't know the first thing about us, does he? No one crosses a Bay woman. And you're one, too, kid. I'm telling you, Cooper's going down for this."

A determined look spread across Sunny's face. "Can you believe I was feeling sorry for him? Until I found out I might get expelled."

As Sunny shook her head in fresh disgust, she glanced back at the pair walking toward the surf. "They're not dressed for the beach. Are they guests here? I saw them in town last night."

Several other guests strolled toward the pool, and Shelly pulled Sunny into the kitchen. Poppy hurried after them.

"They're not guests," Shelly said quietly. "But if you hear anything about those two, I need to know."

Sunny made a face. "You're acting weird, Aunt Shelly. What's going on?"

Shelly wasn't sure she should be telling Sunny about Ivy's

business, but she was family. And she'd find out about it as soon as Ivy returned.

"You're not going to believe this. Your mom is selling the inn to that jerk out there. Milo wants to turn it into a high-end playground with a dance club."

An incredulous look sprang to Sunny's face. "Mom would have said something before she left. Are you sure?"

"I don't know, but that guy sure seems to think they have a deal," Shelly replied, bouncing Daisy, who began to cry. "Shh, little one. I know you're hungry. And probably wet."

Sunny blinked. "But where will I go?"

Shelly sighed, holding Daisy a little tighter. "They're probably moving into Bennett's house. You can stay there. Or with me."

"In Daisy's room?"

"You're welcome with me at my parent's place," Poppy said. "You're almost finished with school anyway."

"Well, I thought so," Sunny said, sounding doubtful again.

"We'll figure this out," Shelly said with determination. "Just like we have figured out every single other thing since we came to Summer Beach. You stick with us."

"Let's not jump to conclusions," Poppy added. "We'll carry on and wait for Ivy to come back. Maybe it's all a big mistake."

"But what do we do until then?" Sunny asked, her voice tinged with frustration.

"Absolutely nothing," Shelly replied, trying to keep her cool. "We keep this to ourselves. And we prepare for the inevitable," she added, her eyes meeting those of her nieces.

"What does that mean?" Sunny asked.

Shelly lifted her chin. "We work on Plan B. Poppy, you have your L.A. clients. Sunny, make sure you finish your degree. I can always work on my blog and video channel. Maybe I'll get some sponsorships. Whatever's coming, we'll face it."

While Sunny looked crestfallen, Shelly glanced around the comfortable old kitchen where they'd all shared so many secrets, heartaches, and happiness these past few years. "I sure will miss the Seabreeze Inn. It's been a crazy wild ride."

Poppy ran her hand lovingly along the tiled countertop and looked up. "So will I."

As if Daisy understood, she stopped fidgeting and stared at her mother.

"When Ivy and I landed here, I was starting over, too," Shelly said. "I had been afraid to leave Ezzra in New York. He was a lot like your Cooper, Sunny. Rich, good-looking, could charm the moon from the sky. But if I hadn't followed Ivy, I never would have met Mitch, my soulmate, or have my precious Daisy. We have to trust that she knows what she's doing."

"Or prove that something's not right," Poppy said, crossing her arms. "I'm still having a hard time believing it."

Just then, Daisy's face reddened, and she let out an ear-splitting wail.

"There's my alarm," Shelly said, clutching her. "Remember, we don't tell anyone about this until Ivy returns."

"Not even Mitch?" Sunny asked.

"I'll swear him to secrecy," Shelly said. "If he says one word about this at Java Beach, he's sleeping on the sand."

*a*s the tram eased to a stop in front of the sunny Port de Sóller cove filled with yachts and sailboats, Ivy wondered what Raquel had to say about the Ericksons.

Bennett held out his hand, helping her and Raquel descend from the wooden tram.

"I'd love to hear more about your grandfather," Ivy said. She also wondered how Amelia figured into Mallorca.

They strolled along the beach where people were sunning themselves, having lunch at outdoor cafes, or shopping at the boutiques. Raquel shared some of the island's history before turning to her story.

"At that time, my grandfather had married and was living in France," Raquel began. "He had a friend in Germany who belonged to a family we all knew—and they knew the Ericksons. They had a home here on Mallorca for a while where they would live for part of the year."

"I never knew that," Ivy said, listening intently.

"No?" Raquel seemed a little surprised. "Well, as you might know, thousands of pieces of art from museums and private collections that the Nazi regime confiscated were sold in auctions in Switzerland to other museums and collectors around the world."

Ivy nodded; she had heard about that.

"Amelia's father and my grandfather, who was a young man then, were among a number of people who managed to divert a lot of art destined to be destroyed. More than five thousand paintings that weren't sold were burned. They couldn't save them all, but my grandfather found places where some pieces could be hidden until they could be returned to the owners. If that were ever possible. It all happened so fast."

"And the Ericksons acquired them?" Ivy asked.

"Some they acquired through her father and his connections. As for other works, it wasn't quite that direct, but eventually, they took what they could. Some people brought out small canvases rolled in clothing."

"That was fortunate," Bennett said, walking on the other side of Raquel.

She inclined her head in thought. "That's what was thought at first. For safekeeping, Amelia had explained. But after the war, the works never reappeared. My grandfather assumed Amelia still had them. Times were tough, and he thought maybe she had to sell them to private collectors. Still, it was odd that the art never surfaced. Sooner or later, someone would have noticed. He was very disappointed."

The picture formed in Ivy's mind. "Until just a couple of years ago."

"When that article was published, you can imagine my grandfather's excitement." A smile bloomed on Raquel's face. "And he fully understood the circumstances of Amelia's health challenge."

"We'd love to meet your grandfather," Bennett said. "Would that be possible?"

Raquel's shoulders drooped. "I'm sorry, no. He enjoyed a long, wonderful life, but…" She shook her head. "He left us just a few months ago."

"Oh, I'm so sorry," Ivy said, crestfallen.

"It was expected, but it's never easy." Raquel pressed her lips together, composing herself. "When I heard you talking on the train platform, it was as if he wanted me to be in that spot today to meet you, and it made me feel closer to him." She touched Ivy's shoulder. "You see, I'd missed an earlier train. Little things like that have been happening ever since he passed away. I never believed in such things before, but after meeting you like this, I'm reconsidering."

"Thank you for sharing this with us," Ivy said. "I'm also learning to look at coincidences in a new light." As she spoke, she could feel Bennett's gaze on her.

"Your grandfather loved art?" Bennett asked.

"Oh, didn't I say? He owned a gallery here." She pointed at one across the street. "A cousin operates it now. Our grandfather represented many artists who became his friends. Those included Joan Miró and Pablo Picasso. He acquired art on behalf of many high-profile clients, including Aristotle Onassis, who used to stay at the Castillo Hotel Son Vida in Palma."

"That's where we're staying," Bennett said.

"It's a very romantic hotel." Raquel smiled as if she had her own memories. "Do you have other plans while you're on Mallorca?"

"We'd like to see the island from the sea," Ivy said. "But we don't have time to arrange a boat excursion today."

"No, not unless you know someone," Raquel said. "I'm meeting my brother Carlos here today. We have friends in town, and we're taking them out on his yacht. Would you like to join us?"

Ivy and Bennett looked at each other, delighted at the offer. "We'd love to," Ivy replied, grateful that their paths had crossed Raquel's.

Bennett grinned at the unexpected invitation. "Only if it's not too much trouble."

"Not at all. Follow me." Raquel gestured toward a large

cruiser. "Carlos brought some food from the market, so we'll make lunch on board."

As they neared the yacht, a tall, good-looking man with dark curly hair waved and called to Raquel.

"That's my brother." Glancing down at their soft-soled shoes, she nodded her approval. "You're ready to go aboard."

Ivy and Bennett met Carlos and another couple, who all welcomed them aboard. Bennett asked Carlos a few questions about the boat, and Carlos launched into an enthusiastic explanation that Ivy didn't quite follow.

"Come with me, and I'll show you," Carlos said to Bennett.

The two men disappeared, and Raquel laughed. "That didn't take long. My brother loves to talk about his yacht."

"So does my husband. I think they each found a friend."

A short while later, the two men joined them again, still talking passionately about things Ivy knew little about.

Carlos guided the craft through the mouth of the port and out into the open water. Ivy loved being on the Mediterranean Sea, and Bennett was in his element. He spent most of the time with Carlos, talking about boats and where they'd taken them.

Ivy enjoyed her time with Raquel and the other couple. As they motored past the steep, craggy mountains of Tramuntana from the ocean side, Ivy took more photos to remember the majestic setting. Around every outcropping was a new vista, and the entire experience filled her with thoughts of fresh possibilities.

"It's time for some artistry in the galley," Raquel said. "They'll be hungry before long."

"I'll help you," Ivy said. "There's still so much I'd love to hear about your grandfather. What was his name?"

"Felipe," Raquel said with a fond smile. She went on to tell Ivy more stories about her beloved grandfather.

Ivy helped Raquel prepare the food that Carlos had

brought on board. Raquel selected fresh grapes, pomegranate, and persimmon, fruits in season on Mallorca. Ivy helped arrange a platter of thin Iberian ham, cheeses, and crusty bread while Raquel prepared salads.

After a lazy, relaxing meal and stimulating conversation, Carlos guided the yacht back into the port.

"Please let us hear from you," Raquel said.

"I'll send photos of the artwork we discovered," Ivy said. "Come see us in Summer Beach."

"We might have to," Raquel said, nodding toward Carlos and Bennett, who were still talking.

As the afternoon waned, Ivy and Bennett left their new friends, promising to stay in touch, and boarded the narrow wooden tram to return. They caught their connecting train to continue to Palma.

By the time the taxi deposited them at their hotel entrance, the sun had set. Lights around the castle glowed against the shade of night. To one side, the subtly illuminated pool shimmered like a gossamer veil of sapphire blue under the stars.

Before entering the hotel, Bennett caught Ivy by the waist and brought her to his side. "Wait a moment," he said in a voice as tender as his touch.

Ivy turned to him and smoothed a hand on his chest. "What do you have in mind?"

So far, the day had been full of pleasant experiences and discoveries, from the excursion through narrow mountain passes and the surprising art museum at the train station to a relaxing shoreline cruise with new friends.

And, of course, Raquel's uncanny connection with the Ericksons.

Across the seemingly impossible divide of time, one might even imagine that Amelia had inexplicably orchestrated their honeymoon.

But that was impossible, of course.

"Are you hungry?" Bennett asked.

"Not really." Ivy looped her arms around his neck. She was happy and relaxed. "Not after that fabulous late lunch that Raquel served."

He lifted his chin toward the shimmering pool. "Then how about we skip dinner and go for a dip? Looks like we might have the pool to ourselves."

The glassy azure surface was placid and inviting. "Looks like a perfect ending to the day."

"I might have something in mind after that," Bennett said, nibbling her ear.

"Even more perfect," she murmured, loving their uninterrupted time together.

Although the inn had a beautiful pool, the last time they'd used it was at their reunion when they'd closed the inn for family. Usually, guests were swimming or lounging nearby, and Ivy was busy running the inn. Occasionally, she and Bennett might take a very late dip after an especially hot day, but that had become so rare she couldn't recall the last time they'd done that.

"Let's go change." Bennett tucked her hand under his arm, and they started up the front steps.

Ivy changed into her new iridescent swimsuit that looked like a swirl of modern art. She'd bought it on a whim after she'd left Teresa's office. She slipped the sheer, bejeweled coverup over it and stepped into her low-heeled sandals. She felt good in it, especially here at the hotel. If ever there was a place for glamorous swimwear, this was it.

"Wow, you look fabulous," Bennett said, emerging in his swim trunks with his white terrycloth robe draped over his shoulders. "I've never seen that on you."

"I decided to splurge a little for the trip."

"I'm glad you did. You don't pamper yourself nearly enough."

"That's what I have you for," she said, smiling. He looked

good, too. But no matter what he wore, he still made her heart quicken.

"Always happy to volunteer for that job," he said, sweeping her into his arms.

When they returned to the pool, it was still deserted. Other guests lingered some distance away in the outdoor restaurant over flickering candlelight. On the hillsides around them, lights shone in homes.

Ivy broke the surface and eased into the pool. The water was silky on her skin, and she'd almost forgotten how good it felt. She pushed off, flutter kicking from the edge. "Come on in. This is so refreshing."

"Right behind you." Bennett plunged in and floated toward her. Gathering her to his chest, he said, "Happy honeymoon, sweetheart. Are you having a good time?"

"It's been a wonderful trip," she replied with a kiss. "I'm thanking our former selves for seizing this opportunity."

Bennett chuckled. "Our former selves? That was only last week."

"Sure. But who we were then made those decisions, whether last week, last year, or ten years ago. When a decision works out well, I thank my former self."

"How so?" he asked, arching an eyebrow good-naturedly.

"Well, I figure I could have made a different choice, so I acknowledge myself for having made a good decision in the past." Ivy gestured as she spoke. "For example, after renovating the old maids' quarters, every month I say, 'Thank you, former self, for creating the opportunity for additional income.' When I find a great pair of old boots in the back of my closet that I'd forgotten about? 'Thank you, former self, for your classic taste and buying quality.' See how that works?"

"What if you regret that choice?"

She grinned. "Sometimes I ask my former self that. Like why I thought lime green boots were a good idea."

"Shows how far you've come." Bennett wrapped his arms

around her, lifted her, and kissed her. "I have to thank my earlier self for meeting you again."

"Hey, not so fast," she said, playfully pushing him away. "As I recall, you weren't too happy about representing me as a client. You inherited me from your partner when she retired."

Bennett shook his head. "I thought you might be like Jeremy—or worse. But you clearly didn't like me either for some reason."

"Oh, there were many," she said, laughing. "That was a tough time, and I probably took it out on you. But you won me over."

"I did, didn't I?" Bennett swirled her around in the water. "You're the best thing that's ever happened to me, Ivy Bay. I love our life together."

"Even living at the inn?" The idea she had in mind came rushing back to her.

"Especially." Bennett looked quizzical. "You've asked me that before."

"Have I?" Evading his gaze, she tipped her head back, admiring the thousand stars that blanketed the sky. This was a perfect evening, just as it was. She shouldn't have let that comment slip out.

"You have, sweetheart. Are you still happy there?"

He clearly wasn't letting up. "I'm happy with you wherever we are," she replied with a smile.

She wouldn't risk ruining this trip, she decided. He might be ecstatic over a sale, but his comments weren't trending that way. Whenever she thought about it, an odd feeling tightened her chest. Despite problems at the inn, would she be tipping a well-balanced scale?

Their lives might slip off kilter, or they might discover a new way of living. Any decision carried with it an element of risk.

Seemingly satisfied with her answer, he kissed her nose. "Mind if I swim some laps? I missed my run this morning."

"Sounds good. I'll join you."

Side by side, they arched into the water, gliding and keeping pace with each other. Ivy had enjoyed being a lifeguard when she was younger. This was one sport where she could hold her own with her husband or even outswim him.

Yet tonight, she wasn't feeling competitive. She stroked through the water in a companionable rhythm with him, simply enjoying being together.

Being on Mallorca with Bennett was opening her eyes to fresh ideas and unlimited possibilities. If only they were brave enough to seize them.

And if they preferred the life they had in Summer Beach? Now she knew that was also a choice.

Milo was waiting for her reply and decision. However, she wasn't sure what that would be.

18

*B*ennett stretched in the sunshine on the balcony overlooking Palma, the cove, and the sea beyond. He eased into a chair to wait for Ivy, who was enjoying a bubble bath. As far as he was concerned, they had plenty of time. He was satisfied merely watching distant ships ply the waves.

His phone rested on the table in front of him out of habit. A shorebird landed on the railing and peered at the device as if wondering if it might be worth snitching.

"Oh, no, you don't," he said, moving the phone closer to him.

As the mayor, Bennett was accustomed to being on call. He had a talented, reliable team at the city and prided himself on effective delegation. Still, some issues required his leadership. His team looked to him for direction and advice, and he didn't want to let them down.

However, they didn't need his input on everything.

His phone vibrated with a message, and he automatically reached for it before he caught himself. His hand wavered over the phone.

The bird hopped closer as if intent on claiming its prize from Bennett.

"Go on, you." He waved his hand, and the bird skittered, squawking in protest.

Boz and Maeve had assured him they would take care of the issue involving Dirk, who wasn't backing down. Worse, he was digging in for a fight that could be expensive for the city to defend. But they were on to him. Boz had sent him a message about the out-of-towner who'd been fishing for information about the inn. Turned out to be the head of Dirk's company, Redstone Investments. Milo Rivers. That was probably another name like Blaze.

Bennett blew out a breath. He had to trust his team to deal with Dirk and the rest. Boz and Maeve had never let him down. If it wasn't them calling, who could it be?

Someone who didn't know he was on his honeymoon. Unless it was an emergency.

The phone vibrated insistently.

It might be his sister or her husband. Concern tightened his chest. What if something had happened to one of them or his nephew?

As the bird swooped toward the table, Bennett snatched his phone and turned it over to see the message.

Call me.

Dirk Wilder.

Bennett snorted. "Yeah, as if I'd interrupt bliss to argue with you."

Ivy appeared in the doorway. "Who is that?"

"Just someone who doesn't know how to take no for an answer." Bennett silenced his phone and looked up.

Wrapped in her white fluffy robe, Ivy still took his breath away, even with her wet hair slicked back and face devoid of makeup. He pulled her closer and inhaled. Her skin held the fresh scent of verbena.

A half-smile turned up one side of her mouth. "That's what some people say about me."

"All depends on what you're asking," he said, swooping her into his lap. She threw her head back and laughed. He grinned at that, loving the sound of her laughter.

She thumped his chest. "I want everything you've got in that heart of yours," she said, sealing her demand with the sweetest kisses.

"That all depends..." Bennett thought last night was one of the most romantic evenings they'd ever shared. Even more than their sweet lovemaking, it was their emotional connection that he was still savoring this morning. Ivy was his sunlight and joy. His best friend, lover, and partner. He'd been lucky twice in love—more than he'd been entitled to. He thanked his lucky stars every day.

Bennett wrapped his arms around Ivy as if to never let her go. Nuzzling her neck, he murmured, "It could take me a lifetime to fulfill that wish."

Dirk Wilder could wait. Forever, if Bennett had his way.

"Then you'd better get started," she said, snapping the elastic on his shorts.

"Hey, that's where I draw the line," he said, scooping Ivy into his arms and stepping back into the room. This was the woman he wanted to love forever and ever.

BENNETT SAT at a table at the terrace restaurant while Ivy perused the breakfast buffet. They had barely made it in time, even though it was late morning. Everything, including schedules, moved at a more leisurely pace on Mallorca.

He enjoyed that. The server stopped by the table to pour green smoothies for them, and Bennett ordered coffee. Before joining Ivy at the buffet, he sipped his drink and watched her from afar, appreciating every graceful movement.

She was wearing another new sundress he'd bought for

her at a little shop in Port de Sóller while they were waiting for the tram. It was a vivid plum-colored print that deepened her emerald eyes. He'd fallen under their trance years ago on the beach, and her gaze still had that effect on him today. The dress was just above her knees—a little shorter than she usually wore, but he loved her beautiful legs.

He sipped his drink and watched her, considering himself a lucky man.

Before Ivy arrived in Summer Beach, his life had been dedicated to the community. His sister Kendra and Dave had included him as much as he wanted, but they needed their family time, too. His nephew Logan had become a substitute for the child he'd nearly had with Jackie.

His first wife would have liked Ivy, he decided. They were similar in their determination, creativity, and sense of humor, though they looked nothing alike. Jackie had passed away more than ten years ago now. They'd been looking forward to starting their family when the illness had struck her.

In all the years since then, he'd never met anyone who made him laugh like Ivy—or burn with a young man's passion again. Her independence was fiercely attractive and made him want her even more.

He'd always heard you could tell a lot about a woman by looking at her mother. Ivy was more like her mother than she realized. While that adage wasn't always true, in Ivy's case, he thought it was. Carlotta was vibrant and active, and her wisdom, intelligence, and love for her family made her even more admirable. Much like Ivy.

Bennett thought he and Sterling were two of the luckiest men on earth.

His buddy Mitch and his brother-in-law Dave were in that club, too. Shelly and Kendra were pretty special. Bennett had come to love the entire Bay family. When Ivy insisted that his family join the reunion they'd just had in Summer Beach, it solidified his love for her even more.

It was one thing to be married—another entirely to be family. That was deep, he decided, chuckling at himself. Probably too deep for such a sunny day.

Ivy returned to the table. "What's that big smile on your face for?"

He rose and held the chair for her while she sat down. "It's our honeymoon. Do you really have to ask, sweetheart?"

Ivy blushed, and the couple at the next table smiled.

He even loved that he could still bring color to her cheeks.

"Congratulations," the woman said, her English accent evident. "You've come to a wonderful place. This hotel and all of Mallorca—it's our favorite place to visit."

Her husband nodded. "We've been coming here regularly for many years."

"Have you been to the cathedral yet?"

"We're going to La Seu this afternoon," Bennett replied. "My wife is an artist, so we can't miss that." He loved telling people about her talent.

They spoke for a few minutes, and then Ivy glanced back at the buffet. "I think they're waiting for us before they take everything away."

"We were a little late," Bennett said with a wink to Ivy. That earned him another blush and a little swat on the arm.

"It's nice to meet you," Ivy said to the couple, then hooked her arm through his.

"Did you see something you liked?" he asked as they strolled toward the buffet.

"Everything. It's far nicer than our Seabreeze Inn breakfast. Maybe I'll make some changes when I return." She nodded toward tables laden with beautifully arranged platters. "They have plenty of fresh fruit and roasted vegetables. There's a cheese assortment, along with Iberian ham and smoked salmon. At that station, the omelets are made to order. And the pastries look heavenly."

"I'm glad we worked up an appetite," he whispered.

"And had fun doing it," she said softly.

"We'll have to do something extra nice for Teresa when we return."

"I have a couple of ideas," Ivy said as she handed a plate to Bennett. "Teresa has family who visit often, so I've offered to provide rooms free of charge for them anytime. I could also offer the inn for events she might like to have. I could ask Marina to cater food from her café for a luncheon or dinner. Or we could host a pool party or holiday party."

"Those are all good ideas. I could add a cruise up the coast on my boat."

Bennett and Ivy continued talking over breakfast, and the couple at the table next to them suggested restaurants and other activities.

"I could start the day like this every day," Bennett said, lifting his face to the sunshine.

"Sometimes we do." Ivy inclined her head in thought. "We have breakfast on the balcony overlooking the sea when Poppy and Sunny handle breakfast for the guests." She bit her lip and looked down at her plate. "I know it's not often enough. But maybe someday—"

"Hey, that wasn't meant as a complaint." Bennett threaded his fingers with hers. "I'm the one running out the door to City Hall."

"The weekends are when the inn is the busiest. That's when we should be relaxing."

"Who says meeting interesting folks at the inn isn't relaxing? I enjoy that."

"As long as you're not the one serving breakfast," Ivy said.

"If you need help—"

"No, that's my job. You work hard all week."

"So do you. I thought you were happy running the inn. You sure fought hard enough for it."

Ivy gave a little laugh. "I was desperate, remember? But

now, I'm thinking about us." She glanced away, fidgeting a little with her napkin.

Bennett pulled his chair closer to hers. "I've told you before. I like our life. But I'm beginning to think there's something on your mind."

Ivy slid a look at him with a small smile. "Maybe I'm just testing you."

Before he could answer, his phone buzzed. He didn't want to look at it, but Ivy heard it, too.

"If that's important, you should check it."

Bennett flipped over the phone and cringed at the message. Even though he trusted his team at the city, Dirk Wilder wasn't giving up.

"I don't need to answer that now." Bennett again silenced his phone, though he would have to reassess the situation when he returned.

THAT AFTERNOON, Bennett and Ivy went into the village of Palma and strolled the streets, taking in the sights. When they reached the plaza of the Cathedral de Mallorca, they both paused in silent awe, mesmerized by the panoramic view of the ocean and the structure that soared before them.

"Look at how the sun plays off the water at this angle," she said, stopping to take a photo. "Those waves look like they stretch toward the horizon."

"Wait right there," Bennett said, taking photos of her, too. Especially when she laughed at him.

Whenever he was with Ivy, her keen eye for detail captured everything, heightening the experience for him as well. He noticed the air was filled with the scent of the sea, tinged with warmth and the leafy aroma of nearby trees.

"Ready to go inside?" he asked, tucking a stray lock of her sun-kissed hair behind one ear.

"Absolutely," Ivy replied, her face glowing with anticipation.

As they held hands and walked through the giant arched doorway, Bennett watched Ivy's eyes widen in wonder. He loved seeing the world through her artist's perspective, every detail a treasure to be unearthed.

It took a moment for his eyes to adjust to the dim light in the soaring cathedral, often referred to as La Seu.

He turned to Ivy. The look on her face was priceless. "What do you think?"

"I've never seen anything like it," she breathed.

The sheer size of it was astounding, even to Bennett. To think that the structure dated back centuries and had withstood so much strife—even earthquakes—was nearly unfathomable.

"Look at that rose window," she exclaimed softly, her voice tinged with awe. "The colors are absolutely divine. Imagine capturing that level of radiance on a canvas." She followed the light flowing through the stained glass. "See how the sunlight casts a pantheon of kaleidoscopic reflections onto this ancient stone floor?"

He looked up. "It's amazing, but it wouldn't look half as good without you. The fine points often escape me."

"I could say the same about you, but on different topics," she said. "You and Carlos lost me when you were talking about boats. But when I'm out with you on the water, it's heaven."

"I guess one plus one does equal three."

Ivy laughed, and the sound of her laughter rang out. She clamped her hand over her mouth. "Good acoustics, too."

Ivy turned her attention to the intricate pillars and the gothic arches. "The architectural elements here are stunning, too. See the blend of styles? Gothic, of course, but there are traces of Baroque and even some Modernisme influence—like

Gaudi's wrought-iron candelabras. Construction began in the 13th century but took almost four hundred years."

"Imagine doing that in Summer Beach."

"Sometimes I feel renovating the inn might take long," Ivy said. "A hundred years from now, someone will still be repairing that plumbing."

Bennett chuckled, but he was still struck by her ability to discern subtleties that he would have overlooked. "This place is a testament to human creativity and dedication. Much like what you do with the inn and your art."

Blushing at the compliment, Ivy leaned in to give him a soft kiss, their lips meeting briefly. "I love that you appreciate what's important to me."

He thought he detected an undercurrent of meaning in her words, but maybe he was mistaken. He waited, but she didn't elaborate.

Squeezing her hand, he said, "Whether it's understanding the nuance in a stroke of paint or your determination and passion that drives you at the inn, I'm forever fascinated."

Ivy sighed, clearly touched by his words. "Even after our honeymoon, I hope we can still see and appreciate each other with a sense of wonder."

"Let's remember this." Bennett's throat caught as he spoke. "This has been an eye-opening adventure."

She smiled up at him, and he felt a surge of love. With her by his side, he was ready to face any problem or embark on any adventure. Yet the greatest magic of all was the love they shared.

His phone vibrated in his pocket, and he reached in and stopped it.

As they stood together, marveling at the sight and surrounded by centuries of artistry and devotion, Bennett put his arm around Ivy's shoulder. He imagined their love was also a sort of sacred architecture meant only for them, a structure they would spend the rest of their lives creating, defining, and cherishing. They would open these doors of their hearts, welcoming family and friends together.

Discovering all this felt like more than enough on this trip. Bennett stood a little straighter, internalizing the majesty of this space. Glancing at Ivy, he wondered if she truly understood how much he loved her.

If only he could put his thoughts into words without sounding silly. But that's what love songs and guitars were for.

Ivy turned to him to say something and then stopped. Instead, she reached out and swept a tear from his cheek.

"I love you, too," she whispered, kissing his cheek. "You don't have to say anything. Just promise we'll take these feelings back to Summer Beach with us."

The last days of their honeymoon were rushing toward them, and he wanted to make every moment count.

*a*s the boat Ivy and Bennet were on maneuvered into a secluded cave, she felt as if she were entering an enchanted world. The nearly enclosed space muffled the sounds of birds and other boats outside the rugged coastal area, cocooning them in a hush of silence.

"This is utterly magical," Ivy whispered to Bennett, sitting close to him in the bow of the small craft. They had set off early that morning to explore the caves off the coast of Mallorca.

The cave was nearly soundless, save for their breath and the lapping of underground pools of water. When the boat captain illuminated the darkness, their small group gasped. Overhead, stalactites dripped like icicles, shimmering in the light. Stalagmites rose from beneath as if reaching for their skyward counterparts.

"I've never seen anything like this," Bennett murmured.

Ivy slipped her hand into his, awestruck at the other-worldly scene. "Neither have I."

Against limestone walls, mineral deposits of iron and copper splashed rocks with impressionist strokes of red and green. She fixed that in her mind, trying to remember everything that mere photos couldn't capture.

All day, they had been exploring hidden caves hugging the coastline. One was so dark that phosphorescent minerals glowed as if by magic, reminding them of the ethereal blue bioluminescence off their coast in Summer Beach. The effect was surreal. Another cave was brightened with filtered sunlight and mossy rocks, like a pastoral scene from Xanadu.

In this one, still, crystal-clear water formed a natural pool where the limestone had eroded over the centuries. The boat captain invited people to swim. Some took photos, and other others simply gazed in wonderment.

"Want to take a dip?" Bennett asked.

"You know I do," she said, slipping off her coverup and sandals. This was such an intriguing place, unlike anything else they had experienced.

Taking a deep breath, Ivy slid into the crystal pool of water, feeling the water envelop her. Bennett followed her.

The water was so clear she felt as if she were swimming through liquid glass. She could see so far, and the rock formations beneath the water were fascinating.

After a while, they surfaced refreshed, eager to put on snorkeling equipment for a better view. Another couple joined them in the water.

"I never expected what we've seen in these caves," Bennett said, shaking his head in amazement. "What a surprise."

Ivy pulled on a pair of goggles, preparing to explore more. "This entire trip has been full of the unexpected." They pulled on flippers and re-entered the natural pool.

Marveling at the submerged world, they explored, watching fish dart between the stalagmites.

Ivy floated in slow motion through the water, reveling in the experience of being in a natural, isolated environment. Clarity, calm, and wonder suffused her soul, and she felt genuinely at peace. She reached for Bennett's hand, and he swung his mask toward her. She held out her hand, her fingers curved in half a heart. Without hesitating, he matched hers, completing their symbol of love.

When they finally surfaced, Bennett had a broad smile of enchantment on his face. "This is amazing." He hugged her, his heart beating in rhythm with hers.

They returned to the boat feeling exhilarated. After wrapping themselves in towels, the captain reversed course. Soon, they were blinking against the bright sunshine again.

Ivy shielded her eyes, thinking about the last few days, a blur of indulgences. She loved all the experiences and treats they'd had, from massages at the spa to delicious little tapas with local wines. At small cafes, they had *panades*, a savory pinched pastry filled with peas, onions, and lamb or *sobrasada* sausage. They also enjoyed the *coca mallorquina* and *coca de trempó*, rustic flatbreads topped with vegetables, meats, or seafood.

That made her hungry just thinking about it.

They had explored the hilltop village of Deiá and snorkeled off the coast, sunning themselves on outcroppings of rocks. Ivy even golfed with Bennett, though it was far from a serious game.

Most of all, she simply loved being with her husband. Relaxing into a languid pace, they had the time to share their innermost thoughts and aspirations. She had nearly accepted the strange coincidences that had accompanied them on this journey. However, some things were still better kept to herself.

And now, it was almost time to return.

"Can you believe it's already our last day?" she asked as they disembarked from the vessel.

"I'd rather think of it as a new beginning," Bennett replied, catching her hands as she stepped from the boat with the other passengers they'd met. "Let's walk a while."

Ivy smiled at him, tapping the brim of his straw hat. His swim trunks were still damp, and a T-shirt stretched across his broad shoulders. She tied her ocean-blue sarong over her one-piece swimsuit.

As they strolled along the soft sands of the Mediterranean shore, the remaining water droplets evaporated from her skin in the warm Mallorcan sunshine.

Bennett's arm around her was reassuring. His presence had grounded her in the swirl of new experiences this past week.

"That cave tour was something else, wasn't it?" he said, his eyes still sparkling from their adventure.

"Absolutely magical." Ivy loved the ocean's endless variety; it was her touchstone, her inspiration for her art. "I've never seen water that clear. I felt like a mermaid in a hidden world."

"My green-eyed mermaid," Bennett said, laughing. He raised her hand and twirled her around, her skirt fluttering around her legs. "But you're far more valuable to me than any pirate treasures those caves might hold."

Ivy's heart swelled with love at his words. Feeling wistful, she added, "It's beautiful here, but I've also missed our Summer Beach."

"And all the chaos that goes with it," he said, looking out at the horizon. "Despite that, it is our slice of paradise. And we'll see it tomorrow."

Ivy nodded, and a strange mix of relief and melancholy overtook her as thoughts of what she'd been putting off floated to the surface.

"Is something on your mind?" Bennett asked, clearly picking up on her shift in mood. "You've seemed a little distant at times, as if you're contemplating a momentous decision."

"Maybe I get lost in the moment." How well he knew her. She had resolved not to bring up the property offer until after their honeymoon, yet it had been tugging at her. She squeezed his hand a little tighter as if that physical connection could keep her secret at bay.

Bennett glanced at her, perhaps not entirely convinced. "I understand what that's like."

Ivy felt her resolve wearing down as they strolled along the water's edge. This man beside her, her new husband, had been steady in his love and support. She owed him the truth, although she wasn't sure which side he would take. This decision about the inn was technically hers to make, but it would affect him and others she loved.

Still, if there was anyone who could navigate a difficult conversation with grace, it was Bennett. His diplomatic skills often united formerly quarrelsome residents. She smoothed wisps of hair from her forehead, reconsidering.

Maybe some issues were better aired on distant beaches.

"I've been thinking about how we live at the inn and what the future might hold for us." She tightened her clasp on his hand, willing his support and understanding. "A few days ago, you suggested we look at everything in our lives and make fresh choices."

"Something like that, yes."

In the silence between them, Ivy could feel waves of curiosity emanating from him. She cleared her throat to go on.

"We've been living in the old chauffeur's quarters with guests coming and going at all hours. A few times on this trip, you talked about how much you love living at the inn, meeting interesting people, and honoring the history of Las Brisas del Mar in the community."

"All that is true."

"And for me, too."

This week had given her distance from the dated plumbing, leaky roof, and pending repairs. Every home needed repairs over time, she realized. Nothing was perfect.

"Still, my days are consumed with more and more work." She drew a breath, centering her thoughts. "I've wondered if there might be another way. I want to look at the inn with fresh eyes."

"You juggle a lot, darling." Bennett stopped and turned to her, gently brushing windswept tendrils of hair from her face. "If you're worried, I'll help you consider all your options. We can brainstorm together. It's good to get ideas out of your head and talk about them."

Ivy rubbed her brow with relief. That was all she needed to hear for now. The weight of her decision seemed lighter when shared with him.

"Thanks for listening," she said. Feeling a surge of love and gratitude, she twined her arms around his neck as the sea lapped at their feet.

"Hungry?" Bennett asked. "I could go for some tapes and wine."

"I'd like that," she said, thinking of *pa'amb oli,* rustic bread rubbed with garlic and tomato, drizzled with olive oil, and sprinkled with salt.

By the next afternoon, they would be home in Summer Beach, cooking in their kitchen and walking along their familiar shoreline. There, she would tell him about the offer, and she hoped they could discuss it calmly.

20

*T*he sun shone bright in Summer Beach as the car Ivy and Bennett had hired at the airport approached the Seabreeze Inn. At the sight of it, Ivy's heart leapt. They'd had such a long return trip, and she was eager for a good night's sleep.

Looking equally weary, Bennett leaned forward. "Turn in the back behind the main house. We'll unload in the car court."

In the back seat, Ivy traced Bennett's hand with a feathery soft touch. "This trip was everything I imagined and more. It's meant so much to me, darling."

"And to me as well," Bennett said, kissing her on the cheek. "We both managed to step out of our lives and make time for each other."

"I know you have a lot of city business waiting for you."

"My team has taken care of most of it. If there was a true problem, they would have contacted me."

"And the same here, I suppose." Ivy wondered how Sunny was doing with her petition to avert expulsion. She was ready to step in to defend her daughter, but she hoped Sunny had at least started gathering the material she'd asked for.

Bennett swept her hair over her shoulder. "I wouldn't have traded this time with you for anything. We needed this. Mallorca was incredible, and even the mishap in San Francisco turned into an adventure with you."

Ivy removed her sunglasses. "This was the trip we were meant to take."

"Just like us," Bennett said, bringing her hand to his lips for a kiss. "Meant to be together."

They'd had a good talk on the beach, and she'd shared more than she had planned. It felt good to unload some of her worries. While they didn't settle anything, he understood her frustrations about the inn, and he had made a few suggestions.

The driver eased to a stop, and just then, Shelly bounded down the rear steps from the kitchen, wildly waving with Daisy perched on one hip.

"Looks like we were missed," Ivy said, stifling a yawn. "I hope they don't need any decisions made right away." She was too tired to do the math, but with layovers in Frankfurt and San Francisco, she thought it totaled about eighteen hours.

"If you don't mind, I'd like to turn in early," Bennett said. "I didn't get much sleep on the plane."

"Welcome back," Shelly called out.

Poppy and Sunny were right behind her. They were all dressed as if they'd been to a party. Maybe they'd had an event here Ivy had forgotten about.

The driver opened the door for Ivy, and she stepped out of the car.

"Mom," Sunny cried, racing to meet her. "We've all missed you so much."

"I missed you, too. But it was only a week." She hugged her daughter and then searched her face. "Are you doing okay with that situation at school?"

Sunny glanced back at Shelly and Poppy, who had followed her down the rear steps from the kitchen. "I'll tell you all about that later."

Bennett retrieved their bags while Ivy greeted everyone. There were hugs all around. Then, Mitch appeared and whisked the luggage upstairs despite Bennett's protests.

"So, how was it over there?" Shelly asked, guiding her toward the kitchen steps.

"Fabulous," Ivy replied, still basking in her feelings for her husband. "We have so much to tell you." She cast a look back at Bennett.

"We have a lot to tell you, too," Sunny blurted out. "Why didn't you tell us you were selling the inn?"

Ivy stared at her daughter. How could she have known? She searched Shelly's face for answers, but her sister looked mortified.

Shelly shook her head at Sunny and mouthed, *not now.*

Bennett's lips parted in confusion, and he turned to Ivy. "Is that what you've been trying to tell me? I thought you were feeling overwhelmed, not preparing to sell the inn from underneath us all."

"I'm only considering it as one of the options," Ivy said. Suddenly, she felt light-headed with remorse. Maybe she should have told Bennett everything, but she didn't want to burden him on their honeymoon.

She turned back to Sunny. "Where on earth did you get that idea?"

"The buyer and his assistant were here checking out the house and the grounds," Poppy quickly explained. Her forehead creased with worry. "They plan to turn the ballroom into a dance club. I don't think the neighbors will go for that."

Sunny's eyes widened. "Oh, my gosh, Mom. Darla will be calling the police every night."

"Is that what all those remarks on the beach were about?" Bennett folded his arms. "You should have told me. It's your property, Ivy, but this is our life."

"And our jobs," Shelly said pointedly.

Poppy nudged her. "We talked about this. Aunt Ivy can do

what she wants. It's her house. And we both have side businesses."

"Don't worry about me," Bennett said, sounding weary. "But you should have told your family before your buyers arrived on the doorstep."

Sunny looked forlorn. "I just want to know where I'm going to stay."

"Oh, honey, don't worry about that," Ivy said, hugging her daughter. How had this gotten so out of control? She was now in a different frame of mind after their time on Mallorca. "I haven't signed anything. This guy only asked if I was interested in selling."

"Did he send you any paperwork?" Bennett asked.

"A letter of intent," she replied. "I was going to show it to you when we returned. But now, I don't think——"

"He's moving pretty fast," Shelly said, twisting her lips to one side. "He wants to come by again tomorrow." Even Daisy looked like she was going to cry.

Bennett narrowed his eyes. "Who are we talking about?"

"His name is..." Poppy hesitated and shot Ivy a look. "I guess I should let you tell everyone, Aunt Ivy. But can we make it quick?" She glanced nervously toward the rear door.

"His name is Milo Rivers," Ivy said, wondering what was going on inside the house as she spoke. "He told me his company invests in hospitality projects."

Bennett put his hands on his hips. "Would his company be Redstone Investments?"

"That's it. Have you heard of him?"

He flexed his jaw and scuffed a heel on the pavement. "Have you met with him?"

"Not yet," Ivy replied, growing defensive. His demeanor had suddenly shifted. What had happened to their loving interactions on Mallorca? "I wanted to talk to you about it first."

She was surprised and concerned over Bennett's reaction.

He looked like he was about to burst. "It was an option, but I thought I should consider it. Remember how much trouble it was to find a buyer? And he's offering much more than it was originally listed for."

"Of course, he is." Bennett let out an exasperated sigh. "But I guarantee it's not enough. You've built and transformed this old house into a thriving business. Don't let it go cheap just because you're feeling overwhelmed."

Ivy bristled at that. She welcomed his advice, but she wasn't ignorant. "I'm quite aware of what we've done here. I wouldn't have made any decisions before consulting an accountant and attorney. This is my only asset. What do you take me for?"

Just then, Mitch loped across the courtyard, his flip-flops slapping the pathway. "Hey man, why does everyone look so tense? I thought this was supposed to be a welcome home party."

"Hush," Shelly said, shaking her head.

"We just spent a week together," Bennett said in a low, measured voice. "When were you going to tell me?"

"That was our honeymoon," Ivy replied, raising a finger. "We agreed not to talk about business."

Bennett smacked his forehead. "This isn't just business. This is our way of life, Ivy."

"But you wanted to move back into your home."

"It's an option that's available." Bennett glanced around. A couple talking by the pool had looked up to see what was going on. "Let's take this inside."

"Sweetheart, we're both exhausted. Can't it wait?" Ivy turned back to Sunny, Poppy, and Shelly, who all looked awkward. "We should get some rest."

Mitch turned to Shelly. Crestfallen, he asked, "What should we tell everyone inside? That the party's over?"

As Ivy sucked in a breath, Shelly quirked a smile. "It was

supposed to be a surprise, Sis. We thought it would be fun. And maybe one of our last chances before…you know."

"Teresa is inside," Poppy added. "She wants to hear all about your trip. Many of your friends are inside. Imani, Jen, and Leilani. Paige from the bookshop and Louise from the Laundry Basket. Marina brought a cake from the cafe; her grandmother Ginger made it."

Mitch shifted uncomfortably. "Even Darla. She was excited to make something special for you."

Ivy threw a look at Bennett. "It was a long return trip, but we should see everyone."

"Oops, we didn't think about that," Shelly said, hoisting Daisy higher on her hip. The baby was wide-eyed now, seemingly following the conversation.

"We can make coffee," Poppy offered.

Bennett threw up his hands. "Okay, let's do this. But of all people, Milo Rivers with Redstone?"

Ivy raised a finger to him. "I will not take that sort of talk from you tonight," she said, restraining her temper. Something in the tone of his voice made her snap, and she was hurt. "I put up with a man's lousy attitude for years, and I won't do it again. Maybe I should have told you earlier, but you have no right to denigrate me for merely taking a phone call of interest."

"We're both tired." Bennett raked a hand over his cropped hair. "But that you would even consider it without my input is what I have a problem with."

"Really, man?" Mitch folded his arms and shook his head.

Bennett turned back to Ivy and spread his hands in a conciliatory gesture. "Okay, I see your point, and I'm sorry. But you should know that Milo Rivers works for Dirk Wilder. Redstone is Dirk's investment company."

Ivy had a sinking feeling in the pit of her stomach. "I had no idea. If I had, I would have told you immediately. He never said anything about Dirk or the club on Main Street."

"No, he wouldn't have," Bennett said, sounding tired and frustrated. "They're shrewd, and they're trying to buy up property around here."

Ivy crossed her arms, still sensing an edge of anger in his voice. "So, blame him, not me."

"Hey, you guys," Mitch said, intervening. "Sounds like the jerk is having fun playing you guys. Don't let him get to you. You had a long trip. Come on in, chill for a while, and say hello to everyone. You guys can fight about this tomorrow."

"Talk, not fight," Shelly said with a pointed correction.

"Is that what we call it, babes?" Mitch grinned and swept his arm around Shelly. "Whatever, we always work it out. You guys will, too."

Mitch's words sank in, while the force of Ivy's feelings, combined with her travel weariness, left her depleted. She cast a longing glance at her husband. "I suppose…"

"Me, too," Bennett cut in, taking her into his arms. A heartfelt apology was etched on his face. "Truce?"

"Never separated," she said, twining her fingers in his. She rested her head on his shoulder. The steady beating of his heart calmed her frayed nerves.

"Certainly not by the likes of Dirk Wilder and Milo Rivers." Bennett lifted his chin toward the others. "Do you want us to act surprised?"

Shelly rolled her eyes. "What do you think?"

"That would be nice," Poppy added, flipping her hair over her shoulder. "They've been sitting in the dark while you've been arguing. Everyone pitched in for this."

21

Ivy thought about their argument as they threaded their way through the kitchen. As attractive as the offer sounded, she wouldn't have committed to any deal without Bennett's input—or professional advice. She'd learned that after the tangled mess Jeremy had left behind. Bennett should have known that about her.

She supposed they still had more to learn about each other. But she'd also learned a lot about herself on Mallorca. The inn had a host of problems, but it was more than a house to her.

The scent of barbecue filtered from the dining room, and before they pushed through the door to the butler's pantry and beyond, she realized how hungry she was.

With his arm around her, Bennett squeezed her shoulder. "Smells good. I think we were just *hangry* back there. I'm starving for something other than airplane food."

She smiled at him. Hungry plus angry equaled hangry. "I really didn't commit to anything. I wouldn't without talking to you. But it was our honey—"

Bennett kissed her. "You were right, sweetheart. I wouldn't have wanted that guy invading my headspace there—any more than he already was with the trouble he's making at the city. I would have had to charge to your defense right away."

She liked hearing his protectiveness. "Thanks for saying that."

"We'll talk about it tomorrow and decide what's best for you," Bennett said. "I've grown attached to this old house, but it's yours. Any help I can give you, I will. And I promise to respect your decision. You were probably thinking about everyone else, too."

She was. What Bennett would want, where Sunny would go, what Shelly and Poppy would do. Her cognitive thinking had been snarled with questions, like a malfunctioning computer.

Poppy flung open the door, and the light flashed on.

"Surprise!" Familiar faces emerged from the darkness in greeting.

"Welcome back, lovebirds!" Teresa called out.

"Oh, my goodness, what a surprise," Ivy exclaimed. Despite knowing, their friends' thoughtfulness struck her. She teared up, pressing her hands to her chest.

Mitch escorted them inside, beaming. "I figured you'd want to eat. I have burgers, veggies, and shrimp fresh off the grill."

"We're not just hungry. We're *hangry*." Ivy winked at Shelly and Poppy. "You didn't have to do all this."

"We absolutely did," said Teresa as she stepped forward with a chilled bottle of cava from Spain. "A honeymoon like yours deserves a proper welcome home."

Ivy hugged her. "From the bottom of our hearts, thank you."

"We'll never forget this," Bennett said to Teresa. "This trip was beyond anything we could have imagined. It was wonderful."

"I'm so glad you had a good time, even though it was a little rocky initially," Teresa said.

Ivy smiled at Bennett and took his hand. "We were just saying that."

Imani joined them, with Chief Clark by her side. "Hey, lady, how was Mallorca?"

"So beautiful and relaxing. You would have loved it." Ivy hugged her friend.

"Maybe we'll visit soon," Imani said, tucking her hand into the crook of Clark's arm. Her eyes shimmered with happiness.

"Oh?" Clark looked surprised until Imani jabbed him. "Oh, yes, ma'am. I'd be up for that."

Ivy laughed and arched an eyebrow at Imani. "Sounds like we need to have lunch and catch up."

"You're on," Imani said. "I want to hear everything. Well, maybe not every detail—you can keep the you-know-what parts to yourself."

Her friend Marina, who ran the cafe at the Coral Cottage, was slicing a cake. Ivy greeted her with a hug. "What a beautiful cake, thank you."

"My grandmother's carrot cake," Marina said. "You have to come by for lunch soon. It's been too long, and Ginger would love to see you, too."

Just then, a clattering sound rippled through the room, and Ivy spun around. "Pixie, come here," she called out.

The Chihuahua raced back to her, its tiny nails tapping on the wooden parquet floor.

Ivy scooped her up. "I even missed you, you little kleptomaniac. Steal anything lately?"

Gilda came panting after Pixie, her pink hair standing on end. "When she heard your voice, she took off. We were coming to greet you anyway."

Ivy hugged Gilda. "It's good to see you. And if you ever write an article about Mallorca, we have plenty of stories."

"I'll bet you do, traveling with the likes of that guy." She jerked a thumb toward Bennett and winked.

As they laughed, the front door creaked open. It was their neighbor, Darla. "I could hear that screech all the way outside, but if it's okay with your guests, I guess it's okay with me. My casserole took a little longer than I thought it would. I don't cook much anymore."

Ivy had even missed Darla's crankiness. Now, she assumed it was only a defense mechanism from having suffered the loss of her son. "How thoughtful, thank you."

Mitch took the warm pan from the older woman. "That sure smells good, Darla. How do you make it?"

Darla beamed up at him. "I take spaghetti—cook it so it's almost mushy—then add chicken, a can of mushroom soup, and a can of peas. I like to add olives to make it fancy. Spanish olives, this time, in honor of your trip. Then, I grate yellow cheese all over it, bake it, and toast it under the broiler flame for the last few minutes to give it a nice color. It was my son's favorite, you know."

"Well, now it's mine." Mitch slung his arm around her.

"You could put it on the menu at Java Beach if you want," Darla said shyly.

"Sure," Mitch said. "We could serve as a special one day, so all your friends can try it."

"No, they hate it." Darla shrugged.

Ivy suppressed a chuckle at that while Mitch inhaled the aroma and smiled. "There's no accounting for some people's taste, is there? We'll enjoy it, and I hope there's some left over for me to take home."

Watching them together, Ivy loved how Mitch had welcomed Darla into their lives. "Mitch knows good food, so I'll be sure to try it," she said warmly.

"What's this?" Bennett asked, joining them. Peering at the casserole, he said, "Looks mighty good."

Darla narrowed her eyes. "Mallorca, huh? Must be nice, Mr. Mayor. Glad you're back so you can deal with that Dirk fellow. I saw him snooping around here the other day. Parked right out in front with another shady character."

Bennett exchanged a quick glance with Ivy. "It's sure good to be home. There's always something in Summer Beach to keep us busy here."

Darla eyed Teresa. "I suppose you're the one who sent them gallivanting off."

Teresa chuckled. "Guilty as charged."

Mitch tilted his head toward Shelly and Daisy, who was cooing in Darla's direction. "I think your grandbaby wants to see you."

Darla's pout morphed into a smile. With open arms, she made her way toward the little girl.

Just then, Boz stepped up to congratulate them. He looked like he had something to say to Bennett.

"If you need to talk, I don't mind," she whispered to Bennett.

"I promise you it won't take but a minute," he said, running his hand along her arm. "That's all I can handle."

As the two men stepped from the room, Sunny appeared with a glass of Teresa's bubbly cava. "I thought this was better than coffee, Mom. Especially if you're really going to try Darla's dish."

"I am, and so are you. And thank you for this." She kissed Sunny's cheek. "I've been concerned about you. Have you made any headway on your issue at school?"

Sunny tilted her head. "Let's just say that Cooper is regretting his actions. Have a good time, Mom. I think I'll have some casserole."

Ivy smiled at her daughter, who seemed different tonight. More confident, more grown up. "Bring me a plate, too."

Sunny did, and Ivy lifted a small amount on a fork and took a tentative bite.

"How is it?" Sunny asked.

"Not bad," Ivy said, surprised. "Tastes like it was made with love."

Sunny grinned and took a bite. "Sure does."

Across the room, Darla watched them, looking pleased and proud of her contribution.

"Thanks for helping put on this party," Ivy said.

Sunny shrugged. "I didn't do much."

"No? I'd recognize the way you fold napkins anywhere. Pretty fancy."

"Just like you taught me," Sunny said, bumping her shoulder. "At first, I thought it was weird that you took a honeymoon. Being older, I mean. But now, I get it. And I think it's cool." She took her mother's plate and motioned across the room. "Leilani and Jen have been waiting to talk to you. We can catch up tomorrow."

Watching her daughter go, Ivy knew she'd made the right decision to encourage Sunny to take an active lead in her defense. From what Sunny had said about Cooper, she must be on her way to proving his theft of her mid-term paper. Ivy would speak to her tomorrow, but for now, she was relieved.

Ivy moved around the room to greet her friends and neighbors. She stopped to chat with Jen and Leilani about their plans for the upcoming winter season in Summer Beach.

Jen tucked her long, freshly highlighted hair behind one ear. "Besides visiting the new hair salon, I've just put out Christmas decorations at Nailed It. You should come by."

"You know I will." Ivy turned to Leilani. "And we'd like to buy a large tree for the holiday party from the Hidden Garden. How long will you be in town?"

"A few more weeks," Leilani replied. "As soon as the student garden club takes over, we'll tuck in the remaining nursery inventory and head to Hawaii for the winter."

"I hope you won't miss our holiday party," Ivy said. "It's a new tradition." One that would continue for many more years, she hoped.

"Ray and I will be there." Leilani laughed. "It's always a party at the Seabreeze Inn, and you never know what will happen."

"We'll try not to burn down the place this time. No flaming cocktails allowed." Ivy felt Bennett's arm slide around her waist, pulling her close.

Jen and Leilani were swept into the crowd as more people joined the party.

"That didn't take long," she said to her husband. "How's Boz?"

"He's fine, and the team devised a good plan to block Dirk Wilder and his crew. Better than I could have, in fact." He looked over the room with a satisfied expression. "When you returned to Summer Beach, did you ever think we'd land here together like this? Surrounded by all these people who care about us—even Darla, in her own way."

Ivy gazed around the room, thankful that they had so many kind people in their lives. "I always hoped I'd be lucky enough to have a second chapter in my life. But this is so much better than I could have imagined."

Their family and friends were a mosaic of intertwined relationships—some awkward, some harmonious, and they all counted. Ivy glanced around the old house that provided shelter and a place to gather. In that moment, she felt profoundly grateful for each imperfect, beautiful piece of their lives that somehow fit perfectly together.

She half-expected to see the Ericksons walk through the front door. They would be welcome, too, she thought, smiling to herself.

"Sorry I blew up out there," Bennett said. "But no matter what happens, I will never stop loving you."

She grinned. "Is that a warning about tomorrow?"

Bennett held her close. "Let's not think about that tonight," he said, letting his lips linger on hers. "But promise me we won't talk about your options until we've had a good night's rest. And a good breakfast. I don't want to risk getting *hangry* again when we talk about something so important."

"Thank goodness." Ivy kissed him back. "It might not be the Castillo breakfast spread, but we won't starve."

After the party wound down, Ivy and Bennett returned to their apartment over the garages. The moon cast a silvery light over the beach, and they paused at the top of the stairway to look out over the crashing waves.

Bennett held her close. "It's not Mallorca, but it's our paradise, isn't it?"

"Anywhere with you is my paradise."

Before opening the door, Bennett said, "I'm heading straight for bed. I'm afraid I'll be out in thirty seconds, but I don't want to lose the love we rediscovered on our honeymoon."

"We won't," Ivy said, sliding her hand along his cheek. "And for the record, I don't think we ever misplaced it."

He opened the door, and even before he turned on the light, the sweet scent of flowers welcomed them.

Ivy flicked the switch. Roses, lilies, and blossoms of all sorts filled the space. "Looks like Shelly and Imani have been here." She recognized flowers from Shelly's gardens and blossoms that Imani specialized in. A good bottle of Spanish wine sat on the table with two glasses, not that they needed that tonight.

Bennett kissed her. "Our family and friends are the best. Wherever we go, it will always be good to come home." He unbuttoned his shirt. "I'm going to crash. If I'm asleep—"

"I won't wake you. I'll change and wash my face, so I won't be long."

While her husband stumbled toward the bed, flinging off clothes as he went, Ivy opened the door to the rear balcony they'd added on. *Their sweet treehouse.* Bennett was so proud of this. She sat on the sofa where she had a view of the ocean.

While this was charming and comfortable, she thought

about Bennett's house and wondered if he would be happier there. Would he like to be the king of his castle—or the consort in hers?

She sighed, still wondering what she should do.

Her beloved old Seabreeze Inn had become more than a project of necessity for her; it was a way of life. A life that offered her room for her family and new friendships forged over firepits and breakfast tables. But now, as she gazed over the moonlit beach, the same view made her wonder—was it time for a new horizon?

Milo's offer to buy the inn had been tempting, but it was only a tantalizing ticket to a less complicated life. Once she'd found out he was in business with Dirk Wilder, the thought of her cherished inn being transformed into another one of Dirk's loud, overcrowded beach clubs made her stomach churn. She couldn't do that to Summer Beach, to the community she loved.

Or to the memory of Amelia Erickson.

Yet the initial offer had ignited a question. What if she could find a buyer experienced in hospitality known for excellence? Someone who would preserve the inn and elevate it, transforming it into a bastion for luxury beach holidays? Like the Castillo though on a much smaller scale.

Her gaze fell on her easel in the corner, where she sometimes sketched or painted. She could set up a similar spot at Bennett's home. She stood and stretched, feeling tired, yet her monkey brain was working overtime, filled with options.

Bennett's heavy breathing indicated he was already asleep. She slipped off her shoes and tiptoed into the kitchen, checking to make sure everything was turned off—a habit of hers in an old house like this. Shelly had been known to leave on coffee pots or stovetop burners. Not that her sister would have had a reason to turn on anything, but Ivy always liked to make sure.

She stepped onto the front balcony to look back at the

main house. Most of its windows were dark; guests were probably sleeping peacefully. A small light shone in Gilda's window. The writer was tapping away on her computer at the desk, likely writing an article. After the fire on the ridgetop, Gilda had moved in and never left. Always spunky, Pixie poked her little nose at the screen, sniffing the scents on the night breeze.

Ivy rested her hands on the wooden railing, worn smooth over the years.

Could she let it all go?

If she could find the ideal buyer, the money she'd make would give her a sense of freedom, the chance to travel, and the time to focus on her painting.

But just as she began indulging herself in that fantasy, a wave of memories crashed over her. She recalled the laughter of guests and families, the wide-eyed wonder of young, first-time beachgoers padding through the inn, and the welcoming of familiar faces who returned frequently.

Many guests called the Seabreeze Inn their happy place.

The walls of this old home had absorbed the laughter and tears of countless guests and visitors, herself included. She and Bennett were married here. And Shelly and Mitch. There were the holiday parties she had hosted for family and friends, the rooms she had decorated herself, and her art studio just steps from the beach. Could she give up such a unique blend of home and work?

This property was irreplaceable. Would what replaced it truly be worth it?

She'd created more than a livelihood; she'd made a haven for her family. A place where everyone was welcome to come and be part of this life. Could she give up the joy of hosting her family and providing a seaside landing for anyone who needed it?

Ivy lingered before turning away from the old house that had stood for a century.

She'd always thought that if the price was right, she would

sell this property in a heartbeat. After all, she wasn't getting any younger. The place needed work, and money in the bank would be welcome security. She thought she'd be keen to trade this hectic job as an innkeeper for the solitude of an artist's life.

Or would she find herself escaping the maddening silence to gossip at Java Beach? Maybe she would find herself waiting for Bennett to return every day from City Hall. She swept fine sand from the railing and drew in a deep breath of salty air as if it might fill her with the wisdom to decide.

Tomorrow, she might choose to list the inn with Bennett for sale.

But tonight, the only certainty was the rhythmic sound of the waves, ebbing and flowing like the rushing of her thoughts.

Tonight, she had no answers, just a heart full of indecision.

Just then, Ivy heard a soft ping from her phone. She picked it up. It was a message from Shelly.

Hey Ives, you're probably sleeping, but I thought you should know about Milo's plans. I couldn't sleep without you knowing everything.

Ivy sat down to read.

22

When the morning rays seeped through the curtains in their bedroom, Ivy woke. For a moment, she wondered where she was. And then saw Bennett beside her, still soundly asleep.

They were home. She smiled, appreciating their modest beach decor and surroundings.

And then she recalled Shelly's message. A warning of what she'd observed when Milo and his assistant visited. Ivy shook her head, trying to get her sister's picture of a dystopian future for the inn out of her mind.

She had a lot of decisions to make. But not now. Not yet.

After easing from the bed, Ivy crept into the bathroom for a refreshing shower. By the time she stepped out, feeling refreshed, her husband had disappeared, along with his favorite running shoes.

The morning was a little cool. Ivy put on a sundress with muted shades of cornflower and navy blue. Over her shoulders, she slung a cotton sweater, or a *jumper*, she thought, recalling the couple from England they'd met on Mallorca.

She glanced out over the sun-dappled ocean. Even after a trip to such a beautiful island, the view from their quarters above the garage still filled her soul and stirred her imagination.

It was slightly overcast, though the sun was already burning through the haze. Few people were on the beach except for the early surfers and locals.

Just then, Ivy heard quiet footsteps on the stairway and a rustle at the front door. She opened the door. "Good morning, Sunny. What's this?"

Her daughter held out a basket. "We didn't know if you'd make it down for breakfast, so I put a few goodies together. You guys looked totally beat last night."

Ivy was surprised at Sunny's thoughtfulness, yet she tried not to act too shocked. "It was a long trip, and the time change threw us off." She parted the red-checkered cloth, revealing blueberry muffins, oranges and apples, and hard-boiled eggs. "Thank you, Sunny. This was thoughtful of you."

Sunny clasped her hands behind her back. "I saw Bennett take off down the beach. If you have a minute…"

"Come in," she said, sensing Sunny wanted to talk. Her daughter's eyes held a mix of apprehension and…something else. "I'll put on the coffee."

Sunny followed her mother into the small kitchen. Unbidden, she took plates from the cupboard for breakfast. Ivy watched her, surprised Sunny knew where they were, but she said nothing. Her daughter had been under a lot of stress this past week.

Ivy pressed the button on the coffeemaker and turned around. "I'm eager to hear how you're doing with that issue at school. Sit down and tell me." She hated to use the word *expelled*.

Sunny hesitated, then began to unload. "When you were away, you told me to get evidence. At first, I wasn't sure what you meant by that. I talked to Aunt Shelly, Poppy, Jamir, and even Imani, so I started searching my computer. I had saved all my draft documents and notes with time stamps. I even created a timeline of the work I'd done."

"Smart," Ivy said, pouring the coffee.

"It was a lot of work," Sunny said, taking one cup. "Then, I thought about how Cooper might have swiped my mid-term paper. He's not very techy, and I've never seen him with a little thumb-drive, so I tried to think like he would." She drummed her fingers on the table. "He always takes the easy way out."

Ivy sat down and leaned in. "And did that help?"

Sunny folded her arms and grinned. "I checked my email, and sure enough, Cooper had emailed my work to himself using my email account. How stupid is that? He had even tried to cover himself by adding a note that said I'd typed it for him. As if I take dictation or work as his secretary. Seriously?" She rolled her eyes for emphasis.

"So, what did you do?" Ivy asked, pinching off part of the blueberry muffin and sharing it with Sunny.

"I organized and printed out my evidence and that email and took it all to school. I had to wait two days, but I finally got in to show my professor, the assistant dean, and even the dean. Cooper is toast," she added, slapping the table with satisfaction.

Ivy's heart soared with pride. Her daughter had navigated this treacherous situation and handled it appropriately. "I wish I could have seen their faces. Have they made a decision?"

Sunny's eyes flashed with triumph. "They dropped the charges against me, and Cooper was expelled. Now he's furious at me." She shrugged it off.

"Well, he should have thought about the consequences," Ivy said. "You stood up for yourself, faced the problem, and fixed it. All by yourself."

"Yeah, I did, didn't I?"

The transformation in Sunny was palpable. She sat up straighter, and her eyes gleamed not only with relief, but also with newfound self-respect.

Just then, Bennett walked in, his face flushed from his morning beach run. "That sure felt good for the jet lag. What did I miss?"

"Good stuff." Sunny raised her hand for a high-five, and Bennett returned it.

"Sunny fought her battle at the university and won," Ivy said.

"I return to school on Monday." Sunny smiled up at Bennett. "Are you surprised at your stepdaughter?"

"I never doubted you could do it," Bennett replied, ruffling her hair. "You're pretty cool. Smart, too."

Sunny beamed at the praise.

"I'm proud of you, honey," Ivy added, catching Bennett's eye. Maybe she'd had her doubts, but Bennett had believed in Sunny. He'd seen something she missed.

Sunny stood and hugged each of them. "I need to head out, but thanks for being there for me. Love you both." She paused by the door. "Mom, I have some messages for you, too. Nothing urgent. They're at the front desk, or I could bring them up to you."

"I'll get them later, thanks." One was probably from Milo. She didn't even want to look at it.

After Sunny left, Ivy sat back, stunned at her daughter's transformation. "Wow. Sunny grew up while we were gone."

"She didn't have you to fight her battles." Bennett eyed the basket and picked up an apple. "Did Sunny bring this with her?"

"She sure did. That was my first clue something had changed."

"She's becoming a talented young woman. People need to be tested so they can emerge stronger."

Ivy rested her chin in her hand, detecting a deeper meaning in his words. "Is that so?"

"Take that however you want." He tossed the apple and

caught it. "I'll shower, and then we can go somewhere else to talk. How about taking the boat out?"

"You haven't had the chance to do that in some time. Let's do it."

"I learned something on Mallorca, too," Bennett said, looking thoughtful. "Like how to trust people to take care of themselves."

Ivy wound her hair and tucked it into a knot. "Ready when you are."

"I won't be long, sweetheart."

After he left, Ivy sipped her coffee, savoring Sunny's win and the love she felt for her. For Ivy, there were few greater joys than watching her children take confident steps into adulthood. In that regard, Ivy shared her daughter's triumph.

Now, it was Ivy's turn.

When Bennett was ready, Ivy picked up her purse and sunglasses. Sometimes, they stopped in town on their way to or from the marina. "I'm glad we're going, but I'd like to get my messages on the way out. Sunny said she jotted down several for me."

"I can guess who some of them are from," Bennett said.

After their argument last night, she didn't want to go there. Not yet. "Some could be important," she said lightly. "I just want to check to be ready for next week."

"And you're curious."

"Aren't you?"

He ran a hand over his freshly shaven face. "Guess I'm as guilty as you are. I picked up my messages from Nan while I was getting dressed. Shall I meet you in the front?"

Ivy laughed. "See you in a minute."

She made her way through the kitchen, which was quiet now, except for the low hum of the twin turquoise refrigerators, Gert and Gertie, a duo of dependable vintage relics.

So far, at least. Ivy wondered what it would cost to replace those.

She walked through the butler's pantry and wound through the house until she came to the breezy foyer.

Poppy was sitting at the reception desk, tapping on her laptop. She looked up. "Going out already?"

"Bennett wants to take the boat out to make sure she's still running. Sunny said there are some messages here for me."

"Sure. Here they are." Poppy handed her a handful of pink slips filled with scribbled messages.

Ivy thumbed through them. "End of year tax planning, dental checkup time…"

"Those sounded personal," Poppy said. "I picked up the shoe repairs and the laundry since I was going that way."

"Aren't you thoughtful? Thank you." She looked at another one. Milo Rivers. She looked up, and Poppy was watching her.

Ivy crumpled the note and tossed it into the trash. "Won't be needing that one."

"Really?" Relief washed over Poppy's face. "We're staying?"

Ivy's heart cracked at the glee in Poppy's voice, and guilt washed over her. "I can't make any promises just yet…but if Milo calls, I'm out." She would deal with him later.

"Ready?" Bennett appeared in the entryway, keys in hand.

"Almost." Ivy scanned the notes. "Oh, look. Viola called from San Francisco."

"Is that who you stayed with?" Poppy asked. When Ivy nodded, she added, "I took that message. She sounded nice and was very interested in our rates and availability."

"Viola and her niece would like to visit," Ivy said. "Would you check to see when our best rooms are available for them?"

"On it," Poppy said. "What was the Ericksons' house like?"

"Stunning," Ivy replied. "Incredible views, beautifully maintained, with a magnificent library and artwork. Their city style was more formal than their beach house, but it was easy to tell that the same architect designed the two houses." She looked up at the stairway. "Even the staircases were fairly similar."

Ivy turned to the decorative newel post at the end of the stairs. She thought about how many times she had touched the medallion on it for luck, and an odd feeling came over her. She reached out to touch the decorative wooden piece. "Like this. There was a nearly identical one there. I knocked it loose."

An idea seized her. Cupping the old carved piece in her hand, she tried to slide it like the one in San Francisco had.

Poppy and Bennett stared at Ivy.

When it didn't move, she shook her head. "It was a fun thought, right?"

"Maybe it's stuck, Aunt Ivy."

Bennett crossed the foyer. "I'll check it."

Ivy stepped back, still clutching her messages in one hand. "Be careful. It's old, and I wouldn't want to damage it."

Bending a little to inspect it, Bennett tried it again. "There's a lot of dust on it."

"Dusting isn't high on my list of priorities," Ivy said.

"No, it's from decades of accumulation." He reached into his pocket, fished out a Swiss Army knife, and began to flick grime out of the crevices.

"Well, that's embarrassing," Ivy said, stepping back.

"I should get something to clean that up," Poppy said, but she stood rooted to the spot, as transfixed as Ivy.

Just then, Shelly strolled through the front door carrying Daisy in a wraparound cloth carrier. "What's broken now?"

"Shh," Poppy said. "Bennett's trying to open that."

"I see a sort of notch," he said, working at it.

Shelly's eyes widened. "It opens? How do you know?"

"I brushed against one at Amelia's old home in San Francisco," Ivy said. "I thought I'd broken it, but Meredith said I hadn't."

"Another one of Amelia's hiding places?" Shelly gave an excited little hop, jostling Daisy, who giggled with glee. "Oh, please let there be diamonds as big as eggs in there," Shelly said, pressing her hands together. "That's all I ask. Even one would be fine. It doesn't have to be as large as the Hope Diamond."

Smiling, Ivy turned to Shelly. "Got your message last night. Thanks."

"That's what sisters are for," Shelly said with a warning look.

Bennett blew out the dust and jiggled the medallion. He glanced at Ivy. "Feels loose. You should try it. I'll take those papers."

A little shiver coursed through Ivy as she placed her hand on the medallion. The wooden carving was the size of her hand. Taking a deep breath, she shifted it slowly until it gave way and dropped into her hand.

"Oh," she cried. "It's the same."

Bennett flicked the flashlight on his phone and peered inside. Shelly crossed her fingers, and Poppy was shimmying with excitement.

Ivy stretched her fingertips into the narrow enclave, then jerked her hand back. "Ouch!"

Shelly swatted her. "Stop it! I've seen that movie. *Roman Holiday.* Gregory Peck did that to Audrey Hepburn. Scared her half to death. Is there anything in there?"

Breaking into laughter, Ivy reached inside the small cubby again and withdrew a gold, scroll-topped skeleton key. "Only this."

"Well, don't just stand there," Shelly cried. "Are there any locked doors or treasure chests around here? Jewelry boxes, safety deposit boxes? Come on, everyone, think!"

Ivy inspected the intricate key. "I can't think of anything."

Poppy shook her head. "Nope. Maybe it fits an old desk or

bureau, but there's nothing that's locked. We'd know about that."

"Sorry," Bennett said, turning up his palms. "I haven't seen anything like that."

Ivy sighed and handed the key to Poppy. "Well, put it in the desk. Maybe we'll discover something."

Shelly shook her head and looked up. "Just one little break. That's all we're asking for."

"Your words to—" Ivy stopped, remembering something she'd seen. "Wait. I have an idea. It's a long shot, but… I need a pen and something to write on."

Poppy grabbed one from the desk and passed it to her. "What are you thinking?"

"Take this," Bennett said, flipping over one of the messages.

Ivy tried the pen. It was nearly out of ink, but she managed to jot down an address she'd memorized. "Poppy, I need you to send that key to this address. Send it by overnight shipment. I want this to arrive tomorrow morning."

"I'll run it over." Poppy glanced at the time. "I'll have to hurry to make the pickup time. Should I include a note?"

Ivy flipped over Viola's phone message. She had the number in her phone. Shaking the pen for the last bit of ink, she dashed off a short note: *I thought this might fit something in your house.* It was a long shot, but Ivy hoped she was right. She gave it to Poppy. "Here. Try to make it."

Poppy was already dashing for the front door.

"We'll drop you off," Bennett said, racing after her.

"Why would a key here fit anything there?" Shelly asked. "That doesn't make any sense."

"A lot of things around here didn't make any sense," Ivy replied, rushing after them. "Unless you were Amelia Erickson."

23

"*H*urry," Ivy called after Poppy, who sprinted into the post office. Just after her niece slipped inside, the postmaster locked the door behind her. "Whew. She made it."

"Do you really think it might fit something at Viola's?" Bennett asked, looking at her with skepticism.

"Can't hurt to try." Ivy felt it was a kind gesture to show their gratitude to Viola for hosting her and Bennett. She was also curious and could hardly wait to see if her hunch was correct. Maybe it would turn out to be nothing more than a bit of fun. Still, she couldn't shake that feeling that sent chills along her spine. Later, she would try to reach Viola.

Bennett turned toward the marina. After parking and gathering their belongings, they strolled across the wooden planks of the marina toward Bennett's boat at the far end of the slips.

"Hi, Mr. Mayor," Tyler called out. "Welcome back."

Bennett's friend was relaxing on his gleaming yacht with his wife, Celia, who smiled and waved at them. Several young kids Ivy recognized from the school music program the couple supported were on the boat with them.

"Tyler seems like a changed man," Ivy said, recalling the couple's marital problems last year. "He's doing a lot for the kids these days. I heard he's sponsoring a youth sports program at the old airstrip park."

"He reassessed his priorities," Bennett said. "I'm proud of him."

Ivy grew quiet, thinking about that. If her priority was her family, would it be better to sell the inn and provide for them now? Or should she keep it running to provide jobs for them? That is, unless the roof leaked or the plumbing system failed. A knot of unease formed in her stomach.

Thinking about the key they'd found, Ivy thought of her choices like doors to be opened, and she wondered which key she might hold that would unlock the right one.

They waved at a few more people before boarding Bennett's boat. He ran a hand along the stern, brushing away some windswept debris. "She's looking pretty good. Glad we're taking her out."

"I'll help you with that," Ivy said.

It wasn't long before they were underway, with Bennett maneuvering past the breakwater. With sea mist cooling their faces, they cruised the coastline, silent and lost in their thoughts.

A few minutes later, they came to an inlet. Bennett eased off. "We can stop here."

"I remember this place," Ivy said, looking toward the shore. The coastline held many memories for her.

"I figured it would be quiet today." A mother and her children played on the sandy beach but were out of earshot. Bennett sat on a bench on the boat, and Ivy joined him.

"That's good because I've been thinking," Ivy began, her voice tinged with hesitation.

Bennett turned to her, his eyes a mixture of concern and curiosity. "About Milo's offer," he began. "I realize you couldn't have known about him. Boz told me about him only recently, and I had no reason to share that with you. We were away, and I was trying to minimize work and enjoy our time together. I was too hard on you last night, and I'm sorry."

Ivy ran a hand along his arm, enjoying the touch of his skin beneath hers. "And I overreacted. Forgive me if I forget who the real enemy is. As for Milo, I've decided against that offer. That old house and I have been through too much to see it destroyed. He also had the nerve to visit while we were gone; Shelly and Poppy heard his plans. I couldn't allow that in Summer Beach."

Bennett placed his arm across her shoulders and drew her in. "I'm glad that part of the dilemma is settled. There's still more to consider, isn't there?"

She shifted with unease, her shoulders tense with anxiety. "There are the financial implications of keeping the inn in good repair. I don't have the reserves to do it, which means I'm one disaster away from financial ruin."

"That's sobering."

"It keeps me up at night, so I've been thinking about my options. The most obvious one is to try selling the house again, now that we've put a coat of paint on it and made some repairs. It's become a business with cash flow, so that should raise the value. You could list it for sale."

Bennett nodded thoughtfully. "It could take some time to find the right buyer. But the more important question is, could you really let it go?"

"That's the part I'm struggling with." Her heart and mind were warring. "I hope my family would understand that a sale would enable me to help them in the future. And secure my life and retirement if I invest wisely. Maybe we could travel more."

"And you could devote yourself to painting." Bennett's voice held a slight note of resignation.

"I'd like to do a little more of that." However, Ivy thought of the solitude required for that endeavor. "I couldn't do it all the time, though."

"No?" Bennett looked at her.

"And now that I think about it, throwing money at my kids is what Jeremy used to do." She thought of how happy Sunny looked this morning, having accomplished a critical task by herself. "Having Sunny there, seeing how a business is run, how we work together and treat guests, is more beneficial to her."

"But it's not only about her. Put yourself first." Bennett stroked her hand. "That's not something you do often enough."

There was truth in what he said, but that's the way she was built. "My family means a lot to me, and I love having a place where they can gather. But I'm also concerned about us. Wouldn't you prefer your home on the ridgetop instead of living as we do?"

Bennett chuckled and rubbed her shoulder. "You might find it hard to believe, but I'd rather live at the inn with you. Sure, my house is nice, but it was awfully lonely up there after Jackie died. I like being around people and helping. That's why I ran for mayor."

After what Ivy had been through, she could understand why he felt that way about his house.

A shadow crossed his face. "And to be honest, I have some painful memories there. I'd like to change a few things and have you put your imprint on it to make it ours. We could do that after my tenants move. I don't have to rent it out, so we could use it as out escape."

That could work, Ivy thought. But it still didn't solve her predicament, and the tightness in her chest returned. She rubbed a spot beneath her collarbone as she sought solutions to her quandary.

"Listing the inn for sale would be one option," she said. "Maybe I could choose buyers who would take care of it."

He turned to face her and smoothed a hand over hers. "Let me say this, and please, hear me out. You seem torn in this decision to sell. What I advise my real estate clients to do if they're not ready is to wait until they are. They shouldn't feel like they're forced into a decision. Though sometimes they are by outside circumstances."

"That's the position I don't want to be in. But I understand why you say that."

As she thought about it, the truth dawned on her.

She didn't want to sell the inn. Not now, and maybe not ever. How could she say goodbye to the parade of fascinating guests, the familial chaos, and the real sense of purpose the inn gave her?

Even her breath came easier as she accepted this. But something still had to change. "Let's say I don't want to sell."

"Okay, let's look at that." Bennett squeezed her shoulder. "But you've been feeling overwhelmed with the workload."

"I've thought about that, too." Ivy looked out over the water, organizing thoughts that had been zinging through her mind at night. "I could raise the room rates a little. I know we're underpriced, and occupancy has increased, especially in the off-season. Income will grow in the next quarter, but it's still not enough to offset potential repairs."

"Potential—that's the key word," Bennett said. "Unforeseen repairs are always a risk, but there's also a chance you won't have a major repair. At least, not tomorrow."

"What I need are emergency funds I could draw on." She liked exploring options with him. He was letting her take the lead and offering ideas, but not hammering them in.

"You're in business now," Bennett said. "You could talk to your banker in advance. Set up a line of credit you could draw on or a loan to bridge the gap."

"Good idea," Ivy said. That thought appealed to her, even though she didn't like borrowing money. "Forrest told me it was better to plan a renovation than make emergency repairs. Or be shut down by the health department."

Bennett sliced the air with his hand. "Oh, no. You don't want that."

Ivy considered a few more ideas. "Talking about this sure helps."

"I hope so."

"There's a third option I'm considering," Ivy said slowly. "It was something that Viola mentioned. She spoke of putting her house in something like a nonprofit, charitable trust, or foundation so it could benefit the community in perpetuity. I'm not sure about the details, but I can ask her. I also had something slightly different in mind."

"This sounds interesting," Bennett said.

Ivy faced toward the horizon. "We host a lot of community events at no charge. I've been looking into it, and I think some people might be interested in donating to a preservation fund. Not everyone, but if there are enough, it will help."

"I can think of a few local residents you might approach," Bennett offered.

"So can I." As Ivy pieced ideas together, she grew more confident. "In searching for information, I also came across something about tax credits for historic property restorations. I think the inn would qualify."

"That might cover the repairs."

"That's what I'm thinking."

Ivy lifted her face to the sun. She was beginning to feel hopeful, although she would still have to put in a lot of work. "I'll ask Viola for advice, too."

A slow smile spread across Bennett's face, and he looked at her with renewed admiration. "I have to give you a lot of credit for your creativity and willingness to learn."

"As if I have a choice."

"Everyone does. They just might not like the choices. But you have the courage to face them."

Ivy appreciated that. "Here's what I have so far; tell me what you think." She ticked her fingers. "First, to maintain my sanity, I'll find a part-time bookkeeper and a housekeeper, and increase rates to pay for them. Then, more sponsors for events, especially another art show on the grounds. Maybe a nonprofit preservation fund or other type of funding campaign. Finally, tax credits and a line of credit for emergencies." She blew out a breath. "That's a lot to do."

"Business can get complicated, but you can figure it out to your advantage. You have a good team to run the inn. You could delegate more to free up your time." He paused and grinned. "If I recall, that's what you told me to do."

She laughed. "It's always easier to see someone else's problems." She tapped her fingers, thinking. "If I can figure this out, we could keep the inn as it is—without the faulty plumbing and leaky roof."

"Will you have time for painting?" Bennett asked, creasing his brow. "I worry about you having a creative outlet. And your work is gaining a following."

"I need that outlet more than I thought I did," Ivy said with a sigh. "But with the extra help, I could schedule my painting time. Especially now that I know the gallery in Sausalito wants more pieces."

Bennett drew back, looking at her with renewed admiration. "You're seeing your problems in a fresh way. That's good."

Keeping the property still felt like a gamble to Ivy, though more calculated. "Do you honestly think this is feasible, or am I deluding myself? If so, I should sell now." She squeezed his hand. "Be honest."

Bennett smoothed a hand over her hair and kissed her forehead. "You have potentially viable solutions. And enough of them that some are bound to work."

Ivy laughed at that, but she also saw the wisdom in it.

"I also know that you can figure out whatever you put your

mind to." He pulled her a little closer. "I've seen Ivy Bay in action. You're a force, and I mean that in a good way. That's part of what I love about you."

"Right back at you, hubs," she said, smiling. Already, she felt lighter, as if a pathway were opening. All she had to do was take one step at a time, just as she had when she opened the inn.

Ivy threaded her arms around Bennett's neck and kissed him. "Your opinion means a lot to me. I know this was my decision to make, but you've been a huge help."

"I want nothing more than to see you spread your wings and succeed," Bennett said, touching his forehead to hers. "I love you, sweetheart."

"And you're the love of my life," Ivy said softly. A warm glow seeped through her. "I think I always knew that, somewhere deep inside, even when I was seventeen."

They languished in the boat a little longer, reliving memories of their trip, until finally, Bennett started the engine.

As they cut through the waves heading back to the marina, Ivy felt more confident about her decision. Going on that trip had helped clear her mind, so she wasn't bouncing from one problem to the next. But the most important part of their honeymoon had been their time together.

She would also call Viola tomorrow for advice—and to see if the other woman had received her package.

24

*S*itting in the library, Ivy pressed the phone to her ear, waiting for her call to San Francisco to connect. Shelly and Poppy were gathered around the table with her, eager to find out if Viola had received the intricate gold key and what it might fit. Her daughter was pacing the hallway outside and listening in. Sunny had volunteered to watch Daisy in case she got fussy.

A man's smooth, deep voice rumbled through the phone line. "Good morning. Standish residence. Who is calling, please?"

Ivy recognized Leon's voice and asked for Viola.

"Hello, Viola," Ivy said when the other woman came on the line. After exchanging a few pleasantries about their trip, she said, "I sent an overnight envelope to you yesterday. Has it arrived?"

"Why, yes, dear." Viola sounded surprised. "It was delivered this morning. A lovely key—how deliciously mysterious. Your note was rather brief. Rather like an Agatha Christie novel."

"I thought you might remember our conversation." When Viola didn't respond, Ivy went on. "In Mallorca, I saw photos like yours of Picasso and Miró. I also noticed a partial view of a woman in one. She was wearing a key on a chain around her neck. It attracted my attention because my grandmother also did that."

"That's interesting," Viola said. "You such have a good eye for detail, but then, as an artist, you're trained to notice details. What was your grandmother's key to?"

"It fit the desk where she kept her valuables," Ivy replied. Nervous energy sparked through her. "I took photos of those old photographs in Mallorca as well. Later, when I compared the images, the print on that woman's dress was identical to Amelia's in your photos." She held her breath, hoping Viola would follow that.

Across from her, Shelly and Poppy looked at each other with surprise, and Shelly crossed her fingers.

"Wearing a key like that wasn't unusual at that time," Viola said slowly. "It was also a mark of status that one had items worthy of protection."

Ivy let out a breath. Maybe this would amount to some-thing, or maybe not. "We couldn't think of anything here the key might fit. And then I thought if Amelia had worn the key, maybe it traveled with her from her home in San Francisco. The photo quality was poor, so I couldn't make out any details. I don't know if the key I found is a match. That's why I sent it. Maybe it will fit something there."

"Perhaps," Viola said, although she sounded skeptical.

Ivy was afraid the other woman might hang up. She had to take her shot. "Maybe it would fit that box I admired."

Viola sucked in a small breath of surprise. "That was thoughtful of you to remember, but I doubt it will. We've tried so many over the years. Still, one moment, please."

Ivy could hear her speaking to Leon, asking him to find Meredith.

Viola came back on the line. "Meredith is outside garden-ing. When she returns, we'll try it together."

All they could do was wait. It was just a lark, anyway. "If you have a few more moments, I have another question."

When Viola agreed, Ivy quickly outlined her idea. "You mentioned that you've created a nonprofit entity for your house. I want to protect this house, fund repairs, and offer it to the community for events. It has a historic designation, but other than that, I'm not sure where to start. I'd like to create a structure to meet these goals."

Shelly pumped her hands in a silent cheer, and Poppy bounced in her chair.

"Meredith and I were talking about that after you left," Viola said. "All sorts of strategies could help you retain the property. What a shame to sell it to just anyone. I firmly believe providence selected us to care for these properties."

Overhearing that, Shelly whispered, "Providence has a wicked sense of humor. I think her name is Amelia."

Viola continued, speaking with her usual air of confidence. "You should contact my advisor. She's very knowledgeable in these matters." Viola rattled off a name and number that Ivy jotted down. "But by all means, check with your advisors as well."

Ivy hung up, feeling a measure of relief.

"I wonder if that's how the jeweled key trend originated?" Poppy mused. "I heard keys can symbolize love, luck, or spirituality. I saw some at Tiffany's once. Some were in plain sterling silver, and some were diamond encrusted. They were so elegant."

"Daydreaming much?" Shelly asked, grinning.

"I was with my cousin," Poppy replied. A twinkle of excitement danced in her eyes. "Elena was checking out her jewelry competitors in Los Angeles. We saw eye-popping pieces you wouldn't believe. I'd be afraid to go out wearing some of that. Remember when that awards show party was robbed, and Elena's jewels were stolen?"

Ivy remembered. Her sister Honey's daughter had nearly

been arrested for the theft. "Let's hope something comes of this for Viola and Meredith. It would be fun for them to unlock a treasure. Maybe they'll call back."

"Aunt Ivy, what was that you asked Viola about?" Poppy asked. "About the future of the Seabreeze Inn?"

Ivy tapped her pen. "I need to talk to you all about the decision I've come to."

Sunny also stepped inside the open door, holding Daisy on one hip. The little girl was listening wide-eyed.

"We're staying. What else do we need to know?" Shelly happily exclaimed. "It's back to business as usual."

"Not quite," Ivy said, shaking her head. "Let me put it another way. I *intend* for us to keep the inn. But to do so, we must get creative. We've got to find solutions to the repairs we need. That's part of what the phone call to Viola was about."

"I wondered," Poppy said. "Are you thinking of accepting funds to preserve the structure?"

"Something like that," Ivy said. "We'll have to be set up for donations. Or maybe run a funding campaign, like a Kickstarter. I have a list of other ideas, starting with a slight room rate increase."

"We've been way under market rates since we opened," Shelly said. "That's how we booked up so fast that first summer. Now people know they love staying here. I say, go for it."

"What will this mean for the business?" Poppy asked, leaning in.

"With a rate increase, I can hire a part-time bookkeeper and someone to change the rooms," Ivy replied. Just saying these words felt good. "The Seabreeze Inn has come this far; we're not giving up now."

"Woo-hoo!" Shelly cried, pumping her fist. "I told you Ives would work it out."

Sunny beamed as she gave Poppy a high-five. "Finally, our least favorite parts of the job will be gone."

"Mostly, but I will need everyone's help," Ivy said. She turned to a new page on her pad of paper.

Poppy nodded with enthusiasm. "If that's how we stay together and keep this place out of Milo's clutches, then we're ready to do whatever it takes."

"Daisy is sleeping through the night," Shelly added. "So, I'm back, Ives. Tell us what you need."

"We'll make a plan and figure it out." Ivy shared her ideas as she wrote them down. "Others form these entities to raise donations and preserve historic places. We can, too. That's what I'll talk to Viola's advisor about. And Imani. And whoever else might be able to help."

Ivy had learned that if she asked enough people enough questions, the answer would materialize. "First, it's important we plan another art exhibit on the grounds next year. Poppy, will you oversee that?"

"I have the list of artists, guests, and booths from the last one," Poppy said. "As soon as we decide on a date, I can send out hold-the-date emails and start getting the artists on board."

"Would you also carve out booth space for young artists?" Ivy asked. "I'd like to work with the school on identifying and promoting young talent. Sort of like what Celia and Tyler do with the music program."

"Good idea," Poppy said. "The second time around will be easier. We can probably attract more people."

Ivy went through her list. "We've all learned a lot since arriving in Summer Beach."

"Especially me," Sunny said, looking pleased to be part of the planning. "You've all worked before. This is my first job, and I've learned so much from all of you. Mom, Shelly, Poppy. Not just about how to wash sheets and towels—"

"Always a good life skill," Shelly said, cutting in. "Just wait until you have kids."

"Not any time soon, I promise." Sunny flicked a private

look at her mother and laughed. "But I also learned how to treat people and run a business. You all gave me the confidence to challenge that rotten Cooper issue last week, too. I would have been expelled if it weren't for you guys."

"You learned how to stick up for yourself," Shelly said. "Don't ever let anyone take that away from you."

Sunny hugged her. "You're the best, Aunt Shelly. You too, Mom. And Poppy." She fist-bumped Poppy and then flung her arms around her mother.

"I always knew you had it in you," Ivy said, smoothing her daughter's hair. Her love for Sunny transcended any frustration or doubts she'd ever had. Her bright, mercurial daughter would make it, and she had the ability to do it on her own.

As she held Sunny, Ivy thought if she accomplished nothing else in life, she would rest easy if she could prepare her daughters for their lives ahead. To teach them how to overcome the arrows of adversity aimed at them. From the Coopers and Milos who would take advantage of them, to the Jeremys who would cheat and mistreat them. Most of all, she wanted her daughters to have good relationships with their families and friends—and recognize when a good man like Bennett walked into their lives.

In the end, the love they shared was all that mattered. Even Amelia Erickson couldn't take anything with her.

Just then, Ivy's phone rang. It was Viola again, so she answered the call.

"Good heavens, Ivy," Viola exclaimed, her voice rising. "You must have a sixth sense."

Ivy's heart leapt. "It fit?"

"Perfectly."

Ivy could hear Meredith in the background, exclaiming over something. "What is it?"

"I'll put you on speaker, dear. Meredith, how do I do that again?"

Ivy smiled as she imagined the scene playing out in San

Francisco. "My sister, daughter, and niece are with me. They'd love to hear this, too. Mind if I do the same?"

When Viola agreed, Shelly, Poppy, and Sunny leaned toward the phone Ivy placed in the center of the table.

"It's Amelia's jewelry box," Meredith said, sounding a little winded with elation. "The one her parents gave her that we could never open."

Shelly's eyes nearly popped. "Is there anything in it?"

Ivy laughed. "That's Shelly, my sister. We've uncovered many things together." She recalled the lovely, jeweled box with its beautifully grained wood, gold fittings, and semi-precious cabochon stones of malachite and lapis lazuli.

"It opened right away," Meredith said. "My aunt told me how you thought the key made it to Summer Beach. I think you solved the mystery."

"Is there anything in the box?" Ivy asked.

"Sadly, no," Viola said. "But it's beautifully lined with black velvet. Where did you find the key?"

Ivy told her about the small cubby behind the medallion on the staircase's newel post and how they discovered the key there. "If I'd never visited you, we wouldn't have found it."

"Auntie, didn't you discover the silver closet key under your medallion?" Meredith asked.

"Yes, after I moved in," Viola replied. "Still, it took me some time to locate the closet, tucked away as it is. Ivy, you can imagine my astonishment when I opened that door."

"Wait a minute…" Meredith's voice changed. "I feel something under this lining. Like a small latch or something…"

Ivy caught her breath, and the others did the same, waiting for Meredith to speak again. They could hear her tugging at something, then an exclamation as the fabric presumably gave way. "Did you find something?"

"A false bottom," Viola said. "Meredith is opening it, and…

Both women exclaimed.

"Why, it's beautiful," Meredith said with awe evident in her voice.

They all leaned in closer. Shelly wiggled her hands. "Can you take photos and send them? We're all dying to see whatever it is."

Meredith laughed. "I'll do that. It's the loveliest diamond necklace. Victorian is my guess. And the center stone is—"

"As big as the Hope Diamond?" Shelly clamped a hand over her mouth to contain a little scream.

"Not quite, but what quality," Meredith replied. "These look like old rose-cut diamonds. This necklace must have belonged to Amelia's mother or grandmother and been part of her trousseau. I must say, the craftsmanship is exquisite. It's nestled in its own case inside the padded false bottom. That's why we didn't hear anything rattling around."

"We were meant to find this," Viola said with conviction.

"I'm sure it will look amazing on you." Smiling with happiness for her, Ivy placed a hand over her neckline, imagining how it might look. "We're also looking at our schedule for when our best rooms are open for you if you'd like to visit the Seabreeze Inn. We'll email a selection of dates and would love to have you as our guests."

"That would be delightful," Viola said. "And I want to meet your friend, the documentary filmmaker, if she is available."

"Megan would be pleased, I'm sure." Everything was coming together, Ivy thought with a sense of satisfaction. "We're all looking forward to your visit."

"And so are we," Viola replied. Then, she added, "Would you hold a moment?"

A scuffle of muffled words floated from the phone before the connection went mute. Ivy tapped the mute button as well.

Shelly rested her chin on her hand. "Why couldn't that have been here? Once again, we lost out."

"Poor Shelly," Ivy said. "Someday, your treasure will arrive."

"And here she is," Sunny said, handing Daisy to her. "Your treasure is wet, though."

Ivy and Poppy burst out laughing, and Shelly checked her baby girl. "Honestly, she's only a little damp. She can wait a few more minutes."

Poppy leaned forward in anticipation. "Viola sounds like a force of nature. What's she like?"

"Formidable," Ivy replied. "And I mean that as the highest compliment." She recalled Viola's support of the arts and local women's groups. "We should all aspire to that. Many women like Viola who've come before us have led quiet lives. Yet they've forged a certain determination to elevate the next generations. Isn't that a wonderful legacy to leave?"

Shelly nodded thoughtfully. "As much as I'd like to bank some real treasure cash, I'd rather see it put back into this property. It's my happy place. Every time I hear one of the kids from Celia's music program playing in the music room, it brings me such joy. And it sure calms Daisy." She hugged her little one.

Ivy blinked back a rush of emotion. "From Las Brisas del Mar to the Seabreeze Inn, this old house has made quite a journey."

"And it's taken us along with it," Poppy said as the small group nodded.

"Even me," Sunny added, perching on the arm of her mother's chair and resting her head on Ivy's shoulder. "I would've been okay if you'd had to sell the inn, but I'm glad you aren't."

"What made you change your mind?" Shelly asked.

"All of you," Ivy replied. She had gained clarity on her trip, and she and Bennett were communicating easily again. "It also helps to step away from your problems to see them more clearly."

Viola's voice sliced through their conversation. "Are you still there?"

"We are," Ivy replied, leaning in.

"The thought that you'd have to sell your property has been troubling us," Viola said. "Your property is a beloved centerpiece of the community. It has a historic designation, and it serves the community. With your plans to support events in Summer Beach, a place that Amelia Erickson loved, we've decided that this precious possession of hers should be put to a use she would like."

"I'm not sure I understand what you mean," Ivy said.

"I will explain." Viola paused, whispering to her niece. "Meredith and I have decided this treasure would never have been found if not for you. A force greater than us meant for you to benefit from it."

To one side of her, Shelly gripped her shoulder, and Ivy choked up.

Viola's strong voice rang out again. "So that you won't have to worry about repairs for a while, we've decided it will be our privilege to make the first donation to your new preservation fund. We'll sort out the details later, but I want you to know that we plan to build an auction around it. Maybe even in Summer Beach. What do you think?"

Tears of joy sprang to Ivy's eyes, and she pressed a trembling hand to her wildly beating heart. "I, I hardly know what to say except thank you."

A thousand words flooded her mind, yet Viola's generosity was so overwhelming she had trouble fishing any words from the flow. Ivy was utterly overwhelmed. This time, in a good way.

After Ivy hung up, the sound of clapping rang out, and she looked up to see Bennett standing in the doorway, his face wreathed with a broad smile. She raced to him, and he caught her in an embrace.

"Did you hear all that?" Ivy's heart was thumping wildly. She was astounded by the gift.

"The part that matters." He buried his face in her hair. "You made this happen; you set the events in motion. I'm so proud of you. Imagine if you hadn't crossed that street in San Francisco."

"Or crossed the country on that flight from Boston." She nuzzled his neck and smiled. "I'm so happy my real estate agent couldn't sell this old relic."

A couple of minutes later, Meredith sent several photos of the necklace. It was even more magnificent than they'd imagined.

"Wow, get a load of those rocks," Shelly said, exclaiming over the photos. "That looks like a new roof, for sure."

"And plumbing," Sunny added, making a face.

Poppy chimed in. "Maybe even electrical. But can we keep Gert and Gertie? They're so cute."

Ivy laughed. "Maybe we'll just take a little load off their turquoise shoulders."

With a deep sense of satisfaction, Ivy realized her family and their shared purpose were what she really loved about the inn. Their location was hard to beat, and the guests were often interesting. With the help of her family, she would find a way to keep her beloved inn.

"This calls for a celebration," Ivy said.

"Sounds great," Bennett said. "I'll fire up the grill, and we can throw on whatever we like."

"I have some squash that survived Milo," Shelly said. "Come with me, Sunny. I'll show you what that looks like. Who's making the Sea Breeze cocktails?"

"I have a new one for you," Ivy said, laughing. "Straight from Spain. Bring in some oranges and lemons, and we'll make sangria."

That evening, Mitch and Bennett's sister and her family joined them. Kendra, Dave, and young Logan brought fresh seafood for the barbecue, and when Darla poked her head over the fence, they invited her, too. Gilda came downstairs with Pixie. Even guests stopped by to share tapas and sangria.

Tonight, everyone was welcome at the Seabreeze Inn.

EVERYONE ENJOYED the impromptu barbecue and shared in cleaning up. The younger people gathered around the firepit to talk. Poppy, Sunny, Jamir, and some of their friends from town lit the fire and put on some music.

Ivy and Bennett paused at the foot of the stairs to their quarters.

"We could join them," Bennett said, glancing back at them. He waggled his eyebrows. "Or we could let them be and…"

"I like the sound of that second choice," Ivy said, trailing her fingers along his arm. "The honeymoon doesn't have to be over just because we're home."

He lifted a strap on her dress. "I notice you're wearing one of the dresses from our honeymoon."

Ivy smoothed the soft, plum-colored fabric over her hips. "I love it. It has such good memories woven into it now." They had returned with memories that would last a lifetime—and so much more. Their marriage was better for the time they'd taken for each other.

She started up the steps, but he lifted her back down.

"Come with me to the beach. Just us."

She laced her arms around his neck and gave him a soft kiss. "I thought you'd never ask."

They left their shoes at the edge of the patio. As their toes touched the sand, Ivy's hand found his, and it was warm and reassuring. Strolling along their stretch of beach could be just as sweet as that of a Mediterranean isle.

Bennett faced the rhythmic waves under the clear, moonlit sky. "Look at all this. I love our life, Ivy. I love the inn, the guests, and even the chaos. It's all part of you, and I wouldn't trade any part of you."

He folded her hand into his and dragged his lips over her fingers. As he did, his hazel eyes captured the moonlight, shimmering with a look of invitation.

A shiver of love swept through her. "Without you, my life here wouldn't be the same. You've brought the joy that was missing from my heart for so long."

Bennett's gaze held hers. "You gave me life again, sweetheart. And to many others in Summer Beach."

Her heart swelled with renewed love and respect for this man, who embraced her sometimes wacky world as fully as she embraced him.

"That was quite a honeymoon," he said, encircling her waist.

She let her lips linger on his with the softest of kisses as every worry she'd had melted away. "I loved every minute of it, darling. It was absolutely worth waiting for."

While the charm of Mallorca was intoxicating, it didn't compare to the life they had right here in Summer Beach, surrounded by family and friends.

As they stood with their arms entwined, watching the waves, Ivy knew they were strong enough to face whatever challenges came their way. Whether it was faulty plumbing, the whirlwind of running an inn, or those who sought to steal their bliss in Summer Beach, they could handle it. Together.

Ivy tilted her head to the stars, grateful for all the blessings in their lives.

"We should take a honeymoon every year," Bennett said, lifting her hair over her shoulder.

"I'd like that," Ivy said, smiling at him. "Let's keep this adventure going."

"There's something else I'd like to do right now."

"What's that?"

Bennett held up his hand in a signal, and at the firepit

nearby, Sunny nodded and turned up the music. A beautiful love song soared across the sands.

Holding her in his arms, he moved to the music. "Remember when you said dancing on the beach shouldn't be a once-in-a-lifetime event? I heard you, sweetheart."

"And I promise, this is just the beginning," Ivy replied, swaying with him barefoot across the sandy beach. "Let's keep this honeymoon feeling for the rest of our lives."

BONUS! Thank you for reading *Seabreeze Honeymoon*. Want to read a little more about Ivy and Bennett? I have an extra scene that didn't quite fit, and I thought you might enjoy it! Visit my website at www.JanMoran.com/SBHBonus. Enter your email address to receive your bonus scenes by email. (If you don't have access to a computer, ask a friend to print these for you.)

NEXT: Want to find out what happens when Ivy throws a gala to auction the vintage Victorian necklace to raise funds? A host of characters descend on quiet Summer Beach, and deep-rooted connections surface. Read *Seabreeze Gala*, the next in the *Summer Beach* series.

SHOP: Keep up with my new releases on my website at JanMoran.com, and don't forget to shop exclusive ebook and audiobook bundles, coffee mugs, and bookmarks ONLY on my bookshop at store.JanMoran.com.

JOIN: Please join my VIP Reader's Club there to receive news about special deals and other goodies. Plus, find more fun and join other like-minded readers in my Facebook Reader's Group.

MORE: Want more beach fun? Check out my popular *Coral Cottage* and *Crown Island* series and meet the boisterous, fun-loving Moore-Delavie and Raines families, who are always up to something.

Looking for sunshine and international travel? Meet a group of friends in a series all about sunshine, style, and second chances, beginning with *Flawless* and an exciting trip to Paris.

Finally, I invite you to read my standalone family sagas, including *Hepburn's Necklace* and *The Chocolatier*, 1950s novels set in gorgeous Italy.

Most of my books are available in ebook, paperback, hardcover, audiobook, and large print. And as always, I wish you happy reading!

RECIPE: SANGRIA DE MALLORCA

On a trip to Mallorca, I enjoyed a few icy libations on the beach under the summer sun. There was no shortage of cooling options, from the sparkling *cava* (blush pink, please), made similarly to French champagne, to the refreshing *tinto de verano*, made of equal parts red wine and sparkling water or soda (often festooned with citrus).

Yet one of my summer favorites is a chilled blend of fruit and red wine often served at casual gatherings, including where I grew up in Texas. Though some high-end establishments might lift their refined noses at it, sangria is a still welcoming concoction that pairs well with barbecue, seafood, and tapas.

One of my favorite ways to elevate this recipe is to use cava or sparkling white wine instead of red wine. For nonalcoholic versions, substitute juice or nonalcoholic wine. You may also use less sugar if you wish. Other substitutions are included below. Enjoy!

Ingredients

Wine Base

1 bottle (750 ml) of red wine (or cava)
(Spanish reds: Tempranillo, Grenache/Garnacha or other)
Nonalcoholic substitute: red grape juice or pomegranate juice
3/4 cup (175 ml) orange juice
1/4 cup (60 ml) lemon juice
1/2 cup (100 grams) sugar (or a sugar replacement, such as
Stevia or Erythritol)

Fruit and Spice

1 orange, sliced
1 lemon, sliced
1 lime sliced
1 peach, diced
1 apple, diced
2 cinnamon sticks
Sparkling water or club soda (a fizzy top-off)
Fresh mint, rosemary, or basil
Hierbas de Mallorca liquor
Ice

Optional Liquor:
1/2 cup (120 ml) brandy
Nonalcoholic substitute: 1/2 cup (120 ml) apple juice
1/4 cup (60 ml) Triple Sec or Cointreau
Nonalcoholic substitute: 1/4 cup (60 ml) orange juice

Instructions

1. Wash all fruit. Slice orange, lime, and lemon into wedges or thin rounds. Dice the peach and apple into small cubes.

2. Combine fruit and wine in a large pitcher or serving bowl and stir. Add 2 cinnamon sticks or to taste.

3. In a separate bowl, mix the sugar or sugar equivalent, orange juice, and lemon juice. Stir until the sugar is dissolved. Add this mixture to the wine mixture.

4. Add additional liquor if desired. Pour into the wine mixture and stir.

5. Cover and refrigerate for 3 to 4 hours or overnight for flavors to blend.

6. To serve, fill glasses with ice. Pour the sangria mixture, including fruit pieces, leaving room for the final fizz.

7. To add fizz, add a splash of club soda or sparkling water. Garnish with a sprig of mint, rosemary, or basil. If desired, add a dash of Hierbas de Mallorca.

ABOUT THE AUTHOR

JAN MORAN is a *USA Today* and a *Wall Street Journal* bestselling author of romantic women's fiction. A few of her favorite things include a fine cup of coffee, dark chocolate, fresh flowers, laughter, and music that touches her soul. She loves to travel, and her favorite places for inspiration are those rich with history and mystery and set against snowy mountains, palm-treed beaches, or sparkly city lights. Jan is originally from Austin, Texas, and a trace of a drawl still survives, although she has lived in Southern California near the beach for years.

Most of her books are also available as audiobooks and have been translated into other languages, including German and Italian.

If you enjoyed this book, please consider leaving a brief review online for your fellow readers where you purchased this book or on Goodreads or Bookbub.

To read Jan's other historical and contemporary novels, visit JanMoran.com. Join her VIP Readers Club mailing list and Facebook Readers Group to learn of new releases, sales and contests.

Made in the USA
Middletown, DE
21 September 2023

38966196R10154